BUILDING FAMILY

BOOK 10 OF THE SEAL TEAM HEARTBREAKERS

Teresa J. Reasor

BUILDING FAMILY
A SEAL TEAM HEARTBREAKERS NOVEL

ISBN-13: 978-1-940047-37-9
ISBN-10: 1-940047-37-4

Contact Information: teresareasor@msn.com

Cover Art by Tracy Stewart
Edited by Faith Freewoman

Teresa J. Reasor
PO Box 124
Corbin, KY 40702

Publishing History: First Edition 2021
Print Edition

TABLE OF CONTENTS

CHAPTER 1

LIEUTENANT COMMANDER HAWK Yazzie scanned the file in front of him for the third time. After six years of excellent assessments, Seaman Owen Morgan had done an about-face. His arrest record read like a man on a mission to sink his own ship.

Last night Morgan was picked up on the beach by the MPs for public intoxication and disturbing the peace, and he popped positive for painkillers during the surprise test Hawk ordered the week before.

Yazzie couldn't ignore a SEAL who was taking drugs on active duty. Their training was dangerous at the best of times, and without a clear head he was a deadly fuckup waiting to happen.

But he wanted to speak with the man before he canned him. The Navy spent a million dollars training this SEAL, and he was an asset until Hawk made the call.

Grabbing the phone, he pushed the button to instruct his admin to allow the man waiting in the reception area to come in.

A few seconds later a quick tap came at the door and it swung open. Seaman Morgan strode into the room and came to stand at attention in front of his desk. Morgan was broad, muscular, and looked as tough as a stone wall. But even the toughest could have their weaknesses. And the one-two punch Morgan sustained during his last deployment and then when he got home were probably responsible for the chink in the wall. But the man wasn't dealing with it.

"At ease. Take a seat, Seaman."

Hawk allowed the silence to seep in while taking in the man's appearance. His uniform was pressed, but his bloodshot eyes attested to either little sleep or a hangover. His broad face showed no emotion. "You already know why I've called you in, Morgan. You tested positive for drugs last week." He looked down at the file he'd already scanned three times. "Pain meds." He'd already talked to Carlson, Alpha team's team leader. Morgan had shown no signs of an injury. "Did you sustain an injury while training?"

"I strained my shoulder. I had some pills left over from an injury I had last year and took some of them."

Hawk could spot the lie a mile off, but he did believe the man was in pain. "Did you go to medical and have it looked at?"

"No, sir."

"If your shoulder's painful enough that you're self-medicating, you need to have it looked at. When you leave here, I want you to go straight to the hospital and have it examined. You're off duty until the doctor has released you."

Hawk turned a page in the SEAL's file. "Your CO told me he suggested you get some counseling."

"I don't find the sessions helpful, sir." The man's jaw clenched and released.

Hawk closed Morgan's file. "I know counseling is a pain in the ass. But you only get out of it what you put in."

Morgan raised his head to actually look at him. "Have you gone, sir?"

"Yes, I have. My mother died while I was deployed. Breast cancer. She never let me know how bad she was... until it was too late. I carried around a lot of guilt because I thought I should have been here with her, for her. She was the only family I had. Talking about it doesn't change what happened, but it helps you release some of the pain so you can learn to live with it."

Hawk picked up the paperweight on his desk and turned it in his fingers. "I've lost men under my command, lost friends, too, Morgan. Too many. I have a list that I try not to take out, but every so often when something triggers a memory…

"You won't forget, but eventually you'll learn to remember the good times and not so much of the bad."

He set aside the paperweight. "As for your other issue. Have you contacted legal services?"

"My wife served me with divorce papers last week."

About the time of the drunk and disorderly. Dammit. Where were his teammates? Had something happened that caused them to keep their distance?

"I'm sorry to hear that." How would he feel if Zoe left him? He couldn't imagine. She was his rock.

He had to ask. "Do you want to remain a SEAL, Morgan?"

"It's all I have left, sir."

That wasn't the answer he wanted to hear.

"Contact legal services and see what can be done about the drunk and disorderly. Be candid with them about your situation. They may be able to plea it down to disturbing the peace." Lieutenant Carlson, Morgan's team leader, mentioned his soon to be ex-wife had cleaned their apartment out and left Morgan only a bed, a microwave, and his clothes. Jesus! "Legal may be able to get some of your personal belongings returned."

"I don't need or want them."

Hawk would probably feel the same. "If you really want to stay in the teams, Morgan, you can't fail another drug test. You can't get arrested for public intoxication. And you have to be at your best during training. What we do is too dangerous to expect any less. I'm giving you an opportunity to walk all those things back. But this will be your only opportunity."

He closed Morgan's file. "I expect to hear that you're attending counseling sessions. I'll revisit this with you next week."

Morgan rose and stood at attention though his mouth was tight and sulky "Thank you, sir." He didn't sound grateful, and was only offering grudging respect.

Hawk controlled his reaction with an effort. He wouldn't make any more allowances.

"This is the only chance you'll get, Morgan. You blow it,

you're gone." He nodded. "Dismissed."

The man strode to the door and out.

Hawk ran a hand over his close-cropped hair. At least he'd taken the SEAL out of the field and lowered the risk of a dangerous fuckup. He called Morgan's Team leader to inform him of Morgan's change in duty.

"I appreciate the effort, sir."

"How long has he been using?"

"I don't know, but I suspect at least a month. I talked to him several times and partnered him with one of the men I trust to keep an eye on him. My hope was he'd pull himself together."

"Has he suffered an injury that could call for pain medication?"

"Not a physical one that I'm aware of." Carlson paused. "Our last deployment... Bravo company lost Seaman Marsh. Marsh and he were tight, had been since high school. They joined the Navy and made the teams together. And when we got back, Morgan's apartment was cleaned out and his wife had left."

Hawk bit back a graphic expletive. He rose and moved to the window until he got himself under control. The guidelines were if a SEAL popped positive, they were out. But this man had taken two big hits in a matter of weeks. "Will he agree to treatment?"

"He was resistant to it when I encouraged him to go."

He'd agree to treatment or Hawk would pass him on for a dishonorable discharge.

"He's been a valuable part of my team, sir. We've all been through several deployments together. I hoped we could turn this thing around. But the loss of Seaman Marsh and this thing with his wife, Tonya, has kicked him hard, sir."

"Has he had any contact with her since she left?"

Carlson shook his head. "She avoided dealing with the fallout and slunk off before we got back. As far as I know, he has no idea where she is."

"I expect you to stay apprised of what's happening with him, Lieutenant Carlson. If he doesn't follow through, let me know." At that point, Hawk would have no choice but to notify command of the man's instability and they'd discharge him for the failed drug test.

After ending the call, he took a moment to forward the drug results to Master Chief Langley Marks along with a summary of everything he and both Carlson and Morgan discussed. Langley kept his finger on the pulse of all personnel, so he might have a suggestion.

Hawk rolled his neck to ease the knotted tension. Zoe had magic hands. He'd get her to massage it when he got home and maybe he could return the favor with a little more than a rub-down. The idea sent blood rushing to areas he didn't have time to think about.

Taking note of the time, he gathered his duffle. "I'm going for my run, Ensign Reins."

He refused to allow the desk part of his duty to affect his effectiveness as a SEAL. Even at his age he might return to action. Five miles in thirty minutes every day kept him in pretty good shape, with an obstacle course thrown in six or seven times a month. And the set of weights in his workout room picked up any slack.

"Your next appointment isn't until two, sir."

"Thanks, Evan." He changed into his running shorts and T-shirt in his office, stretched and loosened up, and went outside to the parking lot. He shoved his sunglasses on to mute the glare of the noonday sun, and, starting out slow, jogged down over the dunes and onto the beach. A crisp breeze rolled in off the ocean, cooling the air and drying the sweat on his skin.

The sand dragged at his feet and worked his leg muscles until the burn turned into the euphoric numbness that allowed him to keep going without issue. The thirty-minute run burned away some of the stress from the morning appointments, but as much as he tried to turn loose of it all, Morgan's situation kept interrupting.

Over the years he'd dealt with numerous issues involving the men in his team, and now in the platoons he supervised. It never got any easier, and it always brought back the last time he saw

Derrick Armstrong, when Derrick tried to kill his girlfriend Marjorie, as well as Zoe and her brother, Brett.

Hawk and his team managed to disarm him and turned him over to the military police.

Derrick had turned his life around, but he'd gone to prison to do it. And as hard as Hawk tried to write the man off, he occasionally drove by the garage Derrick managed to see how he was doing. He was a good SEAL until he wasn't, but then he became dangerous.

Was Morgan headed in the same direction?

Hawk hoped not.

He came up on a group of SEAL Trainees doing log PT on the right. The instructors' voices carried to him as they called out equal parts harassment and encouragement. A mile down the beach another group ran in the same direction. He fell in behind them for a moment before digging in and looping around. The burn in his thighs and calves turned to an easy heat.

Hawk turned toward one of the sidewalks off the beach. He followed it to the main road, then turned back to return to his office. Reaching the side door, he paused to walk back and forth to cool down.

Ensign Reins opened the door and offered him a Gatorade and a towel.

"Ryan, you must have X-ray vision."

"Secrets of the trade of being an admin, sir."

Hawk laughed. "Thanks, I'll be in after I've stretched."

"You still have an hour, sir." Ensign Reins closed the door.

Lieutenant Sam Harding, the Bravo Team leader, came around the corner and strode toward him. Sam had an intensity and focus that showed up in nearly everything he did. The only time Hawk had seen him relaxed was with his girlfriend, Moira.

"Lieutenant Commander. We have a problem with some of our training equipment. I put in a requisition, but haven't heard anything, and it's been nearly six weeks."

"Email me the requisition and I'll take care of it."

"Thank you, sir."

Maintaining access to the equipment the men needed to train with was a major part of Hawk's job. One he found irritating.

He braced a foot against the wall and stretched to keep his muscles from cramping.

"Lieutenant Carlson and I have discussed Seaman Morgan's situation, sir. If there's any way I can help...Seaman Marsh was a good SEAL. He had wit and used it to lighten the situation when things became...intense. All the guys liked him." Sam's expression remained composed, but his eyes shifted away.

Hawk straightened. "Your team has gone through some tough transitions in the past year too, Sam. With Book's accident, Rosenburg's transfer, and now Marsh's death."

"I've spoken to my team and thought maybe some of my guys could reach out to Seaman Morgan. Maybe knowing he isn't alone in this might help."

"That's a generous offer, Sam. And a good idea. Make it happen as soon as you can."

"Will do, sir." He saluted and had taken a step away when he turned back. "Moira and I are getting married, sir."

Hawk straightened and smiled at the same time, then offered his hand. "Congratulations! You're a lucky man, Sam. She has beauty and talent all wrapped up in one smart package."

Sam's smile widened. "She does. And her family has been great."

"That's always a plus. Good in-laws are an asset." Clara, Zoe's mother, treated Hawk with as much affection and unconditional love as she did her own children. "Zoe and I went to the gallery in Little Italy to see Moira's work. It was amazing."

Sam looked like a man in love when he said, "She's sold six paintings there, and they've asked for more."

"I'm not surprised. Think she'll give up her teaching job to paint full-time?"

"I think she's a little wary of taking that final step and cutting ties. The teaching gig is a steady paycheck while selling her artwork can be feast or famine. But it's her dream to make a name for herself."

"What about an artist-in-residence program? If she did one of those, it would subsidize her income and allow her to paint full time on the side."

"There's some travel involved, and right now she's staying close to home, trying to plan the wedding. You probably don't know this, but you were partly responsible for helping her take that final step to submitting some of her paintings to the gallery. Your reaction to the painting of your wife, and what you said about it, meant a great deal to her."

"Everyone who sees it is amazed. Zoe was stunned." And he'd reaped very personal rewards for the anniversary gift. "I wish you both the very best."

"Thank you, sir."

The door opened and Master Chief Langley Marks stepped out. He and Harding exchanged salutes. "Your admin told me where to find you, Lieutenant Commander."

Harding nodded to them both. "Thanks for the help with the equipment, sir."

"I'll do my best," Hawk said.

The two of them watched Harding walk away. "Problem?" Hawk asked.

"No. Just thought I'd come by and talk to you about Morgan." Langley was creeping up on his twenty-fourth year with the Special Warfare Command, and he knew more about personnel than anyone else on the base. It was his job to.

"What did you find out?"

"Yeah. The guy got a raw deal, but there may be more to it than meets the eye. He was showing some ragged edges before this last deployment."

He experienced a déjà vu moment with that one. "What kind of ragged edges?"

"The marriage was rocky, and there were some disturbances at the home. The wife may have been justified in leaving."

"He's not stalking her, though, because he doesn't know where she is."

"No. His duty has kept him here on base."

And he had just given him sick leave. *Shit! I should have listened to my instincts!*

"You and I both know how hard it is to hold a marriage together under the strain of training and deployment schedules," Langley said.

"Roger that."

"By the Grace of God," Langley murmured. They nodded in unison.

Hawk twisted off the top to the Gatorade bottle and took a deep drink. "He popped positive for painkillers this week. Said he strained his shoulder and took some pills he had left over from another injury. I didn't believe him and sent him to the hospital to have the shoulder examined."

"If the doc doesn't release him back to active duty..." Langley said.

Hawk ran fingers through his sweat-dampened hair. "I won't have another Armstrong on my watch."

"Even if you charged him, he'd still be relieved of duty and have an opportunity to respond." Langley's lantern jaw clenched. "And that would give him time to take action against the wife if he's leaning that way."

So, it was a catch-22 situation. "Damn it! I'll send him on an off-duty training to keep him under observation until I know for certain what's going on. It'll keep him here on post, but out of the field." Hawk glanced at his watch. "I'll have Ensign Reins type up the orders and send them out via email and text this afternoon."

Langley's heavy, expressive brows rose. "That...just might work. I'll mosey back to my office and email you the list of available trainings."

"Mosey... Really?" Hawk said with a bark of laughter.

"I save my five-mile runs for the weekends while I'm charging up and down the basketball court with Tad. He's running rings around me."

"Because he's four inches taller."

"Yeah. And a hell of a lot younger. He's filling out college applications now, Hawk."

"You didn't really expect him to stay home with you and Trish forever, did you?"

"God, no!"

Hawk laughed.

"And the rest of the time I'm scaring boys away from Anna. She's fifteen going on twenty."

Hawk chuckled.

"Yeah, go ahead and laugh. When you have a boy, you only have to worry about where one hormone-crazed pecker is going. When you have girls, you have to worry about them all."

Hawk laughed. "Anna is too much like Trish to put up with any hormone-crazed anything. She'll tie a knot in it and send it on its way."

"Jess is a little more tender-hearted. That worries me *a lot*. And she's thirteen."

"She has a brother. She knows boys. She may not be as gullible as you think. Besides, you've got Trish as backup. She'll chop up any little pissants who nose around her girls and feed them to the fishes."

Langley's grin flashed. "Yeah. Ain't that the truth... Thank God."

Hawk glanced at his watch. "Ooops. Gotta go. I have another meeting in thirty minutes and I have to shower."

"I'll forward that list to you as soon as I get back to my office."

"Thanks."

ZOE FOLLOWED SEAMAN Kevin Chalmers as he walked the few steps to the therapy table. SEALs weren't the most patient convalescents. Living with Hawk gave her an insight into the young SEAL, but she couldn't help Chalmers heal more quickly than his body would allow. If the man pushed too hard, he might do more damage to an already-fractured hip.

"Seaman Chalmers, take a seat on the table."

Zoe grasped his gait belt and steadied him. The man out-weighed her by a hundred pounds, but he only needed a small redirection as he shifted his weight from the injured side to the other.

As soon as he stepped up on the bench and planted his ass on the therapy table, he focused on her with fierce attention.

Zoe picked up the clipboard she'd left on the table with Chalmers's therapy plans. "I'm Zoe Yazzie. I'll be working with you throughout your therapy."

He tipped his head to her. "Ma'am."

She flipped the top sheet over, pulled free the pen fastened at the top, and drew a side view of a male body.

Leaning back against the table next to him, she said, "I need to give you an anatomy lesson."

He raised one brown brow that nearly disappeared into the out-of-control curls hanging over his forehead. "Okay." He had a sculpted beard, but he'd let his hair grow, giving him a wholesome farm boy look.

She darkened the bottom of the hip area of her drawing. "This is the pelvic floor." She went through the position of each organ and how the injury he sustained could affect each of them if he rushed the healing process and did more damage. When she said the words incontinence and impotence, his smirk quickly transitioned into clamp-jawed, laser focus.

"You'll get back to top physical shape and move on with your team, Kevin. May I call you Kevin?"

"Yes, ma'am."

"You can't push through the pain with this. You have to listen to the pain, pace yourself, and let your body tell you when it's ready."

She paused to search his young face. "I have a plan that's go-ing to get you back to where you were before this ever happened, but it's going to take a couple of months at least. You'll need to turn all that SEAL determination toward healing and forget about being the Superman all you guys think you are."

Arnold's smile grew cocky and he chuckled. "How many

SEALs have you treated?"

"In the nine years I've worked at this hospital, twenty counting you." Twenty-two if she counted her brother and husband.

"How many went back to their teams?"

"Seventeen. Three had to move on because they weren't able to recover completely."

"Because?" he pushed.

"Two lost legs during deployment and one was paralyzed from the waist down from an accident, but by the time all three left me, they were physically and emotionally ready to move on."

"Not a bad record as percentages go. What about your leg?"

She was used to patients asking about her injury. "I was seven when a drunk driver ran over me while I was riding my bicycle. It took numerous surgeries, skin grafts, and nearly a year of physical therapy to learn how to walk again."

"Shit," Chalmers breathed. He fell silent for a moment. "If you can take a year of it at age seven, I can do a couple of months."

She smiled, relieved. "Let's get started. I need you to lie down on your back on the table. Move slowly, and I'll help you raise your legs."

Their hour passed very quickly, and she paused to give him a chance to relax before helping him sit up and giving him the packet from his folder on her clipboard. It contained printed step-by-step directions so he could continue the exercises at home.

"Today wasn't bad," Chalmers said.

"We're just starting, first building up your muscles around the injury to protect it and head off any complications. Should you have signs of any unusual pain or any of the complications I laid out for you, contact your physician and come in."

"Roger that."

"And don't overdo the exercises. We're going to start with three times a day for the first five days, then move them up to five times a day. These are going to be a walk in the park compared to what you're used to, but that doesn't mean you should rush things."

"Roger that. See you on Thursday." He offered his fist and she smiled as she met it with her own.

Tank, one of the physical therapy aides, wove around tables to bring up the wheelchair. The man fit his nickname. He was six foot six, two hundred fifty pounds of muscle, and could help lift large patients as if they were babies. He also knew when hands off worked better, and allowed Seaman Chalmers to maneuver into the wheelchair on his own.

Zoe gathered her paperwork and turned toward the office.

"Hey, Zoe," Chalmers called.

She turned back to look over her shoulder. "You any relation to Lieutenant Commander Yazzie?"

"He's my husband."

"Dodged a bullet. I couldn't figure out how to ask you out while you were telling me how to squeeze my ass cheeks together so I don't break wind."

Tank's deep hoot of laughter blended with her own.

Zoe pointed a playful finger at him. "The women you date after this will thank me for that."

Kevin laughed and threw up a hand. Tank wheeled him out of the unit.

Zoe was still chuckling as she went into her office, settled behind her desk, and pulled up the schedule for the next few days. Elizabeth wouldn't be back for another month, she wouldn't see Holly for two more weeks, and the triple duty she'd been doing for the last two months was wearing her down.

She'd interviewed several physical therapists to fill the two spots temporarily, but they'd all been looking for full-time positions or were searching for placement to work on their residency to finish their accreditation. She couldn't take on the extra paperwork or work along with them and still accomplish everything else.

Glancing at her watch, Zoe shut down the computer, turned off her desk light, gathered her purse and lunch bag, and left the office. The other therapists were either already gone or finishing up with their last appointment of the day. She raised a hand to wave good night to Norma Gannon, and passed Tank coming back from taking Seaman Chalmers to his transportation.

"They get younger and younger every day, and they still hit on you," Tank commented with a grin that flashed white in his broad, handsome face.

Zoe shook her head. "It's a reflex, like someone hitting them on the knee with a rubber hammer. I'm touching them, nurturing them, and they're drawn to me because I make their pain go away, like their mothers did when they were children."

Tank shook his head. "You're getting better with age, Doc."

Zoe laughed. "I'll tell Hawk you said that."

"I know what I'm talking about. Thirties are a woman's best years. Just ask my Rosa, she says she's strutting her stuff until she throws out a hip."

Zoe laughed again. "We're done here tonight. Go home to her and the kids and have a good night."

"You too."

She wove her way through the hospital, caught an elevator to the maternity wing, and entered the locker room to stow her purse and lunch bag. Fifteen minutes later, dressed in a sterile gown, gloves, mask and a hair cover, Zoe tapped on the door to the nursery.

Head nurse Shelley Abrams opened the door. Her dark, curly bundle of hair was barely contained by the hair cover, and her eyes shone with a smile above her mask. "She's waiting for you."

Zoe shook her head. "She isn't old enough to know who I am."

"Sure she is. She recognizes the sound of your voice. She's waiting for her bottle." Shelley handed it to Zoe.

"I'd better not keep her waiting."

A row of bassinettes sat before the viewing window. Zoe scanned each one briefly, pausing to eye the biggest baby, nearly nine pounds, and winced in sympathy for the mother. Had she carried A. J. to term, he might have been larger, since Hawk was a very big man. As it was, A. J. was in the 90th percentile for his height and weight. At ten he was almost as tall as she was. Though he was affectionate, he no longer let her cuddle him. And when she dropped him off at school each morning he leaped out with a, "Later, Mom," instead of the quick kiss he gave her through preschool and kindergarten and even first grade.

The last bassinette held the smallest baby. Five pounds, two ounces, and eighteen inches long, she'd fit in a shoebox. Her cry sounded like the mew of a kitten.

She was Lily. The name suited her. Her fair skin looked as soft as the petals of the flower she was named for. Her small mouth puckered pink as a rosebud. Dark hair clung to her scalp.

"Hello, Lily," Zoe breathed softly as she scooped the baby up and cradled her close. A burst of longing almost brought tears to her eyes. She'd thought volunteering to help feed the babies each afternoon would somehow ease that longing and stymie it. It hadn't worked. If anything, it strengthened the need.

She settled into one of the three rockers, removed the protective cap on the bottle, and offered the nipple to Lily. The baby latched on and her jaws worked, getting the milk flowing.

Zoe remembered the feeling of having a baby nurse from her own breasts. She'd never felt so close to another human being. It had seemed so natural, so perfect, to hold A. J.'s tiny body in her arms and nourish him with her milk.

A. J. was growing up, becoming more independent every day. And he seemed closer to Hawk now than to her. It hurt. But the same time, she didn't begrudge Hawk the bond they built between them. She was grateful he had a father who spent time with him, teaching him things, talking to him, guiding him toward becoming a respectful, responsible person.

But at the same time she felt she'd been sidelined. She was only a backup when A. J. needed something Hawk couldn't provide. Clean clothes, his lunch, new shoes, a ride to a friend's house. She'd been relegated to a taxi service and a maid while Hawk did the fun stuff.

She asked herself countless times if A. J. pulling away was what had given birth to these longings for another baby. And she just didn't know. It was certain to have played a part in it—as well as the fact she was going to be thirty-five in a few months.

If she was going to have another child, she needed to do it now, while she still had enough energy to enjoy the experience. Hawk would be forty in a few months, and she could only guess what he'd say about this baby idea. He'd freaked out when she gave birth to A. J. because of the precipitous labor. But that happened ten years ago, and there was no guarantee her labor would be like that again.

She'd love to have a baby girl like Lily. She lifted the baby to her shoulder and rubbed her back, then patted it, and was rewarded with a burp. She eased Lily back into position and urged her to finish the last ounce of formula.

Even after Lily was finished eating, Zoe continued to cuddle her for a few minutes, then eased her into her bassinette, sound asleep.

She wanted another baby. She needed to feel Hawk out and see if he was open to them having another. And if he wasn't...she'd try to convince him.

CHAPTER 2

HAWK PUSHED HIS concerns about Seaman Owen Morgan's issues to the back of his mind as he pulled into the driveway. He hit the button to raise the garage door, drove his black SUV inside, and frowned as he eyed the empty space where Zoe always parked. She'd been getting home late for the past month. No, it had been six weeks.

She should have hired someone to take on the added patients instead of dividing them among the therapists she already had, then taking the overflow herself. He worried that she pushed herself too hard. It was the one thing he always worried about— and the one thing she continued to do. Damn it.

He'd made it to the mudroom door before the right garage door rose and her car nosed into the space, so he waited to see if she needed any help carrying things in.

"A. J. decided he wanted to stay with Russell and Mom and have pizza," Zoe said as she exited the car. "I got us Chinese."

Excellent. He could use some alone time with Zoe. He bounded down the steps and went to the car to get the bags.

When they entered the kitchen, she placed the thermal lunch bag on the kitchen counter where she left it every day. "I'll be right back. I have to pull off these clothes and put on something comfortable."

"How about I help with that?" His fingers were already unfastening the buttons of his uniform shirt before she turned to look over her shoulder.

Her smile sent a rush of blood south and he hardened in a nanosecond.

"A. J. isn't here. We don't have to be quiet."

"Yeah." He knew he was grinning like a fool.

Her limp didn't hinder the sway of her hips as she led the way down the hall to their bedroom. She shucked her blouse just inside the door and dropped it on the floor.

Hawk unhooked her bra with practiced ease. She shimmied it down her arms and let it fall. From behind, he cupped her breasts, full and firm, while he found the sensitive spot between her shoulder and neck with his teeth. She shivered and her nipples beaded beneath his touch.

Zoe reached back to run her hands down his thighs while she pressed back against him.

"I've been thinking about this all day," Hawk murmured against her ear.

"I'm so glad you have." She turned to face him and yanked his T-shirt up to his armpits, planting a kiss right where his heart beat strong and fast.

Hawk bailed out of it and tossed it atop her blouse. She opened his brass belt buckle and tugged the khaki-colored belt free.

He kissed her, teased her tongue into his mouth, and sucked. Zoe hummed her pleasure and tiptoed to align her body with his.

They grappled with each other's remaining clothes and tumbled onto the bed, skin-to-skin, their mouths melded. Zoe raised her hips against him, her hands roaming down his back to cup his ass. He thrust inside her, and she made the sound somewhere between a sigh and a moan that drove him crazy every time.

Even after ten years, every time they made love there was a lightning-hot connection that ricocheted between them. They were two puzzle pieces that fit together perfectly. Just touching her stripped away everything but his need to have her.

The way she moved beneath him, the breathless sounds she

made while their bodies strained close, then receded, the love he read in her eyes, drove him closer to release. He lost himself in her ardent response to his touch, his kisses, until his own need overwhelmed him, and his thrust became hard and quick, driving her up and over. Her hips jerked as she climaxed, throwing him into his own.

For long, sweet moments they lay entwined as their breathing and hearts settled. Zoe's fingers stroked his hair, then kneaded the back of his neck, making him realize the stress knotting his back and neck had disappeared as soon as they came together.

"We need to take a few days soon and go somewhere, just the two of us. We haven't done that in at least a year," he said.

"I'll need at least a month, until Elizabeth and Holly are back. Then I can schedule some days off."

He moved to lie beside her and tucked her in close against his side. He needed to broach the subject of her working too much with an easy touch. If he came on too hard, Zoe would blow up at him. She was stubborn as hell. "You're working longer hours."

"Some. But it's not for much longer. One of the girls will be back in a couple of weeks, and the other within a month. I'll be giving them any new cases that come in, and then gradually transition over a few other clients to them. I have another patient close to finishing his therapy, and he'll be moving on, too."

"Good."

She ran a caressing hand over his bare chest. "I'm okay, Adam."

The fact that she called him by his given name instead of Hawk reassured him. From the start of their relationship, she always called him Adam when she was adamant about something.

He pressed his lips to her forehead.

"I've been a little late recently, not because of the added work, but because I've been going up to the nursery at the hospital and feeding some of the babies after my shift."

"Are they shorthanded?"

"No." She fell silent for a beat then two. "I miss having a little one around the house. A. J. isn't a baby anymore."

Words wouldn't come. *Whoa! Where is this coming from?*

He lifted back the long, hazelnut-streaked hair over her shoulder to better study her expression. "A. J. is ten, Zoe."

"Yes. I know. I'm ready to eat, aren't you?" She slid off the bed. The scars on her buttocks from the skin grafts done to cover the damage to her leg gave her ass an interesting topography. He knew the sight and feel of those scars as thoroughly as he did the rest of her. He'd grown so accustomed to them, in fact, he rarely noticed anymore. They were just another part of Zoe.

But as she moved about the room gathering clothes to put on, he studied his wife's slender body. Her shoulders were narrow, her breasts full and high, her waist trim, and her thighs well-toned. But the damaged muscle of her right calf gave her gait an unbalanced limp.

She worked hard to keep the muscles of her injured leg flexible and strong so she wouldn't have to wear her brace, but there were times she had to wear it even though she hated it. In the nine years and change they'd been married, she'd never allowed the injury to hold her back from anything she truly wanted to do.

Physically, despite her disability, there was nothing that would prevent her from having another baby...except his lack of cooperation.

He thought of half a dozen questions he could ask her, but was wary of voicing them. Ten years between kids... He was only a few months away from his fortieth birthday.

She disappeared into the bathroom with her clothes.

With a sigh he rolled out of the bed and fished around in his drawers for underwear, T-shirt, and khaki shorts, and got dressed.

By the time she joined him in the kitchen, she'd changed into a tank top and a pair of shorts. She smiled as she accepted the glass of white wine with a sigh and took a sip, then set it down while she opened the containers of Chinese food and he set the table.

He filled his plate with fried rice, moo goo gai pan, egg rolls, and some fried wontons filled with pork and mushrooms. She'd included all his favorites...a subtle thing, but one he recognized.

She filled her own plate and took a seat while he heated his food in the microwave.

How she could eat everything at room temperature was beyond him.

"How'd your day go?" she asked while they ate.

"It all runs together."

"Mine does too." She reached for her wine glass and took a drink. "You don't have to be in a panic or anything. I haven't gone off my birth control," she said, then bit into an eggroll.

"I didn't think you would until you discussed it with me."

"I'll be thirty-five in a couple of months, and if I'm going to have another baby, I need to do it soon."

He'd been deployed to Iraq and then Afghanistan while Zoe was pregnant with A. J., and he barely made it home for A. J.'s birth. They'd been through eleven deployments to places south and east since then, part of the reason they hadn't had another child. And now A. J. was older, and required less constant care, but he was still a little boy and needed steady supervision.

"You haven't asked A. J. how he'd feel about having a baby brother or sister."

"No. But I'm sure it will be an adjustment. He's been our baby for ten years. He'll continue to be our baby for the rest of his life."

He caught the word *will* and let it pass. "Don't call him a baby in front of him. He thinks he's already a grown-up."

"He wants to be just like you, just like every boy who has a good father. Brett was like that with my dad, too."

"And you feel left out."

"Sometimes."

"That isn't a reason to have a baby."

"No." She remained silent for a moment. "There's just something missing."

Those few words hit him like a punch.

Something in his expression must have alerted her to his reaction, because she rushed to say, "Not between us, Adam, but... It's hard to explain. When I'm holding the babies, feeding them. I feel like a piece slides into place and I'm doing what I'm supposed to do. There's this small baby girl, Lily. Her mother had to deliver via C-section and she's had a hard time of it, so I've given Lily her evening feeding the past four days. They'll be sending her and her mom home tomorrow."

She bit her lip. "She's so tiny and helpless and sweet." The light of tenderness and pleasure in her face hit him like a slap. She was really serious about this. Why hadn't she said something before? Like five years before.

"This is a lot to take in, Zoe. I didn't know you were even interested in having another baby."

"Every time I thought about it, the timing wasn't exactly right." She looked away.

That was a euphemism for he hadn't been home. She'd been here, raising A. J. alone.

They ate in silence for a few minutes.

"I'm a little old for this."

"Men don't really have a biological clock to worry about. You could father a child when you're seventy."

"I'd like to think I'll still be up for things at that age." He gave her a thumbs-up that triggered her grin. "But grandfather will be the speed I'll be moving at by then."

"By then we'll both be enjoying grandchildren, hopefully."

The feeling that he'd failed Zoe settled in the pit of his stomach. But feeling guilty was no reason to agree to another baby.

If he said no, they'd circle it several times, but she'd let it go because she loved him. But would the fact that he denied her something this important stand between them? If he said yes and got deployed again, or transferred to another job that required him to travel... Damn it.

And A. J. was so much less work now. No bottles, no diapers, just feed the kid, play ball with him, or take him fishing, take him to the ball field for his practices and games, play a few video games, spend time with him... No car seats that took an engineer to install, no walking the floors, no whining—or not much.

They'd be starting all over again. He missed a lot of it before.

A. J.'s first step, his first tooth, his first day of first grade. Baby shots, school open houses, teacher conferences, doctor appointments... All the shit details had fallen to Zoe...who took care of it all without complaint.

Which made saying no even harder.

"Do we know anyone with little ones anymore?" he asked.

"Well, we had a little experience with Tess and Brett's twins."

"If you'd ever told me that Tess would take a leave of absence to have a baby, I'd have said you were crazy. You might have to do that too." Which would mean less money coming in. They were doing fine right now, but a hit that large to the budget...

"You mentioned Eric and Rylie Anderson to me the other day," Zoe said.

"Yeah. Jesus! They're so young."

Zoe laughed. "We were once that young too." She folded her fingers over his. "We're not exactly on our last legs. Tank says women in their thirties are at their best."

Thanks, Tank. Hawk met her gaze. "Rylie didn't tell Eric she was pregnant until he got home. She had the baby his first day back."

"That sounds familiar."

"Yeah, I had a déjà vu moment or two when I heard about it. But then I already knew you were pregnant. I just wasn't prepared for labor and fatherhood within hours of hitting the tarmac."

"I imagine Petty Officer Anderson felt the same way. I've never held anything back from you since then."

She hadn't. A. J.'s hospitalization with pneumonia at age two. A fender bender in the parking lot of a grocery store. A number of medical things that had happened while he was away. And all the other inconsequential things that tied him to home in ways she would never understand. Or maybe she did and that's why she shared them.

Zoe rose to put her plate in the dishwasher, then paused beside his chair to slide her arms around his neck from behind. "The chances I'd have labor that fast again are slim. Just think about how fantastic it would be to have a baby in the house." She pressed a kiss to his cheek, then reached for her glass and wandered out into the sunroom.

Hawk finished eating, put his plate in the dishwasher, and poured more wine, sipping while he gazed at the porch doorway. How many doors had he breached with his team during deployments? He'd never counted. He'd never allowed fear to creep in before he led the way. But damn, he was sure as shit wary of walking through that door after her.

He wandered into the sunroom, sat down beside her, and raised his arm to loop it around her shoulders. She slid in close against his side. They sipped their wine. He breathed in the scent of apple shampoo and the floral fragrance that lingered on her skin.

He wasn't too old to father a baby, but he didn't feel young enough to raise one. He'd be fifty before he/she would be A. J.'s age. "I need to think about it for a while."

She looked up at him, and her pale blue eyes held a cautious hope. "Okay."

Guilt gave him a hard pinch. For the first time in their marriage, he just lied to her.

CHAPTER 3

T HE PAINTING WAS a mesh of color and bold strokes that pulsed with life.

Moira rarely painted abstract compositions, but when she did, her style stood out boldly, distinctively. Sam didn't understand how she did it, but he'd have recognized her work anywhere. He had zero artistic talent, but he appreciated hers more and more the longer they were together. and was often awed by it.

He waited for her to set aside her brush before stepping into the room.

"What do you see?" she asked without turning.

He edged in close enough that he could feel the heat from her body and smell the spicy scent of jasmine clinging to her skin, but didn't touch her. Instead he focused on the painting.

It was more than color. The bold strokes he'd seen from over her shoulder were only part of the story depicted on the canvas. It was a portrait, but she'd manipulated the paint in such a way that it dipped and swirled in heavy patches, following the contours of the features with so much movement that it invited the viewer to sink into the color.

Suddenly the face snapped into focus.

"It's Mom. And it looks just like her, but I don't know how you've done it. It's—damn amazing." He rested his hands on her hips, and she relaxed back against him lightly.

"I did a drawing of her, then created a stencil from a sheet of heavy acetate. Took me freaking *hours*."

He grinned at her intensity.

"Then I put the stencil on the canvas and used a spatula to apply texture paste over it to force it into the areas I'd cut. Then I peeled the stencil away, let the paste dry, and added color."

She had the patience of Job. Good thing, since he often tested it.

She was a contrast in color and texture herself. Her coarse, curly, bright red hair could rarely be tamed without the help of a flat iron. Highlights as vibrant as a new copper penny shot through it and flamed against her pale skin. He was moved to explore both, and rested a cheek against her hair while he dipped his head to capture one delicate earlobe between his lips.

She shivered and turned to look up at him. Her blue-green gaze was lit with amusement. "We have to meet your mother in a little more than an hour, and I still have to clean up in here and change."

"It's closer to two hours, and there's time." He worked a hand beneath her extra-large T-shirt to cup her breast, delighted to find she'd already discarded her bra. He toyed with her nipple while he kissed her, his lips and tongue tempting hers, promising fulfillment, then drawing back. Their bodies strained against each other, and he planted a hand against her ass to hold her tight against his erection.

Her cheeks were flushed a berry red when he raised his head. "Still think we don't have time for this?"

"We'd better make it quick." She dragged his mouth back to hers while he chuckled beneath the kiss.

She had a mischievous gleam in her eye as she tugged him toward the bedroom, and they'd barely crossed the threshold when he peeled her oversized T-shirt up and away, then urged her down on the bed. In a quick rush of tenderness, he captured one rose-tinted nipple in his mouth and sucked.

Moira caressed the back of his neck with one hand while she held him close with the other arm.

He slipped a hand beneath the waistband of her leggings and found her with his fingertips.

She murmured his name, her voice somewhere between a whisper and a moan.

He tempted and teased her until she rolled her hips and gripped his wrist. He thrust two fingers inside her, and capturing the rhythm of her movements, drove her over the edge into release.

As she lay still in the afterglow, he dragged her leggings down, bailed out of his clothes, and entered her with a slow, easy thrust. The love and desire he read in her face brought his lips back to hers. Her hands glided over his skin as she rose to meet him in a slow, seductive dance. He tasted her throat, and her jasmine fragrance, light and spicy, filled his head.

Moira slid a hand between them and cupped his balls, then touched him where their bodies fit together. He grew hard as stone and his thrusts became frantic, deep, as he raced toward climax.

"You did that on purpose," he accused moments later as he rested his head on her breast.

"I love that you lose control with me, because you're always in control of everything else."

His thoughts went to Seaman Marsh. No matter how he looked at it, there was no way he could have prevented the man's death. But he still felt responsible.

Members of a drug cartel had ambushed them. The bullet hit Marsh in the armpit, an area body armor failed to cover, but no matter how hard he tried to put the man's death away, it wasn't working.

He hadn't spoken to Moira about it. He'd just gotten back from a four-month long deployment, and he didn't want her questioning his ability to handle any situation. He wanted her to feel secure. To believe he'd always be there for her. But the truth was, he couldn't be, and there was always the possibility that he wouldn't be.

Did she realize that?

Being so involved with her school had insulated her from a lot of the military things she'd become a part of once they were married. She'd be using military hospitals, military medical insurance, she'd have to be issued a military ID to give her access to the PX.

"We need to get dressed. Your mother and brother are expecting us for dinner."

"All my mother will want to talk about is wedding plans," he commented.

"I think we're a disappointment to both our parents since we just want something small and simple."

Sam lifted his head to look at her. "If you want something larger, Moira…"

"No." She cut him off with a finger against his lips. "I don't."

He kissed her fingers. "Then don't let them talk you into anything you don't want. You don't need to please them. It isn't their wedding. It's ours."

"You want your team there, don't you?"

"Yeah. I do." But Marsh wouldn't be there. And though she'd only met him a couple of times, she'd notice. He needed to tell her.

"About the…"

"Oh, shit, we're going to be late, Sam." She scrambled out from under him and pushed free of the tangled bedclothes.

He glanced at the clock. Shit. She was right.

IT ISN'T THEIR *wedding. It's ours.* Moira kept repeating the mantra all the way through dinner, because the subject of invitations for the wedding would come up sooner or later.

Her future mother-in-law, Chelsey, had called and checked on her regularly while Sam was deployed. They met twice at restaurants, and in return Moira had invited her over to her apartment a couple of times for meals. She'd been grateful for the company.

Sam's absence weighed on her heart and mind. His once-a-week calls hadn't come close to filling the vast, empty space he left behind.

To fill it, she threw herself into her painting at night and on the weekends.

"So, have you settled on a guest list?" Chelsey asked as she served coffee and pie for desert.

"Yes, we have," Sam spoke. "We have maybe forty-five, fifty people we're going to invite."

"That's all?"

"Yes. The only people we want at the ceremony are the ones important to us. Family and *close* friends."

Moira relaxed, relieved he said it and saved her from wrestling with it.

Chelsey sighed. "I've had several friends ask me when to expect their invitation, Sam."

"You can tell them this is just going to be a family affair. It will save them from feeling obligated to buy a gift."

Chelsey looked from him to Moira and back again. "You're both serious?"

Moira rested a hand over his. "Yes, we're really serious. If we invited all my mother's and father's coworkers, all yours, and all our own, we'd be up to four hundred guests.

She patted Sam's hand and let go. "It's ridiculous to spend that kind of money on a wedding. I'm certain we'd never be able to afford it, even with my parents' help. This is supposed to be a celebration of our love for each another. We want the important people, the ones who really support us, to be there."

Chelsey remained silent for a moment. "Okay. This is your wedding, and the start of your life together, and if this is what you want, I want it for you. But when I think of all those missed wedding gifts…"

Sam laughed. "After you've bought countless wedding gifts for their kids."

"Exactly! Some will send a gift even if they're not invited. Just don't miss any family members when you send out the invitations. Every one of them owes me at least one gift."

"You don't really mean that," Sam said.

Chelsey laughed. "No, not really. But it wouldn't kill them to send a little cash for your house fund."

Sam's gaze swung to Moira. "House fund?"

"I started the fund a long time ago, when I first started teaching. I put all the money I make from my paintings into it, minus new materials I buy to do others."

"How much is in it?"

"Thirty thousand dollars."

His jaw dropped. "That's amazing, Moira."

"Barely enough to buy a new car these days, but I'll keep working and adding to it until we have a down payment. I'll have a check from the gallery at the end of the month for eight thousand more."

"Jesus!"

"You're marrying a very industrious and talented woman, Sam," Chelsey patted his arm and grinned.

"I knew that already, but…wow, Babe. That's really amazing." Though his tone said one thing, his expression said another. Did he not want a house? Or was it that she was working toward that down payment by herself?

A door shut toward the front of the house. And they all looked up.

"Mom?" The word preceded Sam's brother Trevor's entrance into the living room.

Moira's heart fell at the sight of him. She hadn't recovered from their last meeting many months before. Having him imply she was a whore the first time they met wasn't something she was likely to ever forget or forgive. But she would be part of his family, and he, hers. They'd have to at least tolerate each other.

Chelsey rose jerkily and a strained note entered her voice. "Come join us, Trevor. There's plenty of food left."

"I'm not hungry, but I could use a drink." He passed through the dining room, headed directly into the kitchen, and returned carrying a whiskey tumbler with two fingers of amber liquid and the decanter.

His gaze skimmed over Moira as he sat across the table from her, but settled on Sam. "So, what's the occasion?"

Chelsey answered. "No occasion. Sam just got back from deployment, and I invited him and Moira over for a meal."

"How are the wedding plans going?" he asked.

"We're working on the guest list," Sam said.

Trevor stared into his glass. "Am I on it?"

"You're my brother, Trevor. Of course you're on it."

The tension in the room turned to smothering in a snap, and Moira sucked in a deep breath.

Trevor stared into his drink. "Dad too?"

Sam shrugged one shoulder. "He's my father."

Moira rose and stacked her plate and cup with Sam's. "Why don't I load the dishwasher for you, Chelsey?"

"I'll help." Chelsey stood and gathered her plate and coffee cup.

Moira carried the dishes to the sink and began rinsing the dishes and loading the dishwasher while Chelsey put away the leftovers after emptying the pots and pans, which Moira washed as soon as they were available.

Chelsey took out a dishtowel and began to dry them as she washed. "Thank you, Moira."

"It takes less time with two working."

"Not for this."

Tears stung her eyes, and she kept her attention on the task. "They need some time together. They're brothers. I never meant to create a rift between them."

"It isn't you who created it, Moira. Trevor caused this, not you. You were an innocent bystander, but you bore the brunt of it. I've never been so angry or disappointed in one of my sons. Or embarrassed. Trevor got what he deserved."

Surprised, Moira glanced up. "Sam broke his nose."

"I know. And as much as I hate that it happened, it may have knocked some sense into him. He was out of control. And losing his girlfriend because of his behavior may have put some weight behind that blow, too. He's been a little more thoughtful since.

Less abrasive. Less aggressive."

Less like his father, then? She'd yet to meet Sam's father. And she wasn't sure she wanted to. But since it was his son's wedding, his father would surely want to attend.

If Trevor's behavior was anything to go by—if he was most like his father—God help them all.

"WHAT'S GOING ON, Trev?"

"Nothing. I just came by to see Mom."

He was here for something specific—otherwise Trevor would have never set foot inside the house while he and Moira were here. Most of Trevor's problems were caused by their father. "What's Dad been up to since I've been gone?"

"He's up to his neck in an estate planning." He looked up. "Did you hear about Jonathan Walker?"

For a moment Sam pulled a blank. Then a memory gradually surfaced of a big, brawny man with heavy features and hands the size of dinner plates. His son had been a year behind Trevor in school. "Hank Walker's father?"

"Yeah."

"What about him?"

"He was one of Dad's clients. He was killed while walking to his truck from his office. They think it was a carjacking." He tilted the glass up and drained half the liquor.

"Jesus. Whoever did it must have been heavily armed. That guy was huge."

"They caved his skull in with a tire iron or something and stole his truck."

"Damn. From what I remember, he was a nice guy."

"Yeah. I thought so, too." Trevor poured more bourbon into his glass.

Something was riding his brother hard. Was all this a distraction? "When did this happen?"

"Last night. Hank called just a few minutes ago. How can you be so calm? I mean... how often is it that you actually know someone who's been killed?"

More often than he wanted to think about.

Trevor's features blanked with shock and his cheeks reddened. "Christ, I didn't mean..." He rubbed the glass against his forehead.

If Trevor was apologizing for being insensitive, something serious dogged him. "Do they have any suspects?"

"We haven't heard anything. But the family has been in contact with us. He just made some changes to his will in the past month or so."

So, what was making Trevor so...jittery? "Have you spoken to Hank about his father? Sent a message of sympathy? I'd think that would be standard procedure when you've done business with the family."

"Yeah, we've done all that." Trevor rose, and taking his glass, went to the window and looked out.

There was something hovering there between them that Sam couldn't decipher.

Chelsey returned to the dining room. "I've fixed you and Moira a goody bag, Sam. Extra pie."

"Thanks, Mom." He got to his feet, and Trevor stood as well. "Tomorrow's Saturday, Trevor. We could meet for lunch if you're up for it. I'd like for you to play a part in the wedding."

"I think you'd better ask Moira about that," Trevor said.

Sam glanced at Moira, who was standing next to his mother.

She studied Trevor for two or three seconds. "Weddings are family affairs. I have four brothers, two older and two younger, but there's room for two more."

Trevor dropped his gaze to his glass again.

Sam thought she might just be the classiest woman he'd ever known. After the way his brother treated her... He caught the glassy look in his mother's eyes as she teared up, then looked away.

"Sam's in charge of all of the men." Moira continued. "You should meet with him tomorrow and see what he needs you to do."

Trevor offered her a short nod.

As they said good night, Sam moved in close to his mother and spoke beneath his breath to her. "Something's going on with him."

She nodded, gave his arm a squeeze, and handed him the bag of leftovers. She reached for Moira and hugged her. "You're a gem."

As they walked to the car, Sam grabbed her hand. He opened the passenger door, set the bag of leftovers on the floorboard, and turned to pull her in close. "If I hadn't already asked you to marry me, I'd do it right now."

Moira smiled and rested her head against his chest.

"I plan on us being together for a long, long time. And that makes your family part of my family. We can't go through every holiday and get-together waiting for Trevor to go off again. It doesn't cost me anything to try and meet him halfway. Once he gets to know me, he might like me."

"I don't believe this new phase will last, but I appreciate the effort." He hoped Trevor wouldn't do an about-face and morph into the raving asshole again. If his brother embarrassed their family and Moira at the wedding, he was going to break more than his nose.

CHAPTER 4

T HE JARRING SOUND of Hawk's cell phone cut through his sleep like the blade of his K-bar. "Anchors Aweigh" blared away like a marching band. That tone rarely rang on the weekends unless something important happened. Immediately alert, he muttered, "Shit!" rolled onto his side, and grabbed the phone off the nightstand. "Yazzie." The dull morning light streamed through the edge of the blinds, painting a geometric pattern of light and shadow across the bed.

Langley's voice came over the line. "He's been arrested again."

"Fuck!" Hawk threw back the bedclothes and swung his legs over the side of the bed to sit up. "What for?"

"Public intoxication. This time it was off-post. They did a breathalyzer, and he was combative with the cops, so he's also charged with resisting. He's been in jail all night, but he's supposed to be released around ten this morning. He'll probably get a fine and thirty days, as long as the cops don't push the resisting charge too hard."

"How did you find out?"

"I had one of his teammates keeping an eye on him. He tried to get him in the car to drive him home, but he wouldn't cooperate, and someone at the bar called the cops when he took a swing at his teammate."

"Shit! I don't have any choice but to slap him with an administrative separation. He'll have mandatory counseling until the charges come before the court. If he refuses to go…"

"I know."

"I'll go into the office this afternoon, fill out the paperwork and notify command." Hawk ran his fingers through his hair. He had to cover his back and Langley's. Follow procedure.

"Okay, Send me a copy for my files."

"Will do." He ended the call and shoved the phone on the nightstand.

"Trouble?" Zoe asked from behind him.

"Yeah." It was tempting to share what was going on, but that would be a breach of Morgan's privacy and regulations.

He lay back on the bed and bit back another frustration-loaded curse.

Zoe curled against his side and rested a hand on the center of his chest. "You take every failure personally, as if they're your own."

"I have ninety-six men on my team, plus support personnel. When one of them falls overboard, it's my duty to recover him."

"Is this guy recoverable?"

"He's taken two hard personal hits and, like all of the team, he's done numerous deployments."

"Counseling?"

"He was required to do some after the last deployment. He's resistant to it."

"Most men are, especially SEALs, since they're used to being part of the solution, not the problem. And God forbid you guys should have to talk about feelings or admit you're not supermen."

He looked into her face. "You don't think I'm a superman?"

"Hmmm."

"My ego's crushed."

Zoe chuckled.

"I tell you how I feel all the time." He turned to face her and tucked a long strand of hair behind her ear. Her pale blue eyes looked as clear as crystal.

"Sometimes. I don't hold it against you when you don't. I think it's a man thing."

Hawk traced the tip of his index finger along her cheekbone and jaw. "There are some feelings too intense, too completely consuming, to put into words, Zoe. That's how I feel about you."

Her lips parted and her eyes glazed with emotion, and she nestled in close to brush her lips against his chest.

That small caress set off a rush of blood south and he hardened in an instant. He cupped her ass and drew her in tight.

"That hasn't changed in ten years, either," he said with a wry chuckle.

"Thank God," she said with feeling.

His lips were inches from hers when a knock sounded at the door. They both groaned. "It's Saturday. Why can't he sleep late just one day?"

Zoe glanced at the clock. "He did sleep late, and so did we. It's past nine, and he has a game today at noon." She pulled his head down and kissed him. "We'll take this up later." She rolled out of bed and limped to the door.

With a wry grin and a sigh, Hawk stretched, then bent an arm beneath his head.

"It's my turn to bring snacks and drinks to the game, Mom." A. J. trotted into the room like it was a jogging path and he was just getting started. He seldom walked anywhere.

The kid was lanky, all long arms and legs, big feet, and shaggy, thick hair as dark and straight as Hawk's own. Being in the top two percent in his age range for his height, he looked older than he actually was, but behaved like a normal ten-year-old.

"How many days have you known you were supposed to bring snacks and drinks?" Zoe asked.

"I don't know."

Zoe shot A. J. The Mom Look that conveyed frustration and disbelief.

A. J. grimaced. "I think Coach told me the last time we had practice."

Zoe braced her fisted hands on her hips. "That was five days ago, A. J."

"I forgot." His best doe-eyed, angelic look didn't seem to make an impression on her.

"I'll have to make a run to the grocery to get everything. You and your dad get the cooler out of the garage and rinse it out. I'll buy some ice." She rushed to the dresser to gather her clothes and disappeared into the bathroom.

With the hope of shower sex nipped in the bud by the trip to the grocery store, Hawk shoved up and propped the pillows behind him. "Not a good move, A. J."

"I forgot."

"You need to do better than that. Mom works her ass off all week taking care of other people at work, and then comes home to take care of us."

"That's what moms do." A. J. flopped down on the edge of the bed.

A. J.'s answer triggered Hawk's frown and a memory at the same time. His mother had tried to instill independence in him. She needed to. With his father dead and no other family close by, it had been him and his mother against the world.

He'd been about A. J.'s age when she started teaching him basic KP duties. A remark he made during an argument— something very much like what A.J. just said—had triggered the lesson. He never took her for granted again.

Hawk ran a palm along his jaw, the stubble rough as sandpaper. "I mow the grass, do some of the cooking, and I put in a load of laundry now and then. Do I do that because that's what Dads do?"

A. J. studied him with an expression that was so similar to one of his own, Hawk experienced a kind of déjà vu. After a moment he coughed up an answer of, "You like to grill."

"But I do it to help out, because it's everyone's responsibility in our family to pull together. It's like being on a SEAL team. Everyone works together so the team is more efficient.

"Starting today, before your game, you're going to take over Mom's job for the next week. You'll be washing your own uniform and other clothes, fixing your own lunch every day to take to school, and making sure you have everything you need for school, including your homework. If you think Mom's job is so easy, then you shouldn't have any trouble doing it."

A. J.'s mouth hung open. "I don't know how to cook or wash clothes."

"I'll show you some things while Mom's making the trip to the store, and you can fix breakfast for us all while we're waiting for her to get back. Go get dressed and get your stuff together while I throw on some clothes."

The stunned betrayal in his son's eyes was almost amusing. Hawk rolled out of bed.

"And you might want to thank your mother when she gets back for making an extra trip to get the snacks and drinks. And don't forget anything you'll need at the game, because Mom won't be double-checking your bag. That's your responsibility from now on."

"Yes, sir." Head down, A. J. loped out of the room in the direction of his own. Hawk attributed A. J.'s slower-than-usual exit to shock.

Hawk hoped he hadn't been too hard on him. The kid needed to learn some survival skills and some appreciation for his mother. He was pulling away from Zoe, which was probably typical for his age. But it had to hurt her every time he dismissed everything she did as something she was supposed to do.

If Hawk could turn that around a little...maybe it would ease this feeling of loss she seemed to be struggling with.

And maybe she'd get over this idea of having another baby.

ZOE STARED AT the front driver's side tire in shock. It was flat. Not just low, but totally flat. *Shit.* She quickly calculated how long it would take her to get to the grocery, buy the drinks and snacks, and drive back home. She needed to leave right now in order to get back in time to get A. J. to his game on time. She rushed back into the house.

Hawk stood at the bathroom sink lathering the lower half of his face, his skin dark against the white shaving cream. Black hair swirled across his chest, cut a thin line bisecting his muscular abdomen, then disappeared beneath the waistband of his pajama pants. Even after ten years, her heart tripped into a faster pace when she saw him like this. The raw, virile maleness he projected totally pushed her buttons.

She jerked her thoughts back to the current issue. "I need to take your car."

He scraped the razor downward from cheek to chin. "Problem?" He rinsed the razor in the partially filled sink.

"I have a flat. I must have run over something."

"I'll take a look at it when we get back from A. J.'s baseball game and take the tire in to be plugged." He cleared another strip along the outer edge of his jaw.

"Okay, thanks." Zoe grabbed his car keys from the dresser.

"Hurry back. A. J. is going to fix breakfast this morning."

"What?" She stepped back to the bathroom doorway. *Did I hear that right?*

"I'm going to teach him how to make scrambled eggs and toast. I think it's about time he learned some life skills."

For a moment she was too stunned to react. *What happened to spark this?* She didn't have time to ask just now, but they'd definitely have a conversation later. "I wish I could stay and watch."

He grinned. "Next time. If he decides he likes to cook, you may have to take over his instruction. My skills in this area are a little limited."

"That's okay. You excel at other things." She ran her eyes down his bare chest and flashed him a smile. His deep chuckle followed her as she rushed out of the room, his keys clutched in her hand.

Once on the road, she wove through the subdivision on autopilot, making several turns before pausing at a stop sign.

While she waited for the slow-moving traffic to clear, she attempted to run through the things she needed to buy at the store, but her thoughts turned to the discussion she and Hawk had about the baby the night before. She was trying to hold onto hope, but there was already a feeling of grief sneaking in. He loved their life just as it was. A baby would throw everything off-kilter financially and emotionally.

Though he had tried to cover for his immediate reaction to the idea with his promise to think about it, she knew him too well. His body language, his tone... He didn't want another baby. And he was humoring her until he figured out how to talk her out of it.

She'd known it last night as she lay beside him, wakeful and already grieving, and she knew it now.

Tears clouded her vision, and she pulled over into an empty driveway, bracing an arm over the steering wheel and resting her forehead there while tears streamed down her face. She had to get a grip on these feelings, because she couldn't very well just get pregnant and hope to force-feed him the idea of another child.

He'd been gone for much of A. J.'s early childhood, and she'd thought, because he missed so much before, he'd be more open to experiencing it with another child. But obviously not.

She tried to clamp down on the resentment, but it remained a hard nugget in the pit of her stomach. All the days, weeks, and months of being alone, raising their son alone, accepting complete responsibility for his every need. Accepting Hawk's absences from their lives. Accepting her cold, empty bed even when she'd needed someone to hold her when things got too overwhelming.

Like it was overwhelming her now. How was she going to accept this and move on?

But she had to. Because no matter how hard things were, she loved him. She loved him so much. And she knew he'd feel guilty for denying her what she wanted, because he tried to make her happy in every way he could. But he didn't want another child.

Why was it that women were always the ones who had to make the sacrifices?

But then he'd sacrificed having a woman with a perfect body when he married her. He'd accepted that once she got older, her mobility issues might get worse. And he still loved her.

She reached for her purse and searched for some tissue.

Nothing. She found some napkins in the door and wiped her face and blew her nose. She breathed through another urge to cry, put the SUV in reverse, and backed out of the driveway.

She'd get past this. She'd gotten past worse things.

She pulled down the street and stopped at the next stop sign.

A sudden, violent jolt from behind, whipped her head back and shoved her car forward while she automatically slammed her foot on the brake, glancing in the rearview mirror, but getting only a dim view of a truck behind her.

The engine revved nonstop and pushed against her bumper, inching her car forward through the stop sign and into the intersection.

"Oh, God!" *What's happening?* She stomped on the gas pedal, shot through the stop sign, and rushed to turn the corner.

She glanced up into the rearview mirror again, just in time to see the driver. A man in a baseball cap, dark hair sticking out from beneath the cap, his beard unkept. The truck raced forward again and rammed the rear of her car again. She fought the wheel to maintain control as the car fishtailed, her brakes screaming while she turned another corner.

A major intersection lay ahead, and she prayed the light would stay green. If she could whip through the light and it changed right after, the truck wouldn't be able to make it. The light turned yellow, then red, and she slammed on her brakes as a line of cars surged forward from her right and left, and she was jerked against her seat belt.

The truck's engine growled as he shot past the turn and turned up the street away from the busy intersection.

She gasped for breath, her muscles shaking with reaction. She reached for her cell phone to call Hawk. But what could he do? Her car had a flat, so he couldn't come drive her home. The man who hit her was gone. All she had was a description of a man with curly hair and a beard in a baseball cap.

She'd call the police and report him and give them a description. But while she keyed in 9-1-1, the husky growl of a truck engine came from behind her again, and she looked up into her rearview mirror barely in time to see it racing at her.

He rammed into her car again.

Her whole body was knocked back by the lash as her phone went flying to the floor.

His wheels continued to spin and scream as the truck pushed against the rear of the SUV and inched her forward. She prayed the light would change in time, even though the lines of traffic continued to whip past.

She pushed with both feet against the brake pedal. The smell of burning rubber was almost choking as the truck continued to lunge forward, again shoving her out into the line of traffic. A green blur shot past, clipped the front of the SUV, and spun it around. The front airbags deployed, and she was blinded by the white plastic and powder.

The blare of a loud horn jerked her head to the right. The huge grill of a truck bore down on her, looming larger by the second in the side window. A moment of déjà vu tore a squeak of fear out of her, every muscle seizing, her hands grappling past the air bag to the steering wheel, instinctively bracing against the impact even as her foot floored the gas pedal to get clear.

The SUV leapt forward, and for a second she thought she might make it—

The impact was an explosion of sound while glass shattered, metal screamed, the side airbags deployed, and for a moment the SUV was airborne as it rolled high in the air on its nose, then twisted.

Her head struck something.

Searing pain wrenched a cry out of her just before black swallowed everything.

"WE'LL PUT THE eggs in a container so Mom can taste them when she gets back," Hawk said as they cleared the table and loaded the dishwasher. He glanced at the clock on the stove.

"It wasn't so hard to scramble eggs. But I sucked at cracking the shells."

"I was your age when my mom taught me. It took me at least

five or six tries before I could do it without getting any shells in the eggs. Every new skill you learn takes practice.

"While I clean up in here, go out to the garage and rinse the cooler out. Mom will have ice to put in it for the drinks." A. J. took off in his usual half run-half walk speed.

Hawk glanced at his watch. It was only five minutes later than the last time he checked. Time was flying, and they were going to be late if Zoe didn't double-time it back from the store.

Where is she?

He finished cleaning up, then retrieved his cell phone from the bedroom. He dialed her number, and it rang, then went to voice mail. She wouldn't answer if she was driving. She had to be on her way back.

He went into the garage to find the door open and A. J. using the hose to rinse the cooler out in the yard as instructed. Hawk found some rags in a storage bag and took them out to dry the cooler.

"We'll leave it out here, A. J. Mom can put the ice and drinks in it, and we'll load it. Go in and put your uniform on, double-check your bag, and get your bat. I'm going to take a look at Mom's tire."

He wondered at the number of instructions he'd given A. J. since Zoe left. Her days were filled with constant instruction. Working with injured people and coaching them through their therapy couldn't be a walk in the park even when they were being cooperative. And then, as soon as she got home, there was A. J. And him.

And though he took part in parenting, the lion's share still fell on her.

He'd learned kids were like computers whose hard drives hadn't been completely programmed. It took a lot of time to get the programming right.

And she wants to do all this again with another kid? Jesus!

Shit! What was he supposed to tell her? She'd given him everything he needed from her for the past ten years. And the first thing she ever asked him for...outside of love...

He kicked the tire in frustration.

It took him only a few minutes to jack up the car and run his hand over the wheel as he turned it. A piece of metal embedded in the tread seemed to be the culprit. It might have been there for some time and created a slow leak. He got the tire iron out, worked the lug nuts free and tugged the tire off its axle. They could take it with them, drop it off to be fixed while they were at the game, then pick it up on their way home.

He glanced at his watch again. They were going to be late. He tugged his cell phone out and hit Zoe's number again.

"Hello," a strange female voice answered.

His stomach clenched. "Who is this, and how do you have my wife's phone?"

"Mr. Yazzie. I'm a nurse at Scripps Mercy Hospital. Your wife has been in a car accident and has been transported to the emergency room by ambulance. We'd like you to come to the hospital."

He didn't have enough saliva in his mouth to swallow. "Is she... What are her injuries?"

"Her doctor will have to discuss that with you when you get here."

"Is she conscious?"

"No. And we need some information from you."

"Get with it. I have to finish changing a flat before I can get there."

The nurse rattled off a list of questions about Zoe's medical history. He answered them while he moved to the back of the vehicle, jerked the carpet out of the way, and raised the compartment to get the spare. In mission mode, he held the phone against his ear with his shoulder while he shoved the spare on and got the lug nuts seated.

"We may have more questions once you get here."

"I'll be on my way in ten minutes." He thumbed through the list of contacts on his phone until he found A. J.'s coach. He explained the emergency and that they couldn't make it.

Though everything in him was shouting for him to hurry, he needed to take his time.

"Dad?" A. J. stood at the garage door. "We're going to be

late."

Jesus. What was he supposed to say to A. J.?

Finish the mission. Get to Zoe. He kept spinning the lug wrench and tightening the nuts, then tossed aside the wrench and started cranking the jack to lower the car. He straightened to find A. J. standing over him, watching.

He had to stay calm. Zoe was going to be okay. "We can't make the game, A. J. I called your coach and told him we're not coming, and his wife is going to take care of the snacks. Mom's been in a car accident, and I have to go and check on her. I'll drop you off at Trish and Langley's. You can hang out with them until I get back."

A. J.'s eyes latched onto his face, searching his expression. "Where is she?"

He didn't have time for this. The need to get to her pushed its way up from his chest and out of his throat like a shout. He fought it back. "They took her to the hospital to be checked out."

"Is she okay?"

It was important to keep A. J. calm. Hawk couldn't deal with an emotional meltdown when he was hanging on by a thread himself. "I don't know. Which is why I need to get to the hospital." He dragged the jack out from under the car and tossed the lug wrench against the wall with it. He lifted the flat tire and carried it around the back and tossed it in.

Fuck! Zoe had the keys. "Do you know where Mom keeps the spare keys to her car?"

"I'll get them." A. J. ran inside the house, his baseball cleats clicking on the concrete floor. He was back in seconds with the keys and his bag. He handed off the keys and hopped into the car. He tugged off his cleats and put on the tennis shoes.

"Fasten your seat belt," Hawk reminded him automatically.

"I'm coming to the hospital with you, Dad."

"I may be there a long time."

"It's Mom. If she's hurt, I want to be there too."

If she was bad, he wasn't sure he wanted A. J. to see her. His mind ricocheted away from the thought. *God, please let her be okay.* "Okay."

CHAPTER 5

S AM CHOSE A table close to the door at McP's and took a seat. The Irish Pub wasn't one of the posh bars Trevor was used to, and he wouldn't be impressed with it, though it was popular with the SEALs and other military personnel.

But by god Trevor'd just have to slum it for an hour.

He picked up the menu the waitress left on the table and scanned it while he sipped his beer. He'd get double orders of nachos with beef and the chicken wings and three orders of sliders for them to share while they talked.

He beckoned to the waitress and ordered all three and a pitcher of beer. Tim, his youngest brother, arrived and was shrugging out of his suit coat before he ever reached the table. He draped the jacket over the back of his chair, poured himself a beer, and drank deeply before he pulled the seat out and dropped into it.

"Tough day?" Sam asked.

"You could say that. I've been at the office going over testimony with a witness. I'm ass-deep in a trial, and everything we're doing is stirring up a shitstorm of emotions. We had a fight break out in the courtroom yesterday, and the bailiffs had to jump in and drag the guys out of the room. Thank lady justice it happened before the jury was seated—otherwise it could have caused a mistrial."

Impressed, Sam said, "That's nothing like it is on television, little brother."

"On television you're dealing with fictional characters. In real life you have angry people who want revenge for the gruesome things that have been done to their loved ones."

"Is this the trial the press has been all over? The one where the woman was raped and murdered?"

"Yes."

"Jesus!" His little brother was all grown up and putting the bad guys away. "Are you winning?"

"I have them dead to rights, but there's never any guarantee. And you can never trust juries completely."

"Getting cynical already, and you've only been at the job a little over a year."

"I worked in the DA's office two years before in a different capacity, so that entitles me to be a little cynical. You don't allow yourself to believe you've won until the jury comes in and the jury foreman actually delivers the verdict out loud."

"When you win, I'll help you celebrate."

"Deal. What are we celebrating today?"

Tim was so much easier to hang with than Trevor. He half wished it was going to be just the two of them. "Trevor's supposed to meet us here."

Tim frowned. "That's not exactly grounds to celebrate."

"He's agreed to come to the wedding."

His brows rose. "Voluntarily?"

"Yeah."

Tim grinned. "Is he charging you an hourly rate?"

"Nothing."

"Blackmail?"

"I don't know anything current about him that I could use, and I know he doesn't have anything on me."

"He actually said he'd come."

"Yeah."

"That's either very good...or it could end up being really fucked up."

Sam laughed, then turned serious. "Why do you think he enjoys being such a prick?"

Tim shook his head. "You can be a prick too."

"But I haven't made it my calling in life."

Tim laughed. "That depends on who you talk to."

"He was different the last time I saw him. He came in at Mom's and was talking about one of their clients being murdered."

"Jesus!"

Sam looked up as the front door opened. "There he is now."

Trevor entered the building and headed for them, then veered off toward the bar instead. Though he was dressed casually, and his clothing was as immaculate as ever, there was an unkept look to him. The shadows beneath his eyes looked like moon craters, beard stubble darkened his chin, and his well-styled hair hadn't been combed.

He turned toward their table with a glass of bourbon.

"He's drinking hard liquor before lunch," Tim said.

"Yeah, I see that." For the first time, Sam's aggravation with his brother was overlaid with concern. He'd been drinking bourbon at their mom's house last night. Since when had he started that?

Trevor came to the table and half-sat, half-collapsed into the chair.

"Hey, Trevor," Tim said as silence stretched.

Trevor raised his glass.

"You didn't drive, did you?" Tim asked.

"No."

"What's going on, Trevor?" Sam asked.

"It's the weekend. I can drink as much as I like on the weekend. I don't work weekends."

"Is this an every weekend thing, or just this weekend?" Sam asked.

"I haven't made up my mind yet."

Sam and Tim exchanged a look.

"Are things not going as planned at work?" Tim asked.

Trevor turned his head and shot Tim a narrow-eyed glare. "Why wouldn't they be?"

Two waitresses came out, each carrying trays of food and saving Tim from having to reply. The men fell silent while the women unloaded the trays and positioned plates, silverware, and napkins.

Sam asked for some water in the hope that Trevor would drink it instead of getting another bourbon. "Dig in, guys. We can eat while we talk."

"What do you expect me to do at the wedding?" Trevor asked. Tim filled a plate for Trevor and set it in front of him since he wasn't doing it for himself.

Sam shot Tim a nod. "Act as an usher, light the candles, and read a scripture about marriage before we take our vows." Sam hooked a slider off the platter and a couple of wings.

"Okay. I can handle that."

Sam exchanged a glance with Tim. They talked about the location, the blue suits they might wear since both had one and Sam would be in his dress whites. Moira's brothers, who'd all be doing things too.

Tim took the bull by the horns. "I'll need you to help me plan Sam's bachelor party, Trev. We're the brothers of the groom, and that's our duty."

"Strippers or no strippers?" Trevor asked.

"No strippers," Sam said immediately. "In fact, instead of a bachelor party, I'd rather have a poker party like we used to have, with food and beer. Nothing too wild."

Sam shook his head. "I've already experienced every kind of bachelor party there is with several of my teammates. The worst one was three years ago, when I was still young and stupid. I woke up with a sequin pasty on my cheek. My mouth tasted like the undercarriage of a Humvee that had rolled through shit, and I had a hangover I thought might kill me. I still have no memory of everything that happened."

Tim and Trevor both laughed.

Tim was still grinning when he asked, "Have you told Moira

about that?"

"God, no." Sam pointed at him in warning. "And she better not hear it from either of you."

Trevor cracked a grin. "I haven't played poker in years."

"Good. That means I might be able to win some cash off you for the honeymoon."

"Where are you going?"

"I wanted to take Moira to Hawaii, but I can't leave the CO-NUS, and I don't know how long it will be before I can. I'm just hoping I don't get orders to deploy before the wedding."

"That would definitely be the shits," Tim said.

Trevor finally set his glass aside and reached for the slider on his plate. "You could take her to wine country. Women like the wine thing."

Tim dropped a chicken bone on the side of his plate. He shook his head and wiped his fingers as he chewed. "Wine country is okay for a weekend, but not a honeymoon. Why don't you take her sailing along the coast and make stops along the way? Just the two of you. What good is having a sailboat if you don't sail it?'

"It's technically called a sailing...yacht, and not a bad idea. I'll have to check on that. Plan out the overnight stops. It would be an okay substitute until I can take her to Hawaii...maybe next year."

Trevor bit into another slider and chewed. "Don't tell her about the Hawaii trip until you have it planned. Women eat up that romantic, extravagant gesture thing."

Since when had Trevor become knowledgeable about what women wanted or liked? He'd blown it with his last girlfriend by being an asshole. Maybe he learned from that experience.

"Are either of you guys going to bring a date to the wedding?" Sam asked.

Tim shook his head. "I hadn't thought about it. I've been too tied up with work to think of anything else. What about you, Trevor?"

"No. I've been dating someone, but it hasn't progressed to the point of bringing her to a family wedding."

"Is she a lawyer?" Sam asked.

"No. She works at a local restaurant as a sous chef."

"You don't look like you've been eating much of her cooking. You've lost a few pounds since I saw you last," Tim commented.

Trevor shrugged one shoulder. "I've been busy."

"How's Dad doing?" Sam asked.

He looked away, reached for his glass, and raised it to the bartender for another bourbon. The bartender nodded. "He's okay."

Real concern nipped at the edges of Sam's mind. As a child and a teenager, Trevor worshiped their dad. And now he worked with him and still emulated him. That had caused some of the issues between him and Trevor. If there was trouble between Trevor and their father....

Tim spoke before Sam could. "Are you going to tell us what's going on?"

A waitress brought Trevor's drink and whisked the empty glass off the table.

"We just have a lot going on."

"Have they found out who killed Jonathan Walker?"

Trevor shook his head. "No. Not that I know of. But the police served our office with a subpoena for the will and other legal documents."

"Did you work on any of it?" Tim asked.

"No. It was all dad's business."

Tim polished off his beer. "They'll be looking hard at the family in case money has anything to do with it."

"Hank was crazy about his dad," Trevor said. "No way he'd have anything to do with this."

Tim gave his brother's shoulder a squeeze. "The family is the first thing they look at so they can rule them out, Trev."

Trevor's features hardened. "It was a freaking carjacking."

"Did they find the car?"

"No. Not yet. It was a truck. And they've put out a BOLO on it."

"How do you know that?" Sam asked.

"Hank called and told us."

"Maybe they'll get footage of the attack, if there are security cameras anywhere close by."

Trevor squinted as though he was thinking hard about something. "Maybe." He shoved his fingers through his hair.

"I didn't know you'd kept in touch with Hank," Sam said.

"He and his family are still members at La Jolla. We play golf together now and then. His dad played with us."

Maybe Trevor was different outside their family. "I'm sorry, Trev."

He nodded, wiped his mouth with a napkin and shoved his chair back to weave his way to the bathrooms.

Tim pushed his plate aside and poured more beer in his glass. "Who'd have guessed? I thought he'd cut all of us peons out of his life after going into the firm with Dad."

"You used to work for Dad too, and you didn't do that," Sam retorted. "But now we know why he's taking it so hard. They must have bonded over golf."

"Or he played golf with him to get his business." Tim raised a brow. "I'd never have guessed Trevor could be sensitive."

Sam agreed. It had been some time since he'd seen any sign of empathy from his older brother. Trust came hard, and he still couldn't completely buy into Trevor's sincerity. He'd played his father's son too long.

"If you can manage it, you could go to the funeral with him and see how he is with Hank and the rest of the family. I can't buy into this just yet."

Trevor returned to the table, and Tim eased into continuing the conversation, "I thought I'd go to the funeral with you, Trevor. When is it?"

"Fuck that, I'm not going to any goddamn funeral."

Aaannnd he's back.

Sam glanced at Tim, and his expression said he was thinking the same thing.

CHAPTER 6

"**W**E'VE DONE A CT scan and other X-rays. She has a skull fracture, a broken left arm, plus multiple bruises and contusions. Her head came into contact with some part of the vehicle, so her brain experienced a trauma and has swelled, so I'm giving her medication to reduce the swelling.

"Her EEG is normal, and there's no bleeding, but I'd rather she remain unconscious, because if she wakes, she'll be in a great deal of pain. The orthopedic specialist has already taken X-rays of her arm, and she has a non-displaced fracture to the ulna. He'll put on a fiberglass cast tomorrow."

The doctor's unemotional listing of Zoe's injuries and his calm voice didn't do a damn thing to ease the anxiety whipping through Hawk's system like lightning caught in a hurricane. One of the nurses said this doctor was the head neurologist and was very good, but wasn't that what they were paid to say? "Do you have any idea how long it might be before you let her wake up?"

"Not until the swelling goes down, Commander Yazzie. I've ordered another CT to make certain we haven't missed anything. Unless the scan shows some other undetected injury, the only thing we can do right now is wait until the swelling subsides, and then we'll reduce the sedative and allow her to wake up naturally."

Hawk's mouth, cotton dry, made it impossible for him to swallow. "Can we see her?"

"She's getting the scan right now. As soon as she's back in her room, I'll have a nurse come get you."

The doctor walked away, and Hawk dropped down into the chair next to A. J. He restlessly scanned the waiting room. Only two other people sat in chairs waiting.

"Is Mom okay, Dad?" A. J.'s voice dragged him back.

God, he should have taken him to Langley and Trish. "She hit her head really hard, and they don't want her to wake up yet. She also broke her arm, but it's a clean break and they'll set it tomorrow."

A. J.'s young features were tense with fear. "Did she hurt her bad leg again?"

"I don't think so. The doctor only mentioned that she has some bruises."

He put his arm around A. J.'s shoulders. A. J. leaned against him and pressed his face against his shirt. "I'm sorry I forgot about the snacks and drinks, Dad." A. J.'s voice cracked, and he started to cry.

Hawk cupped A. J.'s head in his hand and smoothed his hair. "I forget things all the time, A. J. This was just an accident, son. Mom's going to be okay." *She has to be.* He couldn't imagine his life or A. J.'s without her. He wouldn't. She needed to be all right.

After a short time, A. J. stopped crying but continued to lean against his side.

He needed to call Clara, Zoe's mother, and Brett, her brother. But he needed to see her first so he could at least try and prepare them for whatever was to come.

Time seemed to stand still, and A. J. started getting restless. Hawk handed him his phone to play a game on while they waited.

Zoe would have thought to bring things to keep A. J. occupied. Probably his homework. Hawk half smiled at the thought.

When a nurse finally appeared in the doorway of the waiting room, Hawk rose to his feet.

Her attention settled on A. J. "We don't usually allow children in ICU, Mr. Yazzie."

Enough. It took all his control not to snap at her, but the words still came out with the tone of command. "It's Lieutenant Commander Yazzie, and my son is coming with me." He rested a hand on A. J.'s shoulder.

Her gaze traveled back and forth between them. "Come this way."

A. J. gipped his hand while they walked down the hall to the elevators. Something he hadn't done voluntarily since he was six. His anxiety calmed Hawk, and he gave his son's hand a squeeze.

The ICU was like a command center. Computers, monitors, personnel, and the beep of machines. The nurse stopped at a room, glass windows allowing for a clear view of the patient. She stood aside for them to enter. "The doctor will be by in a few minutes. I'll bring another chair."

Hawk approached the bed, but left A. J. at the door to decide when he was ready. Zoe looked like she was just sleeping until he stood by the bed. The whole left side of her face was swollen and bruised. As was the side of her head beneath her long hair. Her left arm was wrapped in protective cotton with an ace bandage rolled tight around it.

Driven to touch her, he placed his hand over Zoe's. Her skin was warm, and he found it comforting. "She's going to be okay, A. J."

Her hand twitched beneath his, and his attention shifted back. Her back bowed and her arm jerked and flailed. An alarm went off as her entire body began to shake.

A. J.'s shrill shout of, "Mom," compelled Hawk toward the door. "She's seizing," he shouted toward the nurse's desk.

He swung A. J. out of the way and held him, pressing his kid's face against his chest while the nurses rushed past into the room.

A WHITE HAZE covered Zoe's vision, like light through a veil. Her stomach pitched first one way, then the other.

Had they finished the surgery? She always felt this way after surgery. She lay very still, hoping the sensation would ease. Had they finished the skin grafts? She'd had so many, and her leg and butt still looked like a patchwork quilt put together by a mad scientist. What was the point of doing any more?

I'm not doing any more. To hell with it.

Nausea rose up to torment her, and she swallowed. She needed to sleep a little longer, until the medication left her system. Until her stomach settled. Only sleep would work. The darkness folded around her, and she drifted back into it.

It seemed only minutes later when she sensed movement around her. She found it too hard to open her eyes, but her leg didn't hurt at all. What happened to it? Had they done more skin grafts? She didn't feel any pain anywhere. No. That wasn't right. Her arm hurt, and her head pounded with every beat of her heart. And her neck was stiff.

"Zoe, can you open your eyes?"

Her mouth was so dry she could barely swallow. "No."

"Open your eyes."

"So tired."

"I know, but I need you to do the things I'm asking you to do. Open your eyes."

She needed to concentrate. She raised her brows and her lids followed. She blinked at the light he aimed at her and turned her head away, and gasped when the pain in her head ratcheted up to pounding agony.

"The nurse is going to give you something for pain…just enough to take the edge off, but not enough to make you sleep again."

She sensed movement again on her right side, where tubes ran into her arm. The woman plunged a needle into the access port and pushed the plunger. Blessedly, the pain eased and she drew a shuddering breath.

She raised her left hand to touch the spot still throbbing dully like a stereo with the bass turned up. Her hand dropped back to the bed, the weight of something on her arm making it too heavy to lift. A peach-colored cast, not much brighter than her skin, covered her arm to her bicep.

That's not right. What happened to my arm?

For the first time, she focused on the man sitting on the side of her bed next to her. He was tall, his hair cropped close to his head, and his intense, dark chocolate eyes settled on her face. He had sharp cheekbones and smooth, mocha-colored skin. "Who are you? Where's Dr. Sterling?"

"My name is Dr. Winthrop. And this is Stella, your nurse." He gestured toward the woman who stood on the opposite side of the bed. Tall, with dark hair, narrow shoulders and wide hips, the nurse's smile was pleasant, and she touched Zoe's arm in a comforting gesture.

"Follow my fingers with your eyes, Zoe." Winthrop raised two fingers.

She followed the movement of his hand as it swooped from one side to the other. "Where is here?" she asked.

"You're in Scripps Mercy Hospital."

"There isn't a Scripps Mercy in Lexington."

"You're in San Diego, California, Zoe."

Had she come out to visit Brett? "What am I doing here?"

He proceeded to take her pulse. While he focused on his watch, he asked, "What year is it, Zoe?"

Why would he ask her that? Her head ached, and she raised her right hand to touch it this time. There was some swelling there. "It's...."

She tried to concentrate, but the pain made it difficult. She couldn't get the date to come.

"What do you do for a living?"

"I'm a physical therapist."

"Where do you work?"

"Courtland and McCabe Physical Therapy."

"How old are you?"

"I'm...twenty...five." Was that right? It seemed... "My head hurts."

"You had a very bad car accident, and you were injured. You hit your head and broke your arm."

"Was anyone else hurt?"

"No."

That was good. It was hard to formulate thoughts. "How long have I been here?"

"Five days."

Five days! The shock of it kept her silent. It must have been a very bad accident.

"Is my brother here? He's stationed at Coronado."

"Yes, he's here with your mother and other members of your family."

Mom flew in? Zoe must have been very sick. "Can I see them? They'll be worried."

"Certainly, after I've done a few more tests."

He continued to ask her questions, and the more quickly he fired them at her, the more uncertain and confused she became. She seemed to hit a wall, and it was like her brain was sluggish and her thoughts were trying to find their way through a fog.

He moved on to her reflexes and had her push against his hand with her right hand and then both feet.

"I'm going to raise your bed so you can sit up."

The closer to sitting she came the more her head swam and her stomach pitched. She closed her eyes. A cold sweat broke out all over her body.

"The nausea will pass in a few minutes. You've been lying flat for several days."

It might as well have been a hundred days instead of… How many days had he said? It took all of her control not to throw up. When Stella placed a cool, wet cloth against her forehead, she shivered.

"It'll pass in a moment," Stella soothed. "Just keep your eyes shut."

It took more than a moment, but the nausea finally receded.

"Get her something to drink and to eat. Let's start out with clear liquids first," Dr. Winthrop said on his way out of the room.

"I'll get the kitchen to send you up something," Stella said.

She knew how hospitals worked. She'd been in enough of them. It would be at least three hours before anything arrived, and it would be Jell-O and clear broth.

Maybe she could get Brett to run out and get her something. She must not be too sick if she was hungry.

"Would you like a ginger ale?"

"Yes. Please."

"I'll get it."

"When can I see my mother and brother?"

"I'll send your mother in as soon as Dr. Winthrop okays it."

She sipped the ginger ale and waited. Her attention moved restlessly around the room. Without anything to distract her, every ache and pain was amplified, and she had lots of them. Her neck was painfully stiff, yet she was afraid to move it for fear it would intensify her headache. The side of her face was tender when she touched it. Her arm didn't exactly hurt, but the unwieldy angle of the cast made her movements awkward when she tried to drag up the lightweight blanket on the bed.

The nurse brought her a tray with another ginger ale, the Jell-O she'd known would be on the list, and beef broth. She ignored the broth and ate the Jell-O and opened the other ginger ale with some difficulty.

A woman appeared at the door and entered the room. Zoe stared at her. She looked like her mother, but older. She'd just seen her mother...when was it? What day was it? The woman who walked toward her had gray threaded through her hair at the temples and a streak of it through the fringe of bangs that brushed her forehead. Though the wrinkles around her eyes and mouth had deepened, she was still beautiful. But the change in her appearance....

Shock held her silent for several seconds. "Momma?" Her voice seemed far away.

"Zoe." Tears streaked down her mother's cheeks, and she rushed to the bed. She tossed her purse aside on the bed, put her arms around Zoe, and held on tight.

Dr. Winthrop entered the room and stood at the foot of the bed.

Enveloped in the light fragrance of Chanel her mother had

worn for years, Zoe let herself to be lulled by the familiarity and comfort, though it was still like she'd been punched. Her mouth was numb as she asked, "What's happened?"

"The injury to your head has given you a severe concussion," Dr. Winthrop said. "You have a fractured skull, Zoe. Your brain swelled from the initial trauma. Though we were giving you medication to keep that under control, it got worse, and you had a series of seizures.

"It's not uncommon for people to have some memory loss after a trauma such as yours. It usually corrects itself after a few days, but it seems you've lost more than a few days. The good thing is it may not be permanent. You may wake up tomorrow and remember everything."

She looked into her mother's face when she eased out of their hug, and touched her hair where it had grayed. How many days had Zoe lost? More than days. Months? Years?

"We won't know how severe the concussion is until we do baseline testing, which we'll start tomorrow. And we'll also do another CT."

"Okay." Just listening to him made her tired. But the feeling that she'd lost her life suddenly washed over her. Panic shot through her system like an electric shock, and for a moment she couldn't breathe. What if her memory didn't come back?

"I'll leave you to visit with your mother. But I'll be back later."

As soon as he left the room, Zoe's attention returned to Clara. She wanted to cling to her the way she'd done as a child. "What have I forgotten?"

"It's going to come back. You have to think positively. But… Have I really changed so much in the past few years?" Clara asked.

Her mother looked ten years older than when she'd… When had she last seen her? She had no concrete memory of the when and where. Surely she should. "It's just your hair." She touched the gray streak in her bangs.

"I've been thinking of coloring it. Maybe when you get out of here you can help me do that.

"I have some pictures I think you'll want to look at." She

reached for her purse and removed a book. "I rushed home and got this when the doctor told us...you were...a little confused. You used to do this with Brett, like flash cards when he was...having difficulties."

Brett had difficulties? "What happened to Brett? Is he okay?"

Clara's expression froze for a moment. "Yes, he's fine. He's waiting to see you, so I can't stay too long. They said ten minutes."

"How much time have I lost?"

"You look through those pictures to see if any of them trigger your memory, then when I come tomorrow morning, we'll talk about it." Clara tucked the photo album under her free arm.

What if she didn't remember her mother or her visit tomorrow?

"Will you bring me a notebook so I can write things down?"

"Yes, I can do that. And your pajamas and toiletries?"

Zoe tugged at the neckline of her hospital gown. "Yes. And underclothes. It's uncomfortable to be naked under one of these gowns." She shifted, her energy depleted. "Will you send Brett in? I'm getting really tired, Mom."

"There's someone else who wants to see you, too, Zoe."

"Is Sharon here?"

"No." Clara shook her head. "She wanted to fly in, but I told her to wait until you woke up."

"Who is it?"

Her mother searched her face. "Your husband."

"Husband?" Her voice sounded distant. She had a husband? *Oh, my God.* This was...surreal.

"Brett brought him home with him one Christmas. Hawk doesn't have much family. Only a few cousins who still live on the reservation. He was Brett's commanding officer at the time they visited. Does any of that ring a bell?"

She shook her head then caught her breath. The movement made her head pound and the room wobbled along with it. While she waited for the sensation to pass, she asked, "Did we get together during that Christmas?"

"No. It was after you finished your degree and your internship. Brett was injured, and you came out to stay while he recovered. You and Hawk fell in love during that time. You've been together for ten years."

Clara clasped Zoe's hands in hers. "That's enough for today, sweetheart. I'll send Hawk in, and maybe seeing him will jar your memory. These past five days have been hard for him. He's been very upset. He loves you very much." Her voice shook with those final words.

Her mother was choosing her words carefully and seemed almost protective of him. He must be a good man to have earned that kind of affection.

"Does he know I don't...?"

"Yes." Clara kissed her.

What would he expect from her?

If they'd been together ten years...

Oh, God, did they have children? She automatically placed her hand over her lower abdomen, but there was nothing there to offer a clue.

"It's going to be okay, Zoe. We're all going to support you, and you're going to get through this."

But what if she never remembered him? Her mouth was dry with fear. She'd never even thought of marriage. Her leg and scars had always prevented her from believing it would be possible. What kind of man would look at her with any kind of desire?

"Okay." Clara hugged her and held her for a moment. "It's going to be okay, Zoe."

But she couldn't promise that. Not even her mother had the power to shield her from this. She trembled with reaction as she waited for her husband to come in.

A man strode into the room with the gliding grace of someone who was very fit. His hair, cut short, lay against his head, pelt black and stick straight. Beard stubble darkened his lower jaw. His gray eyes look startlingly pale against the tanned olive of his skin. They lasered in on her with an unwavering focus. When he reached the bed, his throat worked as he swallowed. "May I hold you for a moment?"

His features, noble, strong, and stamped with his Native American ancestry, were almost too handsome. The taut composure of his features was almost painful to look at, as was the shadow of worry in his eyes. She was so distracted by her study of him she nearly forgot his question. "It's all right."

He sat down on the bed next to her and gathered her close with such care it gave her heart a jolt. His white T-shirt hugged his broad, muscular chest, and she rested her head there. He smelled of laundry soup and something she suspected was uniquely him. Whatever it was, it was soothing.

"We thought we might lose you."

She struggled for something to say. "I'm still here."

"We're all going to do whatever it takes to help you recover, Zoe. You have a team of people who work for you at Balboa hospital, and they're ready to help, as are your mom and brother, and A. J. and I."

"A. J.?"

He eased back to look down at her. "A. J.'s our son. He's ten."

The shock of that barreled through her. Oh, God! How could she have forgotten her own child?

CHAPTER 7

MOIRA WALKED BETWEEN the tables, pausing to study each figure drawing in progress. She stopped, taking in the interesting texture in Tracy's drawing. "I love the texture you've given the pants, but you may want to add just a little more shading in this area to create more contrast in the folds of the fabric." She pointed to an area in the bend of the figure's leg.

"Thanks, Ms. McKee."

"You're welcome." She moved on to the next table, gave a few directions, then moved on to the next. Tyler Hanson was working on a multi-media project and adding the last painted touches to the canvas. The timer went off on her desk, and students got up to store their projects and clean up their work area. As much as they enjoyed her class, they were always eager for the lunch break, so she didn't hold it against them when they rushed out of her room as soon as the bell rang.

She was just as relieved. Two more periods and she'd be ready to go home. She collected her lunch from the pint-sized refrigerator behind her desk and moved against the flow of the crowd while she wandered down the hall to the Math wing, where the hall was deserted since it was lunch hour. She slipped into Maggie's classroom and found a seat at the worktable at the front of the room.

"I swear Jimmy Bushnell can bat those baby blues at any girl in class and they melt like butter at his feet. In all the time I've been teaching, I've never seen anything like it. I'm going to have to call a meeting of all the freshman girls to warn them about the dangers of being starstruck by a pretty face." Maggie's short hair curled around her ears and along the back of her neck in lovely brown waves.

"There's one in every school." Moira pulled a chair out and sat down across from her.

"No there's not. I didn't have any gorgeous bad boys in my class."

Moira fanned her face. "Greg Myers, freshman quarterback, five-ten, jet black, curly hair, pale blue eyes, shoulders as wide as that door." She nodded toward the door she just walked through. "And he was very *mature*. I believe he was developing facial hair as a freshman. He collected panties from his conquests."

"He didn't get yours, did he?"

Moira laughed. "No. He wasn't interested in the shy, artistic type." Plus she'd been fifty pounds overweight back then. And the problem escalated once she got to college.

Moira shook her head. "But I knew several of the girls he talked into donating to his collection, and none of them lasted long with him. By junior year he had developed a reputation and the girls were a little more wary.

"After he went to college on a football scholarship, I heard he got some girl pregnant his freshman year and his family paid support payments until he finished his degree."

"Bad boy and deadbeat dad." Maggie removed a bowl with what looked like sir-fry from the small microwave in her book-case.

"Sounds like it. I want to be a fly on the wall when you try to turn a math lesson into a sex education class. Are you going to do algebra problems calculating the odds of conception when x number of sperm meet one egg?" She opened her bottle of water and unzipped her thermal lunch bag, taking out the small salad with a piece of grilled salmon. She popped open the tiny storage bottle of vinaigrette dressing and sprinkled some on her salad.

Maggie sat down. "I'd probably have parents calling to complain. But I'd really like to wave the girls off. Not because Jimmy's a bad kid. He's polite and attentive in class and besides, he isn't really the problem. He can't help being cute. It's the girls who are being silly."

"Were you boy crazy back then?" Moira forked a bite of salad into her mouth.

"No. I was a geek. Just like I am now."

Moira swallowed. "Geeks can be sexy. Abe must think so."

Maggie smiled. "I think he is, too." Color flared in her cheeks and Moira chuckled.

Maggie's fiancé worked at an engineering firm downtown and was a bit of a geek himself, with his Clark Kent glasses and pocket protector filled with exactly one pen and two mechanical pencils. He was brilliant. She'd seen some of the plans he worked on. And though most of the work he did was on the computer, he would whip out one of his pencils and do a quick drawing or calculation of something when an idea struck. She watched it happen when Maggie invited her over for dinner while Sam was deployed.

She and Maggie had gotten to really know each other in the six months Sam was gone, so now it seemed natural to hang with each other at lunch every day.

Moira had time while he was gone to realize that losing the weight and being with Sam had changed the pattern of behavior drummed into her since middle school, when the bullies used to come out of the woodwork and make her life hell. Being obese made her a target for abuse. But she wasn't a target now. With every pound she shed, she'd found more and more of her self-esteem and her self-confidence.

Sam's unwavering interest and support were the icing on the cake.

Moira checked her watch. They had exactly twenty-five minutes to eat before getting back to their rooms for the next class.

"So, how's Sam doing now he's back?" Maggie asked as she chewed.

"He's good. We're making up for lost time."

"That sounds…exciting," Maggie said and grinned.

Moira raised one brow. "It's very stimulating."

Maggie laughed.

"Will you be my maid of honor, Maggie?" She hadn't meant to just blurt it out, but she'd been dying to ask her for weeks. "I know we haven't been lifelong friends, but I feel we're going to be. And I'd really love for you to—"

"I'd love to," Maggie broke in. "The other night, when you and Sam came over and he and Abe hit it off so well… I was hoping that even though Abe isn't in the Navy, the two of them could become friends."

"Sam has friends outside of the Navy, including two brothers who are both lawyers. Besides, he had a good time the other night."

"Good."

"As for the maid of honor thing. You won't have to pay for anything. I'll take care of the dress and shoes. It's going to be a small wedding." She ate the last bite of salmon.

"Have you found your dress yet?"

"No." The other day, when she pulled out the maroon dress she wore to The Del, she wondered why Sam had ever put the moves on her. It looked so staid and unsexy. "I've been looking but…." She sighed. "I want to look especially good for Sam, and I feel like my fashion sense is still stuck in the before-the-weight-loss era, when I was trying to cover up as much as possible. Now I can't really tell what suits me. I'd love it if you would go shopping with me one day and help me find something."

Maggie pushed her empty bowl away. "How about this weekend?"

"Really? That'd be wonderful. And we'll look for your dress while we're at it. I'd like you to pick something you'll wear more than just this once. Not the traditional bride's maid's dress."

She glanced at the clock just as the bell rang, and quickly gathered her dishes, packed everything back in her lunch bag, and hightailed it back to her classroom.

The phone rang as she entered her room, and she answered to hear Principal Jacobs say, "Moira, I'd like to see you at the end of the day to discuss the plans for our next fundraiser."

Her heart fell. They just finished one that started before Thanksgiving and extended through the first few months of the new year. Only now was the last of the money trickling in and the merchandise they sold had arrived and was being delivered by the students.

The first year she handled everything, and even organized a surprise concert at the end of the year, for which she managed to find a last-minute venue, concessions, and security. Because Sam was out of the country for seven months, she took on the fund raising again to fill the gap, but it had been only a five-month effort, nothing that extended through the entire year. With the current gear-up for end-of-year testing, she was tapped out.

Besides, she had a wedding to plan for, and even though it was going to be a small family gathering, it was still a lot of work. Plus she already promised Sam she wouldn't get swallowed up in this next fundraiser. And to be fair, it was someone else's turn to take on some of the responsibility.

Convincing her principal would be a different matter.

She had her own artwork to think about now, too. It was paying off, and she needed to devote more time to it. Plus she was already doing an advanced art class at the end of the for her more gifted students, helping them earn scholarships by building a portfolio and searching for scholarships, as well as going over options to market and sell their artwork.

She did her best to focus on her classes, but her anxiety rose as time slipped away. Finally she nudged the last of the students out the door and set everything up for her first class the next morning. After filling her bag with the day's tests, she collected her purse, locked her classroom door and wandered down to the office.

When she started to sit down to wait, Emily, one of the secretaries, said, "He's waiting for you."

Moira carried her things with her into the office but left the door open.

Mr. Jacobs was finishing a phone call and rose with the phone in hand to motion her into a seat. He quickly hung up and came around the desk to sit in the chair parallel to hers. "I thought we could get a jump start on the next fundraiser now we're back from spring break."

"Mr. Jacobs, we just finished one. The students and the faculty have become saturated with the extra work and may not want to do another one so quickly."

"This one is for the school, so it will benefit our students directly."

The idea Mr. Jacobs outlined would, at the very least, involve writing a grant, organizing students to do the setup work, and creating an online store to sell the products created in the art department, computer science department, and the greenhouse. And, of course, shipping the products.

"You'll have to get a business license to do this, Mr. Jacobs, and that means taxes, incorporating, and people to work on shipping things out, and other grants to keep things going."

"You can do this, Moira."

"No, I can't. The only grant I've ever written was for that first fundraiser. It took me months. You can't just whip this up in a few weeks. And once this project is up and running, to sustain it will take constant work. You might even have to hire someone fluent in computer science to work it full time. I believe the output wouldn't match the input."

"You're already teaching your students how to put their work online to sell. This is just taking it two steps further by setting up the process to do it here and including all the other departments. We'd take a small percentage to run the thing and pour it back into the departments."

"But what I'm teaching them is how to do all the work *on their own*, Mr. Jacobs. And the amount of money we'd make, and they would make after the markup, wouldn't be nearly enough to balance all the work they'd have to put in. This would mean we'd have to have a work schedule for people to get out of class. That would cut into their class time and lower their test scores. The Board wouldn't go for that at all, sir."

"At least take a look at the grant application. You've done two other projects and done very well with them. You can figure out some way to make this work."

"That's just it, Mr. Jacobs. I've done two others, and it's time for someone else to step up and take over. You might want to think about doing it yourself."

"I have duties as a principal."

"And I have duties as a teacher. You have a building full of people to choose from to work on this. You could set up committees and spread the work out across the whole staff. There has to be someone who has experience writing grants in our building."

He shrugged that aside. "They're all hip-deep in testing."

"So am I, Mr. Jacobs."

He frowned. "They're testing is for the core curriculum."

His words were a slap, and she caught her breath. "My testing is for that, too." She should have developed a thicker skin by now, but when he shrugged aside the importance of what she taught, it hurt all the same, especially in light of everything she'd done to maintain a quality program—on top of all the extra duties he'd piled on her.

She was shaking as she turned in her chair to face him fully. "I had four students earn full scholarships to college last year for their art, four out of the sixteen who were awarded in our building. I have two students I'm hopeful about this year. But art doesn't count, does it?"

"I never said that."

"You just did."

She rose to her feet and gathered her bags. "I've done my share for the school. Find someone else this time." She stalked out of his office, past Emily, down the hall, and exited the building.

In the car, tears stung her eyes, and she took deep breaths to restore her composure before starting the engine. At the tap on the window next to her, she caught her breath. Looking up through the glass, she saw Emily's round, pleasant face. Turning the key, she lowered the car window.

Emily handed her a piece of paper. "That's just an old lunch schedule, don't pay any attention to it. I had to make an excuse to follow you. I'm glad you reined him in and stood your ground. I like Principal Jacobs, but he's working you half to death, leaving you to do the whole thing while he sits in his office playing electronic poker, and then takes all the credit for your work at the Board meetings. Don't let him wear you down. The rest of the teachers in the school will thank you."

So she'd been right that the rest of the staff and the students were exhausted after working on two fundraisers. Though they were good experiences for the students, and benefited the community, they were extra work for the teachers. A lot of extra work.

"Thank you, Emily. I appreciate you saying that." She reached for a tissue in the console when her already shaky composure threatened to dissolve.

"You're a fantastic teacher, Moira. You've proven that with all the students who apply to college and actually get in. What Mr. Jacobs doesn't realize is that the students have to keep their grades up in everything to qualify for art scholarships. And they're doing that because what brings them joy is the art. Keep doing what you're doing."

Tears came for a different reason now. "Thank you."

Emily patted her shoulder before hurrying back inside.

Emily's praise was a soothing balm to the slap Mr. Jacobs just gave her. She dried her face, and, after dragging in one more cleansing breath, she started the car and pulled out of the parking lot.

CHAPTER 8

WHEN SAM OPENED their apartment door, there were no tantalizing food smells, and nothing sat on the stove ready to eat the way it normally did. Music played from Moira's studio. He strode through the living room and down the hall.

The studio door stood open, and he paused to watch her for a moment. Her brush actually sounded like she was scrubbing the canvas hard, and her movements were quick and angry.

Sometimes, when she was upset, she'd attack a painting with a vengeance until she'd exhausted her emotions. It looked very much like she was doing just that.

He couldn't think of anything he'd done that would upset her this much, so it had to be something at work today.

He eased past the door and went into the bedroom to change into a T-shirt and well-worn jeans, then reached for his phone, thumbing through until he found the number for a Greek restaurant they frequented and ordered some of Moira's favorites. The food would be delivered in half an hour. It didn't hurt to butter her up with comfort food if it would ease her mood.

The food had arrived before Moira exited her studio and came into the kitchen. Sam set aside the book he was reading and rose.

She dumped her water containers and brushes into the sink and ran water for them to soak. She washed and dried her hands. "Thanks so much for ordering dinner."

"It's about time I kicked in since you usually cook."

She slid in tight against him and rested her head against his shoulder. Sam held her close and rested his chin against her hair. "Hard day at school?"

"Yeah." She drew away. "Let's eat."

He could hear an undertone of stress in her voice.

It took a few moments to fill their plates, and another few passed while they ate in silence.

"Mr. Jacobs ask me to write a grant for another fundraiser—and, of course, run the whole thing. I told him he needed to find someone else in the building to do it. He said he couldn't because they're hip-deep in testing."

She leaned back in her seat. "I'm doing testing, too, Sam. But to him what I teach doesn't count. One of our secretaries was still there...Emily, you met her some time ago. She said the rest of the teachers would thank me for turning him down."

"Writing grants isn't in your contract. If you've turned him down, he can't push it."

"But he can make my life miserable."

"Even after you donate money to buy materials for your classes?"

"Every teacher does that. I don't know any who don't. School funding is never enough."

He bet not many gave as generously as she did. "What kind of grant did he want you to write?"

"That's what's strange. It was for an online store, so the Art, Computer Science, and Science Greenhouse departments could sell products online. Why would he want to do that? It wouldn't pay enough to make it worth our while. Why not a grant for more tech in the classrooms, E-readers for the library, or one for updated, schoolwide software, or classroom materials or...any number of things?"

Sam shook his head. "If you don't want to do it, Moira, just keep telling him you can't. That isn't what you're paid to do. You're paid to teach. And anyone with even one eye can see what a wonderful teacher you are. The quality of your students' work bears that out. So try to relax. He can't force you to do anything. And if he tries, me and my guys will pay him a visit."

She paused with a bite of food on her fork, her mouth half open.

He laughed.

"I was obsessing, wasn't I?"

Sam reached across the table to cover her hand. "You're a people-pleaser, honey. And that makes you an easy target for assholes like your principal. Don't let him use you, Moira."

"I'm not going to."

He hoped she meant it this time. Because she caved the previous two times.

"What were you working on in your studio?"

"Something that wasn't going very well."

The doorbell rang and they looked at each other. "I'll get it." Sam rose and went to the door.

Tim stood before him, his expression grim. He slid past Sam and into the living room, and, with a jerk, turned to face him.

Moira interrupted before he could speak. "Hey, Tim. We just sat down to eat. Would you like to join us?"

He ran a hand over his hair. "Hey, Moira. No, thank you." He paused to collect himself. "The police have arrested Dad for embezzlement."

Sam's mind went blank. "Jesus." He forced the word out. "Who did he embezzle from?" What did it say about his relationship with his father that he didn't even pause to question whether he was innocent?

"Jonathan Walker."

The reason for Trevor's behavior of late suddenly snapped into clear focus. "Trevor knew, didn't he?"

"If he didn't, I'm certain he suspected it. But that isn't the worst of it. They're trying to build a case for murder."

It took him only a second to connect the dots. "The carjacking."

"Yeah. Jonathan came in recently to change some things in his will, and it seems Dad has been syphoning money from one of

Jonathan's investments. They got into an argument, and Jonathan said he was going to the police. But he was killed later that evening while walking to his truck."

He'd always known his father was a bastard, but he'd never dreamed he was a crook. Was he really a murderer too? "Jesus! If he killed someone, he wouldn't do it himself. He'd pay someone."

"They won't be just looking at Dad, Sam. They'll be looking at us, too."

"Us? You're kidding me."

He'd never seen Tim look more serious.

Tracking his brother's thoughts, he said, "You do realize that I haven't spoken to Dad in nearly seven months. I called him before I left just to tell him I was being deployed." His father never asked when he'd be back and didn't really care.

"They'll still want to know where you were."

"That's the night before we ate dinner with Mother. I came off the beach after training, took a shower because I was caked with sand, changed clothes, came home, and we had dinner. Trevor came in the next night while we were at Mom's house and told us Jonathan had been killed."

"Good. Did you leave at any time during the evening to run out to the store or anything?"

"No." They'd eaten frozen yogurt in bed after making love.

"Good."

"Where were you, baby brother?"

"It just happens that I was with someone."

Sam raised a brow. "That covers us. I suppose you'd better talk to Trevor and see if he's got an alibi. Though I can't see him killing someone for Dad."

"You don't think he might do something stupid out of fear of losing his idol?" Tim asked.

After a moment's thought Sam shook his head. "He seemed too shaken up about Jonathan being killed. He said he's been golfing with him and Hank at La Jolla."

Tim frowned.

An idea came to Sam. "Without Dad, Trevor would gain full

control of the business."

"Once word of Dad's embezzlement gets out, the business will be gone. They'll have to have an audit of every account to see if he's been doing the same with his other clients. Trevor will be tainted by what Dad's done. He'll be lucky if he can find a job after this."

Shit!

"You were working there too, a little more than a year ago. Did you suspect anything?"

"Nothing like this. I suspected he was billing more hours than he worked. And I know he had a..." He glanced in Moira's direction. "Another woman on the side." He released a frustrated breath. "If I'd known about the embezzlement, I'd have confronted Dad about it and walked away from the business sooner than I did. I'd have tried to take Trevor with me, though I doubt it would have worked."

"It wouldn't have done any good." Impatience and disgust gave Sam's tone a bite. "I knew the old man had a side piece. He always does."

"Why don't the two of you sit down, and I'll get you something to drink," Moira suggested.

Sam glanced at her. "Thanks, Moira."

Tim took a seat on one of the overstuffed chairs while Sam sat down on the sofa. Since he'd been through other situations a hell of a lot worse than this, he wasn't too affected. And what did it say about their father that Tim didn't seem too surprised either?

Moira brought beers for both of them. "I'll go to the studio so you two can talk."

"You can stay, Moira," Tim said. "You're going to be part of the family soon enough. And you'll have to deal with this, just like the rest of us."

She took a seat on the couch beside Sam. "I've never met your father. Are you certain he'd actually steal money from a client? It isn't someone else with access to the files?"

Sam looked at Tim and said, "If he's cornered, he'll throw Trevor under the bus. There's no question about it."

"Is he really that…uncaring of his sons?" Moira asked.

"He doesn't call to see if I made it home, Moira. Ever."

Tim exchanged a look with Sam and gave a nod, then said, "Since I left the firm, he pretty much cut me out of his life as well. I haven't spoken to him in over a year."

"Trevor said he hadn't worked on the Walker accounts," Moira said. "If the computers at the office are as password-protected as ours, the only one who will have access to your father's computer will be him."

"Unless someone else knows his password or hacked it. That's what he'll argue."

"I wonder how Jonathan Walker discovered he was taking the money." Moira said.

"He may have had a way of checking it from home, or he gets quarterly statements. A withdrawal of several thousand dollars or more would be cause for concern."

"Why would he do this?"

"Keeping one woman in the style she's become accustomed to is bad enough, but when you're keeping two…" Tim shrugged one shoulder. "Dad has a penchant for high-maintenance women."

Sam was compelled to say, "Mom never was one. She was too busy working."

"When will they set bail?" Moira asked.

He shook his head. "It depends on when he appears before a judge, and how fast he gets legal counsel. I'm on the other team, so I can't touch it. And Trevor doesn't have the experience for this kind of litigation." He tilted the bottle up and drank what was left of his beer.

"If they freeze his assets, he may not have the money. Wouldn't that be ironic?" Sam said, his tone droll. He leaned forward. "Have you told Mom yet?"

"No, she's my next stop." Tim rose.

Sam followed and was hit by a thought that made him grit his teeth. "Don't let her bail him out. And she'll be tempted, because she'd be doing it more for us than for him. I'd rather see him rot in jail until he comes to trial than let her give that bastard a single dime. *Not a dime, Tim.*"

"I'm of the same mind, Sam. Dad made his bed a long time ago. She doesn't owe him anything."

"And neither do we," Sam added as he walked him to the door. "Do you want me to come with you?"

"No, I can handle this." Tim extended his hand.

Tim was much more sensitive than Trevor, and outwardly he might not show much emotion, but since he'd become a lawyer in order to fight the good fight, this was a bitter pill. He'd worked for a year with their father to try and build a relationship, but ended up leaving because of their business practices.

When he finally left the firm, he commented that he knew where all the bodies were buried... Sam jerked him in close and pounded him on the back. "It's going to be hard for you at work. Distance yourself from the whole thing as much as you can."

"I will."

Sam wondered if they'd call Tim in to testify. *Fuck!* He hoped not.

As soon as the door closed behind Tim, Moira moved in to hug him. "I'm sorry, Sam."

He gathered her close and held on. Maybe he was more affected than he wanted to admit. Her comfort felt damn good.

CHAPTER 9

H AWK CLOSED THE door to his office and glanced at his watch. His normal lunch time run needed to be put on the back burner until he caught up on the ten days' worth of paperwork accumulated on his desk, and the dozens of phone calls he needed to return. He'd never thought there would ever come a time when he would welcome the mind-numbing chores.

But these days work was the most normal part of his life. That and taking care of his son. Zoe's absence had thrown both their lives into…not chaos, but a grief-stricken no-man's-land. It was like losing a limb.

He wanted to be with her when she got home, but she told him to go to work and try to get back to normal. And while he listened to her, he glimpsed the same Zoe she'd always been. She cringed away from being fussed over, was unquestionably independent, and never stopped pushing herself.

He saw what was missing too. The love he always saw in her face when she looked at him. There was curiosity, maybe even interest, but the emotion he kept looking for hadn't returned. Not yet. But it would. He'd earn it from her again, even if he had to start from scratch to do it.

He looked at his watch and the paperwork he needed to complete. After the trauma of witnessing her seizure, A. J. needed to see her recovering. Hawk wanted to be there when he got home from school, but it didn't look like it was going to happen.

He worked steadily for the next three hours. A sigh of relief escaped him when his phone rang on his desk and he reached for it. "Yes."

Ensign Reins, his admin, said, "There are two police detectives at the gate to see you, sir."

It had to be about the wreck. "Have them issued visitors' passes and ask them to drive up."

"Yes, sir."

While he waited for the two officers to arrive, he went through the paperwork he meant to file for Morgan's administrative separation, signed his name, and set them aside to be sent on down the chain of command. He'd moved on to the next batch of papers when Reins buzzed him.

He rose as the detectives entered the room and moved around the desk to shake their hands.

"Detective Wilson, sir. And my partner Detective Crider."

Wilson, tall and muscular, motioned to Crider, who was female, to take a seat. Her short blond hair cupped her head like a caramel-streaked helmet around a narrow face with large hazel eyes. She moved like a runner. In contrast, Wilson plodded, like a street brawler, and also had a brawler's heavy features, prominent nose, and thick eyebrows.

Wilson spoke first. "We brought your wife's property with us, Lieutenant Commander. The items were recovered from the car after the accident. We'd like you to look everything over, make sure nothing's missing, and sign a receipt transferring possession to you."

"Thank you for bringing everything to me. I've been at the hospital since the accident." Someone had called, but he completely forgot about it. A sign of how upset he'd been...and still was.

Hawk took the paper bag from her, and, using a letter opener, sliced the tape holding it shut. He lifted Zoe's purse, keys, sunglasses and cell phone out of the bag and set them on his desktop, then opened her small purse and took out her billfold. Her license, proof of insurance, credit card and debit card were all there. Nothing seemed to be missing. He dumped out the rest of the possessions on his desk blotter. Besides the billfold, there was a folding comb, pale pink lipstick, a travel toothbrush, and toothpaste. And a notepad and pen. It was surprising not to see at least a few crumpled receipts or coins in the bottom. He replaced everything and put it all back in the bag.

When Detective Crider placed the form in front of him, he signed it.

"I haven't seen the car since I've been staying at the hospital. Now Zoe's awake, I'm not sure I want to see it."

"It's been impounded as evidence, Lieutenant Commander," Detective Wilson said.

"Evidence?" Shock held him silent for a moment. "Did Zoe do something wrong?"

"No. Not at all." Crider took over. "It's taken us several days to reconstruct the accident and track down witnesses. The truck used was stolen from a parking lot downtown. It was found with the key in it in a neighborhood just a few miles away from yours. It sat there a couple of days until one of the residents called to report it."

Wilson continued. "The truck was towed, and the owner's family notified. He was killed a week ago during a carjacking, and the truck was stolen."

"Jesus!"

There was a back-and-forth rhythm to the way the two detectives handed off the conversation. It was probably very effective while interviewing criminals.

Wilson took up the thread of the conversation and ran with it. "Because we were looking for a silver truck with front-end damage, due to what a couple of the witnesses said, we were notified when it was brought in. We had an analysis done of the paint transferred from your SUV, and it matches. But the interior of the truck was wiped clean, and no one saw the person who parked and abandoned it.

"One witness said the truck didn't even slow down, but instead accelerated before hitting your wife's car. They estimated it was going at least forty when it hit. It struck your wife's vehicle in the rear and pushed it forward out into traffic. The man in a green SUV hit the front end of her car and spun it around until she was sideways in both lanes.

"Your wife did try to avoid being hit. She hit the gas, and the car leaped forward, but the truck bearing down on her hit the middle brace between the front and back door and flipped the SUV. They had to use the jaws of life to get her out. The good news is that, had she not been hit in that location, she might have been hurt even worse or killed. I've seen cars ripped in two if they're hit on the rear door."

Hawk's mouth was dry, and he swallowed with some difficulty.

"How's she doing?" Detective Crider asked.

"She has a fractured skull, a broken left arm, and is having some memory and balance issues."

"Does she have any memory of the accident?"

"No." He didn't know whether to share how bad things really were, but decided to go ahead with it. "Her memory loss is the biggest issue at the moment. She hasn't just lost a few days. She's lost years. She doesn't remember me or our son."

"I'm so sorry." Detective Crider said.

"We hope it's a short-term condition. She's going to be released to go home later today. Even though she can't remember what she's lost, in some way I think she senses how much she has." She'd been so quiet and reserved for the past two days, in a state of perpetual shock. "I don't want to put any more pressure on her than she's already under, but if she should remember anything, I'll call you."

"Maybe when she gets home something will trigger her memory," Crider suggested.

"We're hoping that will happen."

Detective Wilson slid forward in his seat. "We wanted to keep you apprised of the investigation."

"I appreciate it."

"There was just one more thing," Wilson said. "We noticed

there was a smaller SUV registered in both your names, as was the one Mrs. Yazzie was driving during the accident. Was the SUV she was driving her regular vehicle?"

"No, it's mine. She was running to the store for snacks for our son's baseball team. Her car had a flat, and she took mine so I could take the flat off to be repaired. When I was notified about the accident, I had to go to the hospital on the temporary tire and have it fixed the next day."

"To what repair place did you drop the tire off?" Crider asked.

"John's Auto Repair on Balboa."

"How's your marriage?" Wilson asked.

Hawk studied the man for a long moment. Did he really think he'd go out and carjack a truck to kill his wife? "We have a strong marriage. Zoe is a wonderful wife and mother." He felt no guilt about using Zoe's wishes to set them straight so they'd move on and find the person responsible. "Though A. J.'s ten now, we've been talking about having another baby. I'm home more often now than I've been in the past."

"Have either of you been having any issues with anyone in the neighborhood, or at work?"

"I haven't, and I think Zoe would have told me if she was. We talk about everything that isn't off-limits here." His gesture took in the office.

"We'll still need to talk to your neighbors and coworkers," Wilson said, "We'd like to ask them if they've seen anyone following either of you or hanging out in your neighborhood."

"You think this was deliberate, and not that Zoe was in the wrong place at the wrong time?"

Crider and Wilson exchanged a look. "They purposely pursued your wife for several blocks, ramming the rear of her car. She was speeding away from them until she reached the intersection, where the perpetrator shoved her car out into traffic. Even while your wife was applying the brakes, the truck driver continued to rev the engine and push her farther out until cross traffic couldn't avoid colliding with her. There were tire marks from both her attempt to keep the car in place and the truck's tires spinning as the driver of the vehicle kept shoving. That's attempted murder. Their intent was to cause the accident."

"Was this road rage?"

"It may have been, but we have to pursue every avenue."

Who did this? And why? Heat flared in his face as his temper spiked. He was used to maintaining an emotional distance at work, but this wasn't work. This was his wife, the woman he loved. He rose and fisted his hands as he took slow breaths to try and regain control. "There were a couple of days when it was touch and go whether she'd make it. We thought we were going to lose her."

He struggled with the temper that threatened to explode, and his face seemed stiff with the effort. "I want them caught." *And strung up by their balls.* "Do what you have to do. You can request NCIS's help if you think someone on post is involved. I won't be able to turn over the names of men involved in disciplinary matters to you. But I can to them. I'll call them and apprise them of everything that's happened and that you'll be contacting them to share the details of the accident." He went to his desk, hit a button on the phone, and gave instructions for Ensign Reins to provide the appropriate number to the detectives.

"Sounds like a good idea," Detective Wilson rose.

"I haven't seen anyone hanging around or following me. If Zoe noticed anyone, I think she would have said something to me. Now, with her memory issues, unless she suddenly recovers some of it…" he shook his head.

Right behind Wilson, Crider paused before heading out the door. "I'm sorry about your wife, Lieutenant Commander. I hope she recovers."

"Thank you."

He fell back into his desk chair and ran his fingers through his hair as the quick flash of adrenaline leached away. It was good he wasn't involved in finding the asshole who put Zoe in the hospital, because he'd never make it to jail.

CHAPTER 10

MOIRA SHUT THE door and turned off the lights as the last of her fourth period class filed out.

She needed a few minutes of quiet to unwind. For the past week Sam had been restless at night. Being a light sleeper, she woke up every time he left their bed, and right now she needed a nap. Her lunch of cottage cheese with pears and slivered almonds sat on her desk untouched.

She couldn't continue to avoid Mr. Jacobs, and she was already tired of hiding out in her room or Maggie's. Worse, Maggie was out for the latter part of the day due to a doctor's appointment, and the substitute wasn't one she knew well enough to join for lunch.

She dropped into her chair behind her desk, folded her arms on the top of her desk and rested her head on them. She'd get through the day, then go home and take a nap.

A tap came on the door and the door opened. "Headache?" Principal Jacobs asked.

A falling sensation hit her stomach and her pulse rose. Realizing he was waiting for an answer she said, "A slight one. You can turn the lights on."

He flipped the switch, then lumbered to her desk.

Moira pushed her chair back and got to her feet.

Jacobs glanced at her lunch. "I know you don't have much

time to eat. I'll be brief."

He stuffed his hands into his pockets. "I want to apologize to you, Moira. I was out of line the other day." He studied his shoes for a moment. "I got overly enthusiastic about the project I was proposing, and after you left, I realized you were right. It isn't a viable model for us to implement."

He looked away, then back. "I made you feel like what you do here has no merit, and that isn't true. You're a valuable member of our staff, and the students who excel in art probably wouldn't do as well in everything else if you weren't encouraging them to keep all their core content skills up while they pursue their art skills."

He shifted from one foot to the other. "I think you're right that the teachers and students are tired and overextended. We'll put any more fundraisers off until next year."

"I think that's a wise decision, sir. I've had feedback from some of the teachers that supports that decision."

He gave a brief nod. "Then we're on the same page."

"Yes, sir."

He went to the door. "I hope you'll accept my apology, Moira," he said without turning.

She wasn't ready yet. So she stayed silent.

A tap came at the door and Jacobs opened it. "Hello Ms. Morgan. You came at just the right time."

A young woman stood at the door, her body whip-thin, her blonde hair pulled back in a ponytail.

"Come in, and I'll introduce you to Ms. McKee, our art teacher."

"Moira, Ms. Morgan just joined our staff. She'll be working in the copy room duplicating your tests and other teaching materials."

Moira smiled at the woman. "Hello."

"I just came by to see if there's anything you need copied for next week, Moira."

Jacobs left the room and closed the door.

"Welcome to the school. And yes, I have a couple of tests I need copied for next week." Moira moved to her filing cabinet and pulled out the necessary paperwork, sticking post-it notes on each with the number of copies she needed and her name.

"I used to love art in high school," Ms. Morgan said, her voice soft while she studied a drawing on the board. "I never did anything as good as that, but I enjoyed drawing. It was relaxing."

"I'm not sure I'd know what to do with myself if I didn't draw or paint," Moira commented. "Everyone has a gift they need to cultivate."

"It would be a real loss if you stopped." Ms. Morgan moved on to a study Moira did demonstrating weight shift of the human body. "Do you sell your work?"

"Yes, I do." Moira handed her the papers. "What's your gift?"

She was silent for a moment. The woman reminded her of a shy bird that might take flight if anyone spoke too loudly. "It's been a long time since I've thought I had one. I used to love to sew when I still had a sewing machine. In my last apartment, I made all the curtains."

"That's an art form too. What happened to your sewing machine?"

"It was a portable machine, and the table it was on collapsed and it fell."

"That's a real shame. Maybe you'll be able to buy another one soon."

A smile peeked out. "Maybe."

"My name is Moira, by the way." She extended her hand. "You don't have to call me Ms. McKee."

"I'm Tonya. If you need anything else copied, you can call down to the office and I'll come up and pick up the originals."

"I'll try to drop them off early in the morning so you won't have to walk all the way down here."

"Okay. You'd better eat before the bell rings." Moira glanced at the salad.

"I hope you enjoy working here, Tonya."

"Thanks."

AWARE OF HER mother and her mother's husband, Russell, watching her, Zoe wandered slowly through the living room and paused before a picture on one of the cherrywood end tables. Hawk's features were strongly mirrored in A. J.'s. The two were laughing while she had an arm looped around each of them. She recognized the similarity in the upholstery of the couch in the photo. "Who took this photo?"

"You told me Trish and Langley Marks's daughter Jessica took it. Hawk and A. J. were playing around with Tad while they waited for Langley to arrive, when all the guys were going to a ball game while you ladies were going shopping."

These were names of people she was supposed to know, and she couldn't get a single face to come to mind. Her eyes lingered on A. J. Were they really such a happy family? Afraid of voicing the question aloud, she asked, "Are we very close to Trish and Langley?"

"Best friends, both of you. Hawk and Langley have been in the teams together for almost twenty years. Langley has enough years in to retire, but he's staying in for a few more years. He's like Hawk's right-hand man.

"You and Trish hit it off the moment you met. She works for the military and runs a sort of social work network that makes sure disabled veterans receive the care they need and deserve.

"Trish wanted to come visit at the hospital but thought you would already be too overwhelmed. She said she'd call and you can tell her when you're ready for her to come visit."

"Do I have her number?"

"Yes. It's in your cell phone. But I don't know where that is at the moment. Hawk can give you the number."

She nodded.

Russell spoke for the first time. "Don't push it, Zoe. Something will trigger a memory, and then it will be like a cascade, and you'll remember a number of things at once."

It had been such a shock to know her mother was remarried. She never considered the possibility since she remained a widow for so long. She studied Russell's handsome face and kind eyes, his thick mop of white hair, and she understood why her mother was attracted to him. He was strong and protective, and he had the military bearing to go with it. Her father had it too.

She hoped he was right and that she'd remember everything soon.

Her gaze lingered another moment on A. J.'s face in the picture. Why couldn't she remember him? He was her *child*. She carried him inside her body, gave birth to him. Her memory's failure ate at her.

She scanned the room to find something to distract from her gloomy thoughts. A built-in shelving unit held books, baseball trophies, and the television. She'd bet there were movies and video games stored behind the doors at the bottom of the unit.

"Did you come over and clean, Mom?"

"No. Hawk and A. J. straightened up. They didn't want you to have to worry about doing anything."

That made her feel even more guilty. Their love for her was tangible here, while for her it was like there'd been a door inside her slammed shut between them.

She moved on through the living room and past the dining area to the kitchen.

"A few years ago, you and Hawk had a company come in and tear out the walls that divided the living room and dining room, and had the kitchen updated. He did some work on the bathrooms himself."

"Mom, you and Russel don't have to stay. I'll be okay here alone."

"You can't stay here alone, Zoe. The doctor said you have to have someone always with you for the next two weeks at least."

So what if she got a little dizzy if she stood up too fast? Lots of people did that now and then. And if she lost her balance sometimes, that's why they made canes and walkers.

The same thing must have occurred to her mother when she said, "Russell, could you get the walker out of the trunk of the car?"

"Sure." He loped to the front door.

"I know you want to be alone. But it truly isn't a good idea," Clara said as soon as he went out.

"I'm tired of everyone hovering. If something happens, it happens. I have to keep moving forward, Mom."

Clara's smiled even as her eyes shimmered with tears. "I'm glad to see this setback hasn't changed your attitude. But if something does happen, I'd just as soon be here to help, because your family adores you. Hawk and A. J. need you, Zoe. A. J. thinks it's his fault you were hurt, because he forgot to tell you earlier in the week that he needed to bring snacks for the team."

"It was an accident. When I talk to him, I'll try to convince him of that. It was just an accident." Zoe looked away. "I'm going to look around. You don't have to follow me. I'm not about to fall over at any moment. If I get dizzy, I'll sit down."

They said the kitchen was the heart of the house. She probably spent most of her time here when she was home. Everything was organized and clean. She walked around the space but didn't open the cabinets.

When she caught a glimpse of a screened-in sunroom, she went to the glass-paneled door, opened it, and folded it back before walking out into the space. The old-fashioned metal glider beckoned to her, and she sat down and set it to rocking. The hot tub cover lay propped against the wall, the faint scent of chlorine carried on the breeze.

Did she get into the hot tub with Hawk? The idea set her heart to racing while heat flared in her face. He had such a presence and was so…gorgeous.

How the hell had she gotten so lucky?

He must have adjusted to seeing her scars. They had a son, but no other children. Why not?

This was her life, but she didn't feel comfortable about asking him questions. It was like poking her nose into someone else's business. And besides, how could she be sure he'd be completely honest with her if she did ask him questions?

After a few more minutes, she wandered back inside to find Russell in the kitchen drinking a glass of water. "Would you like something to drink, Zoe?"

"I can get something." She moved to the cabinet next to the sink and reached for a coffee cup with Best Mom printed across the front. She held it in her hand and stared at it. How had she known where the cup was?

"It's called muscle memory. You do things automatically because you've done them over and over," Russell said. "You've trained yourself to know where things are."

She moved to an unmarked canister and opened it. The tea bags she'd been expecting were inside. Tears blurred her vision, and she shut her eyes against them. "How can I remember where things are in the kitchen and not remember the people I share it with?"

"The brain is a complex organ, Zoe. Yours has been dealt a substantial blow. It needs time to heal. Just relax and give it time."

Easier said than done. Zoe filled the cup with water, added the teabag, put it in the microwave, then turned it on. "Has Mom gone somewhere?"

"She's picking A. J. up from school."

Zoe would have to learn A. J.'s schedule. "How long before I'll be able to drive?"

"You'll have to talk to your doctor about it, Zoe. But I'd say at least six weeks."

What about her job? What about...*everything*? Weariness suddenly drained the last of her energy. She picked up her tea and went back out into the sunroom. Leaning her head back against the glider, she used a foot to set it in motion.

Thirty minutes passed, and she might have been dozing lightly when she heard, "Mom!" A shout came from the front of the house. She heard Russell's deep, rumbly voice just before A. J. rushed out onto the sunroom. He threw himself down on the glider, setting it to rocking wildly, and his hug was fierce. He smelled of outdoors, boy, and laundry soap, and he looked so much like Hawk it gave her heart a squeeze. She hugged A. J. back, the cast making it awkward.

"Your arm. Does it hurt?" He touched the cast.

"It did at first, but it's getting better."

"You have black marks on your face."

She was surprised how tall he was, his legs nearly as long as hers already. "They're just bruises. They'll go away soon."

"Do they hurt?"

"Only a little, and only if I touch them."

His lashes looked so long and dark around eyes as pale a gray as Hawk's. "Dad said you're having trouble remembering things and you get dizzy."

"Yes. I am, and I do."

"You can ask me things if you don't remember."

She fought against the rush of emotion that brought tears to her eyes. Her one good arm tightened around him. "If I need to, I will. How did school go today?"

"I did good on my math test, but I suck in geography."

"What country are you studying?"

"America."

She laughed. "Living here and knowing where everything is are two different things. We'll look at a map together, and I'll try to help you."

"I'll go get my tablet and look up one."

"Tablet?"

A. J. searched her face. "You bought it for me. It's like a computer, but it's just a screen. You can hook a keyboard to it when you need to write something."

It sounded interesting. "Go get it. I'd like to see it."

"Okay."

"And bring a marker back. You need to sign my cast."

He grinned. "Okay."

The weight of everything she'd forgotten was crushing. But A. J. was her son, and if she couldn't remember the past, she needed to make new memories while she got to know him again.

She did feel a connection between them. It was more like an emotion than a memory, hovering on the edge of her consciousness, but she couldn't draw it completely out.

They were still working on identifying the Midwest states

when Hawk came home. "Hey, you two, feel like a break and something to eat?"

"Yeah," A. J. answered. "I'm starving."

"You just ate a snack an hour ago," Zoe reminded him.

"It was a snack, Mom. Not a meal."

Zoe laughed. "Okay."

A. J. was up and gone in a nanosecond. She heard her mother say, "Go wash your hands first."

The scent of Chinese food made her mouth water. She was hungry for the first time since she'd awakened in the hospital.

"How's it going?"

Zoe set the tablet aside on the wicker coffee table. "He's wonderful, isn't he?"

When he smiled and his shoulders relaxed, she realized how tense he was. "Yes. He is."

"Why didn't we have any more children?"

"I deployed every year. Sometimes for short periods, one after another, and sometimes for six or seven months at a time. Then there were the trainings and other interruptions. You had your hands full working, taking care of A. J., and the house. Time just got away from us. Since my promotion, I've been home more."

So much time lost. Why would she have decided to marry a man in the military when she always said she'd never do it. She wiggled forward on the edge of the seat to stand. He stepped forward and offered her a hand. She gripped his wrist one-handed, stood, and then hesitated while she found her balance.

"I'll show you where your brace is later, in case you need it."

She'd rather fall flat on her face than wear it.

Clara handed her a plate as she entered the kitchen. "Hawk got all your favorites."

Did she at least remember her favorites? She sat down at the dining room table with a helping of fried rice and General Tso's chicken. Three bites of rice and three more of chicken and she was done. She was suddenly too exhausted to eat anymore. She sipped the green tea her mother set next to her, hoping the little bit of caffeine would give her a boost.

Hawk rested an arm along the back of her chair. "You need to lie down?"

She nodded and pushed to her feet. Everyone looked up. "Mom, will you put my food away? I'll come back to it later."

"Sure, honey." Clara smiled.

Hawk stood and shoved his seat back, resting a supportive hand against her waist as he guided her around the table.

Guilt tightened the muscles at the back of her neck. "I hate to see that look on her face."

"What look is that?"

"That she's worried but doesn't want to me to know it. It was like a default facial expression from the time I was seven until I graduated from high school and left home."

"Once a mother, always a mother, Zoe."

"I suppose so." She thought of Hawk's tension when he came out into the sunroom earlier.

"You don't have to worry that I would do anything to hurt A. J. I may not have the memories, but there are feelings he triggers...I can't exactly describe it."

"Losing a few memories doesn't change the person you are, Zoe. I wasn't worried about anything you might do. I was worried he might still be feeling guilty about the accident."

"I'll talk with him about it when I feel it's a good time. It was an accident."

Once in the bedroom, her attention snagged on a painting hung over the bed. She paused just inside the door. It was her, but she'd never seen herself display such self-confidence. She wore a two-piece bathing suit and a wrap. Something she didn't remember ever doing. The wind was blowing the scarflike fabric out behind her. There was such movement and color in the painting. But what held her attention was the serenity and happiness in her expression.

This wasn't the uncertain, anxious woman she was right now. The portrait was of a woman comfortable in her own skin. Confident. And she wasn't hiding her leg or scars.

"I commissioned the painting for our ninth wedding anniversary last year. It'll soon be our tenth."

"But A. J. is already ten."

"He was born before we got married. I was deployed when you found out you were pregnant, and we'd barely adjusted to having a baby when I was deployed again. He was already a year old before we got married."

She moved to the bed. Hawk pulled the bedspread back and she climbed in. When he covered her, her eyes had already fallen shut. "Was marriage always the plan?" Exhaustion softened her voice.

His fingers brushed a long strand of hair back from her face. "Always."

She sensed his nearness and opened her eyes. The heat from his body reached out to hers as he leaned down and brushed her lips with his. Even exhausted, her heartrate sped up and heat raced down her body to settle in intimate areas. She half raised a hand to touch him before she thought about it.

Hawk grasped her hand and drew it to his cheek and turned his lips against her palm.

"Sleep. A. J. and I'll be here when you wake up."

Though exhaustion dragged at her and she closed her eyes, sleep eluded her. Her heart and body seemed to recognize him. Why couldn't the rest of her?

CHAPTER 11

HAWK POURED A glass of cold, sweet tea from the pitcher in the refrigerator, added two fingers of bourbon and squeezed in the juice of a lemon wedge. Drinking had rarely been his thing, other than a cold beer after a mission, but the stress of the day had brought on a craving. Now A. J. was in bed and the house was quiet, he was just grateful to settle into the glider in the sunroom to unwind.

Ten days ago he would have talked to Zoe about the accident. But now, with everything she was going through, he wasn't certain she was strong enough to hear what the detectives told him. Someone had deliberately shoved the car out into traffic so she'd be hit. Did they know who she was? Had they believed he was at the wheel? Surely they could see it was a woman driving, even from behind.

Who would have a motive to do this? He needed to work the problem.

Half an hour later he was still puzzling over it when he heard a sound in the kitchen and got up to look in.

Zoe stuck the plate her mother set aside for her in the microwave and turned it on. When she noticed him standing in the doorway, she offered him a small smile. "Hey."

Sleep pants hung low on her hips, emphasizing how much weight she'd lost in the past ten days. Her T-shirt had a cartoon on the front of a television remote that read, *your remote does not qualify as an exercise machine.*

"Wake up hungry?" he asked.

"Yeah."

"You slept for nearly three hours."

"They don't let anyone rest in the hospital. They woke me up at midnight, three, and six to take my blood pressure, pulse, and temperature. Then just when I finally went back to sleep, they'd come in to do something else. Then there's breakfast, lunch, and dinner, and in between the vampires—sorry, lab techs—drawing blood, and the cleaning crew taking care of the room, and respiratory therapy wanting you to breathe into a machine to make sure you don't develop pneumonia because you're lying around too much…" She shrugged one shoulder "You get the picture."

The microwave dinged, and she went to a drawer, got a potholder, and reached in for the plate. She set it on the island and stared at the potholder like it was something totally foreign.

"What is it?"

"Russell says that muscle memory is why I know where things are in the kitchen."

He looked from her to the potholder. "Could be. Don't push yourself, Zoe. It's your body's way of saying you need to rest to heal."

She set aside the potholder and looked up. "I suppose so. I'm not used to waiting to do anything anymore."

Hawk leaned against the door facing and sipped his drink. "No, but you're really good at explaining to other people why they need to be patient."

"Am I?" She took a bite of her Chinese.

"Yeah, you are. The people you work with at Balboa tell me that all the time."

She chewed, then swallowed. "I want to see them. Talk to them. Since I spend significant time there, maybe a visit will jar loose some memories. Russell said something about muscle memory triggering other things. And my work is a kind of repetitive muscle memory."

"We'll call and talk to your boss. It might be overwhelming for you to talk to too many people at once." And embarrassing and upsetting if she couldn't remember them.

"Can we do it tomorrow?"

"Zoe, I'd like for you to do it at a time when I can go with you, and I can't make it tomorrow."

"When?" She took another bite and chewed slowly.

"Maybe next week."

She ate in silence for a time, then wiped her mouth with a napkin and carried her empty plate to the sink, rinsed it, and loaded it into the dishwasher.

Her silence wasn't encouraging, but as much as he wanted to protect her, he needed to tell her about the detectives' visit. "There's something else I need to talk to you about."

"What is it?"

"Two detectives have been assigned to investigate the accident."

"Detectives? Aren't accidents usually investigated by a special accident recreation expert?"

"Usually, but the truck that hit you was stolen during a carjacking, and the man who owned the truck was killed." He wouldn't tell her she'd been pursued for several minutes before the accident. "It was determined that the person driving the truck purposely pushed your SUV out into the middle of traffic."

"Pushed me out into traffic?"

"Yes."

"Why would anyone do that?"

"They don't know yet. They asked if there were any neighbors we've had a falling-out with, or if there was any reason for someone to follow or attack either of us. And we've never had issues with anyone in the neighborhood as long as we've lived here.

"The police will be questioning the people you work with at the hospital to find out if they're aware of any issues. NCIS will be asking the personnel who've had issues with me some questions as well.

"And since you were driving my car instead of your own, they'll probably be following through with some of the guys on post."

"Why was I driving your car?"

"You ran over a six-inch piece of metal and had a flat. We'd all slept in and were running late, so you took my car to go to the grocery. I was changing the flat to the temporary tire when the hospital called.

"Oh, and before I forget. The police detectives brought your purse to me at the office. I've put your cell phone, sunglasses and the purse on the dresser in our bedroom. I think the charger for your phone is in the nightstand."

"Thanks."

He was used to doing things for her without the barrier a thank-you threw up between them. It made them seem like strangers.

He'd shared a bed with her for ten years, and the loss of that closeness set off an ache every time he thought of it, like a bruise that wouldn't heal. The distance he read in her eyes…

He jerked his thoughts away from that and moved to the refrigerator, poured more sweet tea in his glass, then added a splash of bourbon, and a lemon wedge.

"Do you drink often?"

"No. A beer now and then. An occasional glass of wine with you at dinner when it's just the two of us. We don't usually drink anything but tea around A. J." He turned to look at her. "I'm not likely to get drunk on two cocktails with barely an ounce of bourbon in each."

"Can I have a sip?"

Surprised he studied her. "Only a sip. You just got out of the hospital today." He extended the glass.

Zoe took a sip, held it in her mouth, swallowed, then grimaced. "That is—disgusting."

Hawk laughed. "Want to sit out on the glider for a little while?"

"Sure."

THE SUNROOM WAS becoming her favorite room in the house The April breeze, cool and crisp, carried a hint of freesia and honeysuckle. When Hawk put his arm around her, the heat from his body kept the chill at bay.

"When Brett was injured and you and your mom first came to stay with me, you spent a lot of time out here."

"He told me about being hit on the head and the coma, and how you saved his life."

"He'd have done the same for me."

"I know he would."

She rested her head back against the cushion behind her.

"You spent hours at the hospital doing PT with him to keep his muscles from atrophying," Hawk said. "Standing on your feet for hours made your calf ache. I tried to talk you into the hot tub but you were too shy to get in with me."

"Because of my scars."

"Yes. It wasn't until after I talked you into going parasailing with me that you'd join me in the hot tub."

"I went parasailing?"

"Yes."

She thought about that for a moment. Since when had she gotten to be so adventurous? "I'd like to do it again."

"As soon as the doctor says you're good to go. But the water will be damn cold."

The woman in the painting in their bedroom wouldn't let a few scars or cold water hold her back. But would she let a sore, aching head dissuade her. She ignored the beginnings of a headache and breathed in the smell of soap and man. Hawk's scent hovered on the edge of her memory like a song she couldn't quite remember the words to. She closed her eyes and continued to breathe it in, hoping it would trigger something.

When nothing happened, she asked, "What if I never remember?"

"When you're feeling better, stronger, we'll start over."

"What if I'm not the same person?"

"We all change. We've both changed in ten years."

But what if she didn't fall in love with him again? Or he didn't love her when he got to know her again?

She had reason to wonder about it again when Hawk followed her into the bedroom where she slept earlier. He peeled off his shirt and tossed it in the hamper. His broad shoulders and muscular torso were things of beauty, but when he shucked his pants, a nervous flutter settled in the pit of her stomach while intimate parts of her body tingled with a sensitive heat that made her restless.

She remembered making out with her college boyfriend, but they'd never gone beyond that, had they? She probed at that memory, and something hovered at the edge, something painful she didn't want to touch.

Hawk pulled a pair of sleep pants out of the drawer, and, wearing just his boxer briefs, went into the bathroom. When he came back out, he'd obviously ditched his underwear, leaving the sleep pants to hang low on his hips and accentuating the musculature of his abs and waist. "I'll turn out the lights and lock up." He wandered out of the room.

She hadn't thought to even wonder about their sleeping arrangement, but the idea of sharing a bed with him left her heart pounding and her breathing a little labored.

Was this arousal like the shadow feelings she was experiencing about other things?

Did her body, and her heart, remember the passion they had for each other even though her mind didn't? And how far would that carry their relationship if she never remembered their life together?

Hawk settled into the bed beside her. "I'm a light sleeper if you need me during the night."

She fought against a bout of self-deprecating laughter and managed a soft. "Okay."

She turned her back to him, hoping to block off the lingering feelings and go to sleep.

She needed to remember her awareness of him was a double-edged sword. She had to give herself time to build a connection before they became more intimate.

In a way it was like she was taking over another woman's life. A life already created for her.

She needed to be sure it was the life she wanted.

CHAPTER 12

MOIRA HEAVED A frustrated sigh while she went through yet another rack of dresses.

She hated shopping. When God passed out the shopping gene, he skipped her. Unless it pertained to art supplies. She could spend the entire day at *Dick Blick*, *Michaels*, *Artists and Craftsman*, *Visual* and half a dozen other art supply stores. A good buy on watercolor paper or pre-stretched canvases made her heart leap with excitement.

So, it wasn't surprising when she couldn't find the perfect dress. She didn't have a vision of what it might look like. Maybe she needed to buy some canvas and have it made into a dress so she could stretch it for paintings later. She smirked at the thought.

"Maybe I could just buy some lace leggings and a satin top and strut down the aisle," she said with a sigh.

Maggie paused from browsing a rack of bride's maids' dresses to give her a narrow-eyed look. "Have you seen Sam in his dress whites?"

"No. Only a very nice suit and his cammies." And he was hot enough in those.

"I have yet to see a man who doesn't look drop-dead gorgeous and hot in uniform. And if Sam is going to be handsome and hot, you need to be gorgeous and sexy."

Moira thought Maggie's expectations might be set a little high.

With her out-of-control naturally curly hair and her pale skin, she fell a little short of supermodel material. But she wanted to look beautiful for Sam.

With a sigh she browsed back through the endless row of dresses, and was nearing the end of the size eights and already resigning herself to disappointment when one caught her eye.

It was actually the back of the gown that faced her. A strip of ecru lace stretched down the center of the back where a row of pearl buttons ran. The rest was sheer. She turned the gown. Another band of lace encircled the neck. The bodice of the gown, created of voile and off-white satin, was form-fitting and cut in a sweetheart design. Lace, pearls, and sequins swirled in leaf-shaped designs across the bodice and down into a full skirt with a train in the back.

It was beautiful and sexy, just as Maggie had suggested. But could she pull it off?

She slipped away to the dressing room, turned her back to the dressing room mirror, removed her clothes, slipped on the dress, and asked the attendant to button the dress for her. But still didn't look in the mirror.

"Just an observation," the woman said. "This dress was made for you."

Moira flashed her a nervous smile. "I hope you're right, because this is the second weekend I've spent looking, and I only have six weeks to find a dress." She pulled up her hair to a tail at the crown of her head, twisted it into a messy bun, and stuck in two pencils to hold it in place. Then finger-combed a couple of curling strands on either side of her face.

"We have a hair comb that would be perfect with the dress. Would you like me to get it for you?"

"Yes, please. I'm going to go out and look at it in the long mirrors and get my friend's opinion."

"I'll get the comb and bring it to you so you can try it."

"Thank you."

She exited the dressing room and walked over to the three full-length mirrors. Maggie glanced up. Her eyes widened and her lips parted. She rested a hand on the clothes rack.

Moira studied the warm color of the dress against her pale skin. The copper highlights in her hair gleamed beneath the lights. If she did up her eyes with shadow and more mascara and added a little blush... she might come close to wowing Sam.

When Maggie remained silent, she finally said, "What do you think?"

"I think it's perfect, and it's certainly sexy. And with your back being bare, but covered with that delicate mesh, he'll be thinking all afternoon about unbuttoning every one of those buttons to take off the dress."

Moira laughed. When the attendant returned with the fancy hair comb, she took it and positioned it at the back of the bun. Then turned to look at the back of the dress and the comb.

"It's beautiful, Moira, and I think with a few pins here and there, the comb is all you'll need."

"I'll take it. I'm not certain I want to wear a veil, and I think just having my hair fixed and wearing this will do the trick."

Excited and relieved, she let out a sigh. "Now we have to find something for you, Maggie."

"I've laid out three dresses to try on, but I think there's only one that will work with the design of your gown. It has some small areas that will show my shoulder blades through lace, and has the filmy sleeves similar to yours. Plus it's blue and will match the men's suits. I'll get it and try it on."

Half an hour later, Moira was grinning as they left the store, until Maggie said, "We need to go shop for shoes."

Moira groaned and Maggie laughed. "We can do it another time."

But if she stopped now, she'd only dread doing it until they got it over with. "No. Let's get it done."

They walked down the mall and stopped to get a drink at one of the restaurants at the food court. She'd tried to keep her mind focused on getting her dress and taking care of other things, but the disagreement she had with Principal Jacobs had preyed on her mind all week. He hadn't said anything more to her, but every time she needed to go to the office to pick up paperwork, she grew tense with dread. She sent students in her place several times to avoid any chance they'd meet. But this couldn't continue.

"Principal Jacobs approached me about another fundraiser the other day."

"It's a little soon, isn't it? We just finished one."

"That's what I told him. He was pushing me to write a grant for an online store where the students could sell artwork, electronics, and plants."

Maggie's brows rose. "The logistics alone would be a nightmare. Plus, I'm sure the Board wouldn't sign off on anything like that. It would cut into the students' classroom time."

"All things I mentioned myself. I also told him if he wants the grant written, he'll have to appoint a committee to do it, because I don't have enough experience." Moira leaned back in her seat. "I told him the staff and students were overwhelmed at this point with these extra projects, and if he wanted to do it, he was going to have to find someone else to spearhead it or do it himself. I can't do it anymore."

Maggie's eyes widened. "Wow."

"He then said no one else could take this on because they were busy with testing. When I pointed out to him that I was testing too, he shrugged it off like what I do is nothing."

"Every teacher in the school knows that isn't so, Moira."

Not all of them. Despite the scholarships her students had earned, many on the staff still thought art was a frivolous hobby, not a career.

She dragged her thoughts back to the discussion. "The thing is, I've been avoiding Jacobs ever since. I haven't gone into the office to pick up my paperwork in the mornings, and I send someone down from homeroom to get it for me."

"What makes you think he'll push you about this?"

Moira shook her head. She was still a little wary about going into the office. "He came to my room the other day. The day you were out for your doctor's appointment. He apologized for pushing me to write the grant and said he'd decided I was right.

The project was too ambitious, and the teachers were tired and needed a break."

Maggie nodded. "If he comes back, stick to your guns, Moira. Don't allow him to back you into a corner. You've done enough, and the other teachers and the students are burned out with these extra projects."

There had been something different about the way he pushed this time. But she didn't think he'd come back a second time.

"If he does pressure you, I'll back you up, and I know everyone else in our wing will too. So try not to worry about it."

"Okay." Moira forced a smile. She decided then to continue holding back the news about her future father-in-law's arrest because she didn't want to embarrass Sam or his brothers. They hadn't seen anything in the news about it thus far, but Tim and Sam spoke often about their father's situation. "Are you ready to try on shoes?"

Maggie stood. "Yeah. Let's do it."

Moira tried to put both issues out of her mind and let Maggie's positivity carry her through. They found stylish pumps that matched Maggie's dress, and dressy sandals with a dainty heel and just a bit of bling on them that matched the cream of her own.

"You want to call the guys to come out and join us for a meal before we go home?" Moira asked.

"Abe's catching a plane for New York tonight. I was hoping to jump his bones a time or two before he left."

Moira laughed. "I think jumping his bones is much more important than eating out with us. You need to pick something up on the way home."

"That's the plan. He'll be gone for about 5 days. It's some kind of think tank thing to do with his specialty. He's been working on a presentation for days."

"He's so impressive. So smart," Moira said. "It's a shame you couldn't go with him."

Maggie paused next to a window to eye a summer sweater. "I thought about taking the days off, but he'd be MIA most of the time doing his thing. He says these things are pretty intense. So I couldn't really justify using my personal days and handing testing over to a substitute."

They sidestepped to avoid the large cluster of teenagers rolling down the mall in a wave.

Moira sighed. "We're too responsible for our own good. I've sacrificed personal time for a lot of things since I started teaching. We all do. But I'm cutting back. Sam could be deployed at any moment, and I'd regret not spending time with him when I can. Every minute is precious."

"I don't know how you do it." Maggie's expression held a hint of concern.

"I love him. You just try to stay supportive." The problems with Sam's father came to mind.

Maggie rested her hand on her arm. "You're a strong lady, Moira."

Touched and close to tears Moira patted Maggie's hand and said, "Yeah, I am, because I shopped. And I hate to shop. He'd better appreciate it."

Maggie laughed.

After dropping Maggie off at her apartment with the takeout food, Moira turned toward home. She had just pulled into the parking lot when her phone rang. "Ms. McKee, this is Emily from school."

She never got phone calls on the weekend about school. Concerned she said, "Yes, Emily. What can I do for you?"

"You came by my office on Friday to bring me the fundraiser money, and you and I counted every dollar together. And the receipts. And signed off on it."

"Yes, I remember. And you made out the deposit ticket, put everything in a bank bag, filed the receipts, and printed out the check to send to the charity."

"Mr. Jacobs said he did the deposit at the end of the day. But later that day the money was withdrawn again and transferred into a bogus account. There was more than twenty-five thousand dollars in the account, including other money that came in in addition to the fundraiser funds."

"Who had access to the account information and the password?"

"Only me, and now it's gone and everyone's looking at me."

No way. There wasn't a dishonest bone in Emily's body. "I know you didn't take anything, Emily. If you'd wanted to steal the money, you could have waited for me to leave, taken out part of the money, redone the deposit slip, and destroyed the receipts you filed, and no one would have been the wiser. You've been doing this job for years, and nothing like this has ever happened. No one is going to think it was you."

"But what about the password?"

"Do you have it written down somewhere?"

"No. It's a password that's personal to me."

"Then it has to be someone who's very familiar with you. Someone who's around you all the time. Someone who may have watched you key it in."

Emily fell silent for a long moment. "I'll have to give it some thought." A beat passed. "Thank you for being so supportive, Ms. McKee. I feel much better after discussing it with you."

"I know you didn't do anything wrong, Emily. It's going to be okay. If you need me to stand with you, I will. We both signed off on the count. The police have computer experts who can trace the transactions, and they'll find out where the transfer was done, where it went, and who did it."

"Thank you, Ms. McKee."

"Moira. We've been working together for the last six years. You can call me Moira."

"Thank you, Moira."

"You're welcome. I'll see you on Monday."

"Okay. Have a nice weekend."

"You too."

As soon as she hung up, Moira allowed herself to wonder who could have done this. How was the school going to cover the check to the charity? The charity head office would have gotten it by now and tried to deposit it. What if it bounced?

Surely the school would catch who was responsible and make

it right. That money represented many, many hours of work for the students and teachers. For her too. "Damn it!"

She got out of the car and reached into the back seat to get her shopping bags.

As she entered her apartment, she noticed Sam's gear bag opposite the door and his keys in the pottery dish on the coffee table.

She took her dress and shoes and comb into her studio and tucked them out of sight in the nearly-empty closet there. Though there were some canvases stacked in the bottom of the closet, there was room for both items and would be safely out of Sam's sight.

She kicked off her shoes and wandered down the hall to the bedroom. Sam lay on his back on the bed, his face partially turned away from her, his chest rising and falling in slow, even breaths. He'd been so worked up about his father, he'd been restless at night and hadn't slept well.

She set her purse on the dresser, eased down on the bed to curl on her side, and turned to face him. With his features relaxed in sleep, she caught a glimpse of what he might have looked like as a boy. He frowned in his sleep, and she fought the urge to smooth away the crease between his brows.

Such a strong, fierce, controlled man. But for all his ferocity, he showed her a tender side few had probably seen. And he inspired tenderness in her.

She stifled a yawn. Shopping was more exhausting than teaching, but at least she'd found her dress and shoes, and Maggie had chosen hers. What a relief. Her eyes closed and she was out like a light.

CHAPTER 13

SAM WOKE TO a Perry Mason ring tone and fumbled blindly for the phone on the nightstand.

"They've arrested Dad for murder. No bail," Tim said.

Sam ran a hand down his face, shaking loose the dullness of sleep. "Just give it to me straight, Bro."

"They think he paid someone to kill Jonathan Walker and steal the truck, and said the truck was involved in an accident."

"What kind of accident?"

"The carjacker rear-ended someone and shoved an SUV out into traffic. He caused a pileup."

"Jesus." Sam sat up and swung his legs over the side of the bed. "Anyone hurt?"

"Yeah. Your CO's wife. Zoe Yazzie."

"Shit! How bad?"

"She was in an induced coma for five days. In the hospital for ten. She has a brain injury and a broken arm. Mom asked around, and found out she has severe memory loss, reoccurring dizziness, and it's going to be months before she'll be back to normal, if ever."

"God dammit!" He raked his fingers through his hair. Beating back his rage took all his control. "That bastard leaves destruction in his wake everywhere he goes and inflicts it on everyone he comes in contact with. Family destruction, economic destruction and now Zoe Yazzie and Trevor's lives."

"We don't know if he did this. The embezzlement I'm sure of, but not the murder."

"Who else could be responsible?"

"I don't know. They're doing some forensic testing on the truck. It was stolen from the parking lot and driven through town, then went missing for several days until it was found parked in a residential area not far from the Yazzies' house."

"Jesus!"

"I'm hoping they get some fingerprints or something that will point to the carjacker."

"How did you find all this out?"

"I have friends in the DA's office."

A thought occurred to Sam and his anger spiked again. "You're not catching any shit for this, are you?"

"No. I already have a good reputation here. I'll be okay. But they'll be calling you for an interview soon. They've already talked to me."

"I'll be fine. I'm not involved."

"Be careful. This is turning into a major case. Hundreds of thousands of dollars stolen, one person dead, and another whose life may be changed forever, and their families impacted."

Sam's phone beeped and he glanced at the number. Strangely familiar. "I have another call. I have to go."

"Watch your back, bro."

"Roger that."

He closed out his brother's call and answered the next. "Lieutenant Harding. This is Detective Michael Hart of the SDPD. We'd like to speak with you. When would be a good time?"

"You can swing by right now, Lieutenant. I'm at my girlfriend Moira's apartment. You've been here before."

"Yes. Detective Buckler will be coming with me."

"That's fine."

"You were expecting us to call?"

"My father's been arrested for embezzlement and murder. I'm his son. You have to rule me out as an accomplice."

"We'll be there in thirty minutes."

Sam ended the call and lay the phone back on the nightstand. He turned to Moira, silent and watchful behind him. She rubbed his chest, her touch a comfort. "I'm sorry about your dad. He's really being charged with murder?"

"I'm not so sure I'm sorry. If he's in jail he won't be able to cause any more heartache."

"Are the police coming here?"

"Yes. Detective Hart and Buckler."

Moira shook her head. "They sure get around, don't they?"

"Yeah. They sure seem to." He slid down to pull her in close and kiss her. "How did the shopping trip go?"

"Maggie and I found our dresses and shoes."

"I knew you could do it."

"It was easier having someone along who actually likes to shop."

"Excellent. I don't suppose you want to model the dress for me later."

"It would be bad luck, and besides, I want to surprise you."

He grinned. "Is it sexy?"

"Very."

"I can't wait. Let's get married tomorrow." He kissed her.

"I wish we could."

He searched her face. "I do too. I'm getting antsy. I keep expecting command to throw a monkey wrench in the works and call the team up for a mission. We could slip off and get married in Vegas or the courthouse and still plan the wedding and do the ceremony for our families on the date we set. That way if I get called up, you can go ahead with the reception and everything, but we'll be married."

Her pale blue eyes studied him. "You don't have to worry about me, Sam. If you get called up, I'll wait for you."

"There's a lot of paperwork that has to be done after we get married, so you'll be on my military insurance, and other things."

"Are you worried something might happen to you?"

"No. But if I get deployed right after the wedding, I won't be here to take care of everything."

"I'm not worried about the paperwork. I have health insurance through my job. And I have a savings account to fall back on if something happens while you're gone."

He needed an independent woman, but he wanted to be able to take care of her. "I want time with you, Moira. We've been apart so much already."

"You're not neglecting me, Sam. You're nothing like your father."

Hearing her say it relieved tension he barely realized he was feeling.

She caressed his cheek. "You've watched out for your mom for years. You're a good man, a good son, a good boyfriend, and you're going to be a wonderful husband and, one day, a wonderful father."

"How can you be so certain?"

"Because you've taken your father's transgressions too much to heart to allow yourself to be anything like him."

"If ever I fall down on the job—"

"I'll kick your ass myself."

The idea of Moira kicking anyone's ass made him laugh. "I think that idea is turning me on."

"I think everything turns you on."

"Pretty much anything to do with you does." He slipped off the bed and offered her a hand. "Have you told your parents about him?"

"No. But they won't judge you for what your father's done."

"I know they won't. I just wondered…"

She raised one shoulder in a shrug. "It feels too much like gossiping to tell them personal things about your family. I'll just let them read the papers and find out. Besides, we don't know anything besides the bare bones of the situation."

When she slipped off the bed and stood, he drew her in close. "I never dreamed I'd be marrying a woman as closemouthed as I am."

"I'm not closemouthed with you."

He grinned.

She gave him a pinch on the ass. "I meant I share things with you I don't share with other people."

He chuckled. "Yes, you do."

"Since I seem to be digging a bigger and bigger hole with everything I say, I'm going to stop."

He nuzzled her neck and felt her shiver. "Please don't."

The doorbell rang, and he straightened. "It hasn't been thirty minutes. They must have been on their way here when they called."

Her arms tightened around him. "No matter what happens, nothing your father has done will ever change how I feel about you, Sam."

"Thank God," he murmured. And, grabbing her hand, tugged her out of the bedroom and down the hall to answer the door.

Detective Hart and Buckler looked as careworn as they did the last time he and Moira saw them.

"How have you two been?" Hart asked as he and his partner took a seat in the overstuffed chairs in Moira's living room.

"We're good," Sam answered for both of them.

Buckner didn't beat around the bush. "Your father was arrested for murder today."

"I heard. My brother called me just before you did."

"You don't seem too broken up about it."

"If he did it, he deserves to be arrested. If he didn't, I'm sure the truth will come out."

To listen to him talk like he didn't have feelings and this didn't matter, hurt her, because she knew he wasn't emotionless. He wouldn't be so antsy if he was that detached about what his father might have done.

"When was the last time you spoke to him?" Detective Hart asked.

"Nearly eight months ago, when I went wheels up on deployment."

"But not after you got back?"

"No. My mother called him and told him I was back."

"Did you talk to him then?"

"I wasn't with her when she called. She just said she wanted him to know I was okay."

The two detectives looked at each other.

"Can I speak to you outside, Ms. McKee?" Detective Buckler asked.

Sam fought the urge to look at her and focused on Detective Hart instead.

"We can go into my office if you like, Detective." She rose and led the way down the hallway to her studio.

Sam leaned forward and braced his elbows on his knees. "I'll save you some time, Detective. My father and I don't have a relationship and haven't since I was a teenager. I was twelve when I figured out that he was fucking around on my mother. When he left her for his current wife, I slashed his tires. I was fourteen. He had me arrested.

"When he came to bail me out the next morning, I refused to go with him and pushed his buttons until he punched me. He was arrested for child abuse. We ended up in family court, and I refused to have anything else to do with him.

"Until college. He paid for my education, but only if I went into law. I went to college, got a law degree, and as soon as I graduated, I took the bar and passed. The same day I got the letter, I had a copy messengered to his office with a copy of my enlistment papers. When I left for boot camp, I called him and told him to go fuck himself."

"Where were you Thursday, March twenty-fourth?"

"We had beach maneuvers for an op that got canceled. I was covered with sand, so I took a shower at the base, changed into fresh clothes, and left at eighteen hundred. I was home sometime before nineteen hundred for dinner. We stayed home and watched a movie on one of the movie channels and went to bed."

"How can you be sure?"

"We had dinner with my mother the next night, and that's when my brother Trevor came in and told us that Jonathan Walker had been killed during a carjacking and that the police had come in and taken the Walker files. I figured if my dad was involved, I'd better make sure I remembered exactly where I was."

"How long has it been since you've seen Jonathan Walker?"

"High school at least. Hank played basketball, but he was a senior, while I was a sophomore. I remember his dad as a big guy with huge hands and a big voice. A lot of personality."

Moira returned with Detective Buckler and took a seat next to him.

"Were you surprised when you heard your father had been arrested for embezzlement?"

"No. He always has a side piece. And he always goes for high-maintenance. The money has to come from somewhere." Though Sam tried to keep the bitterness out of his voice, some still leaked in. Moira's gave his bicep a supportive squeeze. He glanced at her and rested his hand over hers.

"What about the murder charge?"

"When Tim called, I was a little shocked. I can see him stealing money, but not killing. He'll smack a fourteen-year-old, but facing off against someone the size of Jonathan Walker." He shook his head. "And stealing his vehicle. I can't picture him doing that at all."

The two detectives exchanged a look and rose in unison.

He and Moira got up to walk them to the door.

As soon as the detectives left the apartment, Moira turned and held him close.

"You weren't gone long in the office."

"I didn't know anything other than that you were with me March twenty-fourth. We've been together every night since you got back from deployment."

Thank God for making up for lost time.

"They don't really believe you'd kill someone for your father.'

He was careful in the way he said it. "I carry a gun. I know how to kill in a number of different ways. They have to ask." If his father had anything to do with Walker's death…

Who better to throw under the bus if he feels the walls closing in?

CHAPTER 14

I N THE UNPROTECTED bleachers at the little league field, the relentless April sun beat down with the heat of July. Hawk wiped the sweat off his forehead with a napkin left over from A. J.'s lunch. He should have brought a hat.

Hawk concentrated on A. J.'s game because he'd ask how he did, and Hawk needed to know details to answer him. But another part of his mind was busy thinking about what would be waiting for him at home. Zoe was getting restless and impatient with the restrictions of staying home with a keeper. Though her memory was still gone, her personality hadn't changed at all. Even recovering from a fractured skull, she was as independent and driven as she'd always been. That's what had made them such a good couple. She could handle everything on her own while he was gone, and she was delighted to turn the reins over when he got back.

He was in charge on post, but when he stepped inside their home, he pretty much did whatever she needed him to and reaped the rewards of being loved and cared for.

She asked nothing of him now. She'd lost the rules to their relationship when that truck pushed her car into traffic.

A. J. came up to bat, and Hawk focused all his attention on his son's form and stance. A. J. popped up a foul ball with the first pitch. The second pitch went wide and was called a foul. The third pitch, he hit the ball solidly and it sailed to left field while A. J. ran around the bases and made it to third before the outfielder threw the ball. He flashed Hawk a grin as he kept a foot on the base and waited for the next play.

"A. J. looks like he's in good form," Langley said as he took a seat beside him.

Hawk leaned forward to plant his elbows on his knees. "He loves baseball. He wants to be a professional ball player—for now."

"He'd make a helluva lot more money than we do."

"That's for damn sure." He braced himself for the inevitable question, and Lang didn't surprise him.

"How's Zoe?"

"She's not sleeping as much, and she's getting restless being at home all the time."

"Not a surprise. She and Trish have more energy than any two women I've ever known."

"That they do."

"Has she remembered anything?" Langley asked.

Hawk shook his head. "Not a damn thing."

"Jesus," Langley breathed. His lantern-jawed features crimped with concern. "Two weeks is a long time."

An eternity.

"How's A. J. doing?"

"He's okay. She's great with him. Sometimes when she looks at him you can tell she's homed in, searching for something. She wants to remember."

"How's she with you?"

"Sometimes the same. Mostly like she was when we first met."

"You've got your work cut out for you. I remember how the two of you circled each other when you first met. Her ignoring you but watching you when you weren't aware of it, and you acting all protective and hands-off even though you had a thing for her."

He eyed Langley in surprise.

Lang grinned. "Trish and I had a bet going on when you'd

finally cave and move on her."

"A bet?"

"Yeah."

At the sound of a ball connecting to a bat, Hawk shifted his attention to A. J. as he ran across home plate and raised a fist in victory.

Hawk raised one in return, then, when A. J. disappeared into the dugout, returned to the conversation. "Who won the bet?"

"I did."

He shot Lang a look.

"Hey, you've never been known for your patience, and I knew you didn't care about her leg issue and that you'd wear her down."

"I have the patience of Job."

Langley laughed.

They fell silent as the little league game continued.

"Trish is missing her. Think you might want to encourage her to call, or maybe you could bring her over to the house for a meal with us tonight. Maybe Trish can shake something loose. A. J. and Tad can battle it out in one of their video games."

"I think Zoe will be thrilled to get out of the house for a visit."

"How about nineteen hundred?"

"That'll be good."

"I'm going to hit the market for Trish. I'll see you all at seven."

Once the game was over, Hawk waited for A. J. to join him at the end of the bleachers while the rest of the parents gathered close to the fence and the other spectators wandered back to the parking lot to their cars.

A. J.'s face was red from exertion, but his smile stretched wide. "I did pretty good."

"You did great." Hawk placed a hand on his shoulder as they walked to the car.

"When do you think Mom will be ready to come back to the games?"

"It's only been a couple of weeks, A. J. I think at least another two weeks at the very least. There will be a lot of parents who'll want to check in with her, and it'll be hard for her unless she can remember who they are."

A. J. was silent until they were in the car. "Do you think she'll ever remember us, Dad?"

"Yeah. I think she will. We just have to be patient."

"She tries hard to make me think she remembers."

"What do you mean?"

"She tells me she loves me, but how can she love me if she doesn't remember me?"

Jesus! "You're her child, A. J. Her baby." At the word baby, his son's eyes rolled with an outraged frown that would have been funny any other time. "There's an emotional connection between you that nothing will ever change. She may not have the memories, but she still has the feelings and the need to care for you."

"Are you sure?"

"Positive." He cupped his son's sweaty head, then gave his shoulder a squeeze. He could only protect A. J. to a certain extent. Children were supposed to be resilient, but A. J.'s concerns were reasonable.

He nearly sighed out loud when A. J. changed the subject. "Langley came to my game."

"Yeah, he had to leave after it ended to run some errands. He was impressed with your hit."

AS MUCH AS she loved her mother and everything she did for her, some small part of Zoe resented the need to have her as her guardian. And she hated herself for that resentment. Her mother was taking time off from her own life to stay with her. But when had her mother become the master questionado?

Clara didn't just ask one question, she asked many, many, many questions. She questioned everything Zoe wanted to do. And her favorite question was, "*Has your doctor approved that?*"

And Hawk had gotten just about as good at it as her mother.

"What's Hawk's favorite meal, Mom?"

"Roast beef, gravy, mashed potatoes, green beans, and homemade rolls. Pecan pie for desert."

Her mother laughed at her slack-jawed look. "I know. I can feel my arteries clogging just smelling it cook, but he's so active and in such good shape, I doubt that it hurts him the few times a year you fix it."

"I'd like to fix him something special, and I'd like to have an evening alone with him—without A. J."

The hopeful look on her mother's face had her cheeks heating.

"He's been so good to me these past couple of weeks, and I just want to thank him for everything."

"Don't fix his favorite meal for that. He may read more into it than you intend. Fix something else."

So her mother had noticed how she and Hawk were dancing around each other like—not strangers but...she wasn't sure. Husband, father, good guy, hunk, Navy SEAL... Stranger. She was getting to know him, getting used to him handling her like she was someone he knew and loved. Getting used to waking every morning to find him holding her.

Though he hadn't pushed her for anything physical, mentally she was in constant conflict. Emotionally and physically her reaction to him was embarrassingly intense. And she felt his erection every morning, though to his credit he tried to redirect.

She turned away to hide her reaction and reached into the cabinet for a glass. "What would you suggest?" She went to the refrigerator for chilled water.

"Maybe something on the grill."

"I'll look in the freezer and see what we have."

"I can take you to the grocery store."

"I don't remember my pin number for my debit card or the password for the bank so I can check my account balance." Every small thing she ran up against seemed overwhelming. Since when had she become such a wuss?

"You can ask Hawk. I'm sure he'd know."

"It's really weird, but it feels like I'm taking money from a stranger."

"It's your money, Zoe. You worked for it."

She went to the refrigerator and looked in the freezer. Seeing a package of pork chops, she removed them and set them on the drainboard at the sink to thaw. "I want to go to the hospital and see where I work. It's been two weeks since I got home, and it's time for me to see where my life is." Hawk continued to resist taking her there.

"Has your doctor said anything about that?"

Zoe bit back the words that threatened to rip through her control. Her doctor was more concerned with healing the injury to her brain than he was with getting her memory and life back.

Her mother frowned at Zoe's silence, correctly reading rebellion into it. "You need to rest and take things easy."

"I have to move on, Mom. I want to go back to work. I need something to occupy my time." And she needed to be able to walk around the block without someone holding her hand.

"You'll be back to work in a few weeks."

She'd be stark raving mad by then.

She looked at the clock again. Hawk was due back with A. J. by four.

"What will you do with A. J.?"

"He can stay the night if he wants to since it's the weekend."

"What do you do when he stays?"

"We go for walks to the nearby park. He plays ball with some of the neighborhood children there. Russell makes him milkshakes. And we watch science fiction movies. He's into aliens and all sorts of creatures. And superheroes. We've seen all the superhero movies, and he and Russell have really bonded."

"I can tell. They were playing a video game the other day and got into a philosophical discussion about why one superhero's power was creating things out of his imagination and the other was based on strength, and why one was better than the other."

Clara laughed.

"A. J. may be hungry from playing sports. I'll fix him something to eat." But what did he like? She settled on peanut butter and jelly with slices of apples and raisins on the side.

"Have you fixed him this before?" Clara asked.

"I don't know. His not allergic to peanuts, is he?"

"If he was, you wouldn't keep peanuts in any form in the house, would you?" Clara asked.

Zoe breathed in and out slowly to control her temper while she covered the food with plastic wrap. She went out into the sunroom, then rushed out the side door into the yard.

Her mother hadn't meant anything by it, but she was talking to her like she was a ten-year-old. That was what was driving her crazy. She had a brain injury, she recognized that, but she wasn't…incompetent.

When she heard Hawk's car pull up, she let herself out the back gate and limped around the side of the house to the driveway.

She met A. J. in the driveway as he got out of the car. She moved to hug him immediately, but when Hawk stepped out of the car, she shook her head at him. "Don't get out of the car." She turned her attention back to A. J. "Grandma is going to take you home with her for a little while. If you don't want to stay the night, call and we'll come pick you up. Remember to take your toothbrush, pajamas, clean underwear and a change of clothes if you're going to spend the night."

"Okay."

"I love you." She meant it. He was her child.

A. J. hugged her hard, and she returned the embrace.

Zoe watched him walk toward the house for a moment, and when her mother came to the door and stepped out on the porch, she raised a hand, and slid into the car. "Please drive."

"Where to?" Hawk asked.

"I'll trade sexual favors if you'll just drive away from this house and my mother and not ask a single question for at least five minutes."

Hawk gave a single bark of laughter, then tried to cover it with a cough. He threw the car into reverse and backed out onto the street.

Zoe breathed a sigh of relief as the house disappeared from view while Hawk wound his way through the neighborhood at a slow, steady speed. The houses they passed were similar in size to theirs, the lawns all manicured and raked. There was a sense of security in cruising the neighborhood and a realization of how boring it was. She supposed security was more important than adventure.

"My five minutes are up, and I'm going to ask a question."

She sucked in a deep breath. "Okay."

"What kind of sexual favors?"

Zoe laughed then covered her face with her hands. "I can't believe I said that."

"You looked ready to hit someone or blow up."

Suddenly close to tears, she looked away. "When they told Mom I had a brain injury…" She closed her eyes and swallowed. "She thinks I'm brain-damaged, and questions everything I do. She talks to me like I'm A. J. instead of a grown woman."

Hawk's good humor faded, and he remained silent for a moment. "I'm sorry, Zoe. We'll make other arrangements."

"No. We're not making arrangements at all. Starting Monday, I'm on my own. I can't live like this." *Not again.*

"It could be dangerous for you to stay by yourself."

"The dizzy spells have stopped, and I'm getting stronger." Though she still needed to rest and sleep a lot. But that was the point. She knew when she needed to rest and when to sleep.

"What about the headaches?"

"Those are going to be with me for a while." Maybe always. Like her leg. "I've learned to adapt. I'll do it again."

Hawk came to a halt at a stop sign and paused with his right blinker going. "Your mom said you get a little anxious in heavy traffic."

"When did she say that?"

"After your first follow-up with the neurologist."

Why was her mom tattling—on top of questioning everything she did? "I'd only been out of the hospital a few days. What did she expect?"

Hawk fell silent again.

She tucked a stray strand of hair back off her cheek and tossed her long, braided tail over her shoulder.

Hawk turned the car toward a busy intersection and stopped at the red light. The vehicles sped past in packs, like they were jockeying for position in a race. Two transfer trucks lumbered by, their engines revving.

She hid her urge to flinch by keeping her eyes on the nose of their car. She looked into the side view mirror at the vehicle behind them. It was a compact car, not a truck, and she relaxed a little though her knee bobbed. It was like she was swallowing air instead of breathing it in. It wasn't triggered by a specific memory, but by the sounds and frenetic movement.

"Is this the first time you've been here since the accident?" Hawk asked.

"Yes. Mom avoided this intersection when she took me to the doctor."

He reached for her hand and gave it a squeeze.

The light turned green, and Hawk replaced his hand on the steering wheel and turned right.

A few minutes of silence passed and her shaking eased. "There's a disconnect between my memory and my emotions. And right now my emotions are running the show."

"What do you mean?"

"Even though I don't have memories of things, I have emotional reactions to them. When I met A. J., I wanted to hold him, though I didn't remember him. The first time I smelled him, it triggered a protective emotion."

"How does he smell?"

"Like outdoors, boy sweat, and him."

Hawk chuckled and shook his head. "Have you spoken to the doctor about it?"

"He's only interested in making sure my brain is healing and that I don't overdo." He'd probably say being delusional was part of having her brain slammed against her fractured skull.

Hawk cut through the traffic and wound his way to Highway 1, where they followed the coast for a time, just enjoying the scenery. Zoe rested her head against the seat back and drifted off.

When she woke up, everything was still and the car was parked. Hawk was outside, leaning back against the hood. His broad shoulders looked so strong. He had been a rock for the past two weeks, and he deserved better than what he was getting.

She clicked open the release on her seatbelt, and he turned when she shut the car door and joined him.

He offered his hand. "Let's walk on the beach."

Walking on the sand was difficult for her, and when he automatically tucked her right hand through his arm, offering her extra support, her heart seemed to turn over. No one had ever taken such care of her without calling attention to her leg. And now she had an arm in a cast too...They wandered down to the waterline where it was easiest for her to stroll without struggling. The breeze surrounded them with the tart scent of the sea and plastered their clothes against their bodies.

There were few people enjoying the stiff breeze or the sighs of the surf as it rushed in and then was dragged back out. The horizon line looked blue-violet, with dark clouds congregating in the distance.

"Is it going to storm?"

"It will storm out there, but we'll probably only get a little sporadic rain."

They continued to walk. Hawk's companiable silence relaxed her as much as the short nap she'd taken in the car. When the water came in too close and nipped at their feet, he guided her farther up the beach to drier sand and found a spot to sit. He drew her down between his legs and used his larger size to protect her from the brunt of the wind.

"Langley asked if I thought you might be up to going over to their house tonight for dinner."

Anxiety brought an instant rush of uncertainty in its wake. What would the real Zoe do? There was no doubt. "Okay. You told me that Trish wants me to call her when I feel ready. It might be easier to talk to her in person."

"Stop pushing, honey." He put his arms around her and held her lightly. "As much as I want you to remember...I don't think pushing is going to help. Just try to live for the moment and enjoy it. Once you've begun to relax and you've healed a bit more, it will happen."

And if it didn't... She would never understand why he loved her like he did. Their shared experiences were what had built their relationship into something strong and resilient before. She was so afraid of hurting him and A. J.

She rested against him because whenever he was close, she wanted to be closer. More than wanted. But she was afraid to give in to it.

They had built a family together. Added to the one she'd already known. What if she couldn't get it back? It wouldn't just hurt Hawk and A. J. It would hurt them all.

CHAPTER 15

"J UST RELAX AND enjoy the moment," he reminded her when they pulled into the Marks's driveway.

"What about A. J.?"

"Your mom is going to keep him tonight and take him to church with her and Russell in the morning. He has everything he needs."

"Okay."

She hadn't relaxed since she opened her eyes in the hospital. He could practically see the tension working its way across her shoulders now.

He caught her hand to stop her before they reached the door. "These are friends, Zoe. Langley and I are tight. Trish and you talked every day before the accident. She thinks of you as a sister."

"I know I'm blessed, Hawk. I know I have so many people in my life who care about me. But I can't stop thinking that...that... I'm not the same person they care about. I haven't become that person yet. I don't remember the experiences that made me that person. I'm not certain I'll ever be that person again."

With every word he felt the devasting punch of her loss. And his own.

She'd lost herself.

She might not ever be his Zoe again.

She might never want to be his wife again.

The pain stole his breath and nearly brought him to his knees. The hurt ricocheted through him, chewing up his insides. He swallowed, though his throat was dry, and for a moment his control teetered.

As he rode that cruel, cutting edge, Zoe touched his cheek. But he needed to look past the concern and empathy he read in her face. Otherwise he'd lose it completely.

He cleared his throat, but his voice still came out hoarse, squeezed by emotions he couldn't hope to suppress. "I don't ever want you to be anyone but who you are, whoever that person might be, now or later, Zoe."

The front door opened and Langley stepped out on the shallow slab that created the porch. "Everything okay?"

"Yeah," Hawk said. He moved forward, and Zoe tucked her hand in the crook of his arm.

He was relieved Langley's attention shifted to Zoe as soon as they made it to the front door. "Hey, lady, how you feeling?" Langley asked, giving her a brief hug.

"I'm okay." She looked up to study his face and smiled. Langley's homely, lantern-jawed face inspired smiles from kids to dogs and everyone in between.

"Trish has been cutting things up for a salad and has steaks to go on the grill. Tad has run to the store for the sour cream for the potatoes that I forgot, but all the girls are in the kitchen waiting to see you."

Hawk hung back a short distance while Langley directed Zoe from the front door, through the living room, and into the kitchen. He heard a squeal as the girls converged on her, hugging her and exclaiming over how good she looked, though she was thin and pale.

Langley turned, his good-natured grin falling away as his gaze fell on Hawk's face. "You look like you need a drink. Come outside and I'll get you a beer."

Once outside, Hawk brushed past him. "I need a minute." He followed the concrete surround alongside the pool to the grassy area of the yard out of view of the kitchen. He spent several minutes pacing and shoring up his defenses even while the doubt and grief still throbbed inside him.

When he joined Langley, he offered him a bottle of beer. "Take your time. I'm going to clean and light the grill."

With his first drink, it seemed like his throat might actually close, but the sensation finally eased. He needed to shake this off. There was nothing he could do. She had to find her way alone. But he could try to sway her in his direction. He might be wounded, but he was still on his feet and in the game.

Langley went back into the kitchen, and after a few minutes returned with the steaks.

"How are they doing?" Hawk asked.

"They're getting to know one another again."

"I'm getting to know her again, too."

Lang put the steaks on the grill and closed the lid. "How's that going?"

"She's anxious all the time. Like she's waiting for something bad to happen at any moment. And her mother, though she means well, keeps asking Zoe questions she doesn't know the answer to, and it's driving her crazy." *She doesn't know who she is anymore.*

"What about you?"

It was like having a limb removed without anesthetic. "I'm taking it a day at a time." He looked away in an attempt to hide the doubt that had taken root even as he was shoving it away. "Losing her isn't an option, Lang."

"She's going to work through this, just like she has other injuries in the past. She's going to be okay."

She would be okay, but would he? He'd come to several realizations....

The longer she couldn't remember him or their life together, the more difficult it was for him to trust that she would ever do so.

He couldn't force-feed her the past from his perspective and hope to trigger her memories. She needed to remember on her own.

She wanted to move forward with her life, but in order to do that she might choose to leave behind the people who loved her most.

It was the last possibility that would maim him.

Searching for a different topic, Hawk asked, "What's going on with the Morgan situation?"

"Legal aid has gotten involved. His teammate refused to press charges and the bar didn't want to hang him up, so that situation went away, but the resisting arrest charge is still an issue. The earlier drunk and disorderly was dropped to disturbing the peace."

"That doesn't end the issue of the drug test, either. What did the doctor say about his shoulder?"

"There was some inflammation. Instead of pain meds, he put him on an anti-inflammatory."

"I've already filed the paperwork for an administrative separation. He'll still have to go through the process and present the doctor's findings."

"Actually, I asked Ensign Reins to hold that until I could update you on all this so we wouldn't have to walk it all back."

What the fuck? That was two weeks ago. "We still don't know if Morgan is going to stow his shit and toe the line, Langley."

"I think we need to give him another week. I believe he's turned a corner. He hasn't had a drink in the last two weeks—not even a beer—and he's been busting his ass in training."

"You're sure about this?" Hawk eyed Lang.

"As sure as I can be after I interviewed him, talked to his team leader, and read the doctor's evaluation. I ordered another surprise test this week, and he was clear."

Hawk raked fingers over his close-cropped hair. His instincts were to push the paperwork through. "Any sign of the wife?"

"No. She's still MIA."

"No one's seen or heard from her since he returned from deployment?"

"No. But his team leader went to his apartment and said the place was barren. The minimum of furniture. A recliner and television in the living room, a bed and nightstand in the bedroom, and a microwave in the kitchen."

He had a bad feeling about that. What if something else was going on? "One more week." He hoped he wouldn't regret this, but he thought it was time to contact NCIS and ask them to check on the wife.

TRISH AND THE girls emerged through the sliding glass door laden with plates, silverware, and salad. Zoe followed with a stack of plastic cups. With the cast on her arm, she couldn't carry much of anything else.

Trish and the girls' delighted welcome had brought a quick rush of tears to her eyes.

Or had it been Hawk's expression of pain and loss she kept seeing? She'd hurt him. But worse, she'd snatched away some of the hope he was clinging to. She'd allowed her frustration with her mother to spill over onto him.

And now she didn't just feel guilty, even if every word she said was true, it twisted her up inside to know she could hurt him so badly.

He wanted his life back. The life he'd been living before the accident. And she didn't blame him. From what everyone told her, it was almost idyllic. She wouldn't mind a life like that. But she couldn't promise him anything, not yet.

Anna placed the pitcher of tea on the table. Zoe stacked the cups next to it. The stack toppled and one fell over the side of the table. She bent to pick it up, but it rolled out of reach. She knelt and reached for it. The distinctive scent of chlorine and suntan lotion wafted to her, and she was struck by a powerful moment of déjà vu. She must have smelled those scents a thousand times here.

"I'll get it for you, Zoe," Anna, Trish and Langley's youngest daughter, said and crawled under the edge of the table. Zoe looked up to see long, tanned legs at that end of the table.

For a moment she thought she saw a knee brace on the right

one and crutches helping him keep his balance. A mixture of emotions bombarded her. Anger, frustration, and attraction.

Her eyes swung to Anna. Strawberry blonde hair cupped an elfin face with a fine dusting of freckles across her nose. The slender-limbed thirteen-year-old wasn't who she expected to see. The hair wasn't blonde enough, and her eyes shone a paler shade of blue. Who was the child she'd been with under the table? And why had they been under there to begin with?

Anna touched her arm. "You okay, Zoe?"

She tucked one long, sun-streaked lock behind Anna's ear. "Yes, I'm fine."

Anna picked up the cup and handed it to her. The girl scrambled out from beneath the table.

Zoe's eyes traveled up the long length of Hawk's legs as he extended a hand to her. Her movements awkward, she swung around on her bottom, braced the toe of her right tennis shoe against his and allowed him to lever her to her feet.

She'd ask him later. Maybe something else would come while she was here.

Though she caught Trish's eyes resting on her several times, the open hope and expectation weren't as obvious, but they were there. The steaks were done to perfection, the potatoes flaky and rich with sour cream or butter—or both—and the salad crisp and colorful.

With the Langleys' children there to keep the conversation going, Zoe didn't feel pressured to join in.

"The kids baked you a cake. Well, Tad helped a little," Trish said as the kids cleared the table.

"He cleaned the icing bowl with a spatula and ate what was left. If you can call that helping," Jessica said with a wry smile. The fifteen-year-old had Langley's sable hair and hazel eyes, but her mother's beauty and attitude.

"I helped clean up, and I set the oven timer," Tad said.

Zoe laughed while Trish shook her head.

"Be more helpful and bring out the ice cream to go with the cake and the desert bowls and spoons," Trish instructed.

Tad's grin was a mirror of Langley's, though the shape of his chin was his mother's. He sauntered into the house with his sisters.

"Are they always so helpful?" Zoe asked.

"For the most part," Trish answered.

"We had them just so they could take care of all the crap details we didn't want to do anymore," Langley said, in a satirical tone. "Like mow the grass and do the laundry. The only bad part of the deal is we have to feed, clothe and board them, and they even expect an allowance."

Zoe laughed again. "They're really great."

"They are." Trish rested her fingers over Zoe's wrist for a moment and her eyes were suspiciously bright. "I'm so glad you decided to come tonight."

"It's good to get out of the house and spend time with other adults." She didn't want to ask her mother about those few fragile wisps of memory. If she asked Hawk it might give him a little too much hope. But she had to know. She leaned forward and lowered her voice. "When did Hawk have a knee brace and crutches?"

Trish's fingers tightened against her wrist. "He was injured saving Brett's life. When they got back to the states, he had to wear a brace and walk on crutches for several weeks."

"Were we here when he had them?"

"Yes, it was the second day you'd been in San Diego. Your mother, sister, and Katie Beth were here."

It had to be Katie Beth she'd been under the table with. "Don't tell him. I want to remember more first. I don't want to disappoint him."

Trish blinked as tears pooled in her eyes. "Okay." She swallowed. "You may not be able to remember, Zoe, but it hasn't changed you. You're still the same."

Was she? Zoe glanced toward the end of the table, where Hawk sat talking with Langley. If he found out she had remembered something and didn't tell him... He'd be hurt again.

The teens came back out with the cake and ice cream and gave her an opportunity to ignore the situation...for a while.

She realized how tired she was when they rose to leave. The doctor had warned her she wouldn't have the energy she once had, and it was true. The cast on her arm seemed to weigh ten pounds, and she cradled it against her as they said goodnight and walked to the car.

Hawk opened her door for her, and she got in. Once inside the car, he helped her fasten her seat belt.

"I'm sorry to be so much trouble." Her stomach tumbled with his attention focused on her.

"If I were paralyzed, had a missing limb, or was disfigured, would you say I was too much trouble?" he asked.

All things that could have happened to him during deployment. "Never."

"I think I can handle fastening a seat belt." He inserted the key and started the car.

Her mind wandered as he turned toward home. She'd wasted the past two weeks trying to force memories that wouldn't come. The only thing she knew was her emotions were all tied up in Hawk and their son. There was an instant bond with Trish, and she found Langley funny and endearing. Their children were affectionate and sweet, and so mature.

Could she even hope to do as well with A. J.?

She'd opened herself completely and behaved as a mother to A. J. even if she didn't remember how that went... Why couldn't she do the same as Hawk's wife?

If she let herself accept her role and embraced it, would she find her way back?

The house felt empty without A. J. there to greet them. Hawk locked up while she went into their bedroom. She looked through her dresser at the nightgowns, sleep pants, and tank tops the other Zoe preferred—and realized they were things she would have chosen herself. She chose a cotton gown with tiny flowers embroidered across the yoke and soft lace following the seam where the yoke and gathered fabric of the gown met. It wasn't sexy, just feminine.

"I remembered something at the Marks' house."

Hawk's head came up and he swung to face her.

"You had a brace on your knee and crutches."

"That was when Brett was injured and in the hospital."

"It was just a flash, but then I hit a wall again. Was I angry with you about something then?"

Hawk got his pajama pants out of the dresser, then sat next to her on the bed. "I couldn't tell you anything about the mission or anything about how he was injured. You were pissed about it. You thought you deserved to know. And you did. But I still can't tell you about it, even now."

She unbraided her hair and combed the fingers of her one good hand through it. "I know I upset you earlier. I was anxious, and I took it out on you. I was worried about Trish's expectations. You said she's one of my best friends, and I was afraid I'd disappoint her."

"No one else is worried about you disappointing them, Zoe. They just want you to be okay. Even if you never remember."

She closed her eyes against the burn of tears. When she thought she had her emotions under control, she opened them again and sucked in a deep breath. "A. J.'s gone and we're alone. What would we normally be doing right now?"

Hawk's gray eyes settled on her, and a wolfish grin stretched across his face while he shook his head. "What married people do when their kids are out of the house. Because we don't have to be quiet while we're doing it."

Heat climbed into her face, while saliva pooled in her mouth, and she swallowed. "I don't remember ever...."

"Your first time was with me. We've been very...compatible."

Her face heated again, and her entire body seemed to go into sexual hyperdrive.

"What are you doing, Zoe?"

"I'm trying to find a way back to my...our life. When A. J. comes home from school or he's getting ready to leave for school...it helps me to go through the motions of being a mother. It's helped me make a connection with him, and helps the feelings I have for him feel more legitimate. He's my child, I want to love him and be a mother to him."

She looked up at him. "Do you think doing the same with us will help me find the way back?"

"I don't know, honey." He tossed aside his pajama pants and

put an arm around her. She leaned against him and put her cast-covered arm around him. "As much as I want you, which is all the time, I'm not in any hurry. I don't want you going through the motions. I want you to be a wife to me because you want to be. And if we have to start from the very beginning again, that's where we'll start."

The tears came despite her attempts to stifle them. "Okay. What would be the beginning?" She quickly wiped them away.

"Date night."

"Isn't that what we just had?"

"I guess it was. But I didn't get to kiss you good night."

Nerves fluttered in her stomach. He'd brushed her lips with his, but he hadn't really kissed her.

Hawk's hand cradled the back of her head. His pale gray eyes looked dark, his pupils expanding as he lowered his mouth to hers. He kissed her lightly, gently, once, twice, then came back for more. The pressure of his lips urged hers to part, and his tongue traced the opening.

Her stomach tumbled, and a heated ache she couldn't ignore settled in intimate areas. Her nipples beaded. She raised her right hand to grip his shirt and draw him closer while their tongues came together in a sensuous battle that went on and on until she thought she might melt from the need that pulsed between her thighs.

When he raised his head, her heart beat a heavy rhythm that stole her breath. His cheeks were flushed, his eyes dark, his masculine features sharpened by need. "I'm going to take a shower."

Her mouth went dry as her breathing quickened. She swallowed with difficulty.

He rose and gathered his pajama pants and a T-shirt and went into the bathroom.

When he said they were very compatible physically, she had no understanding at all of what he meant. When she suggested going through the motions of acting like a wife, she had even less.

How was she going to be able to sleep next to him and resist the urge to reach for him?

CHAPTER 16

MOIRA CLEANED THE brush and set it aside to dry. Palettes, containers and brushes filled the dish drainer and cluttered the countertops as she cleaned and dried them. She returned to the studio with a load, and organized everything in the new cabinet she and Sam just bought. It gave her a feeling of accomplishment to stay organized.

Sam had his own idea of organization, and she tried to allow for that. Luckily he wasn't a slob. Otherwise they might have some adjustments to make.

It was about time they moved in together. After all, Sam had spent more nights at her apartment than his own before deployment. And after he returned, they hadn't wanted to be apart. Now his lease was up and they were within five weeks of getting married, it was time.

She went to the large chifforobe she'd emptied and stashed Sam's seabag inside along with several pieces of equipment. She hoped he wouldn't regret the sacrifices he made. Aside from his clothes and the recliner from his living room, he'd opted to put his furniture in storage and use hers.

She hoped he'd feel welcome when he got home. She'd tried to blend his possessions with hers so he'd feel this was his home as much as hers. He even insisted on paying his share of rent and utilities, something she hadn't been concerned about in the least.

She hung his framed commendations on one section of the wall in the living room, and made it a grouping in a spot that would attract people's attention as they entered the room.

She went into the hallway and straightened one of the photographs of his grandfather she just hung. A younger Sam stood on the bow of the yacht, his hair longer than she'd ever seen it and wrecked by the wind, and his T-shirt and cutoff shorts were grimy. His grandfather stood next to him, a coil of rope dangling from his fingers. The older man had the same blade-straight nose, sun-streaked brown hair, and piercing brown eyes as his grandson. He was a very masculine man, just as his grandson had grown to be. Both men had a commanding presence about them.

Would her and Sam's sons, if they had sons, look like these two men, and have that presence? She hoped so. And what about their daughters? She tried to imagine Sam's features on a daughter and actually laughed. The guys wouldn't have a chance, because she'd intimidate the hell out of them.

She moved into the bedroom and studied the painting she did for Sam and just this afternoon hung in the bedroom. He stood at the wheel of his yacht, sunglasses obscuring his eyes, his brown hair windblown, and the sun glancing off the warm tones in its texture. A slight smile tilted his mouth.

She remembered the day she took the photo. They'd been slightly at odds with each other, but not at that moment.

A door opened and closed in the living room, and nerves fluttered in her stomach. If he'd rather not hang the painting in the bedroom, they could put it in the living room.

She wandered down the hall to join him.

"Hey, it looks like you've been doing some reorganizing." His attention homed in on the cluster of commendations on the wall, then moved to the recliner she'd positioned in line with the television. "I've brought the last of my clothes. They're out in the car."

"I've bagged up some of my old things and will drop them at a local clothing bank after school one day next week. I should have done it a long time ago, but I had more motivation to do it today. So there's plenty of room in the closet for your things."

Suddenly nervous, she went into the kitchen. She stacked the dry palettes, hooked her fingers in three of the quart-size canning jars she used for water, and took them back to her studio to put on the large table where they'd be handy.

"You want these in the same place?" Sam asked, both hands full of jars.

"Yes, please."

She crossed the room to the new chifforobe, saying, "I put some of your things in this cabinet." She opened the door and showed him where his equipment was.

"And I have all your underwear, socks and shorts stored in the new dresser."

He caught her around the waist and pulled her in close. "And you hung my family pictures in the hallway."

"Yes. I want you to feel at home."

"I appreciate it." He brushed his lips against her forehead. "All I really need to feel at home is you, Moira." His brown gaze, heated with gold, delved into hers. "When I'm on deployment and I'm not focused on a mission, all I think about is you."

Her face flushed and she rose on tiptoe to kiss him. "I think about you all the time, too. I have something else I want to show you." She caught his hand.

"Is it something I've seen before?" He grinned.

"No." She laughed. "Close your eyes." His grin widened.

"Come this way, just a little," She positioned him at the foot of the bed. "Okay. Open your eyes."

The thirty-six by forty-eight-inch painting stretched nearly the width of the headboard. While Sam's eyes were on the painting, Moira's were on him. She read surprise, then his eagle-eyed concentration kicked in as he studied every inch, then a smile almost identical to the one in the painting tilted his lips.

He slung an arm around her shoulders and pulled her in close against his side. "It's amazing, Moira. You're amazing. Thank you."

"Do you like it in here?"

"Yeah. I wouldn't want people staring at me in the living room."

"I liked the idea of having you there above the bed. It will help me feel as if you're watching over me when you're gone on deployment."

His expression shifted to include a hint of sadness. He moved in close and held her, his fingers gently massaging her neck as he held her. "I love you very much, Moira."

He showed her in a hundred different ways, but rarely said the words. She found herself tearing up.

She'd missed him so much while he was gone. Ached to have him home. She pressed closer, aligning her body to his—

Her phone rang at the same time his did.

It had been happening more and more of late. While it was wonderful having family and friends, the more comfortable they were about calling or coming by, the more they interrupted.

"It's a conspiracy. They have binoculars trained on the apartment," Sam said jerking his phone out of his back pocket.

Moira laughed and reached for the cell phone she'd left on the dresser.

"Moira could you meet with me at school?" Emily's voice sounded tense and wobbly. "I think I know who stole the funds, but if I look at it alone they won't believe me. They'll think I'm just trying to cover for myself. I want a witness."

Moira looked at Sam. It sounded like he was talking to his brother. "What time do you want to meet?" she asked Emily.

"I'm on my way to school right now. So if you could come now, I'd appreciate it."

It would only take her a few minutes. She knew Emily's anxiety level about this theft was in the stratosphere. News of the missing money had spread like wildfire through the building, and the woman was falling apart before the staff's eyes.

She didn't deserve this.

"Okay. I'll be there in about forty minutes."

"Thanks, I'll be in my office waiting for you."

Sam hung up and looked at her. "Tim wants to come by for a

few minutes."

"Emily, the secretary at school, needs me to run over to the school and help her with something. I have a ham and potato casserole fixed in the refrigerator. Turn the oven on to three-fifty and set the timer to sixty minutes. Tell Tim to stay and eat with you. I'll eat something when I get back. There's salad in the refrigerator. I don't think I'll be gone very long. We're just going over some financial stuff to do with the last fundraiser."

For a moment she debated on telling him briefly about the situation with the funds, but it was so similar to what was happening with his father… She just refused to add to everything he was already going through.

She led the way back into the living room, got her keys and purse off the console table, and stretched up on tiptoe to brush a kiss across his lips. "I'll be back as soon as I can."

"Having someone to come home to has some serious perks," he commented. "My recliner in the prime spot for watching the games and there's real food in the refrigerator. I may never be the same."

Moira laughed. "Enjoy it while you can. This whole thing is going to be a fifty-fifty split once you're settled in."

"I can handle that. But I doubt you're going to like my cooking."

"That's why I have a list of local restaurants handy. There's always takeout."

SAM SLUNG THE load of hanging clothes over his shoulder and shoved the car door shut with his hip. Once upstairs, it took only a few minutes to hang them in the area of the closet Moira had cleared for him.

She had made it too easy for him to move in, and he felt like a goldbricker for doing so little.

When a knock came at the door, he sauntered over to answer it, and Tim barged past him and into the apartment, saying, "The

DA has dropped the murder charge. They don't have the evidence to back it up, and the judge has thrown it out. But he was with the side piece when Jonathan was killed, and the woman backs him up. And his cell location confirms it. The embezzlement charges stand, though. They've reinstated dad's bail and he's gone home."

Sam shut the door and went into the kitchen. He opened the fridge and removed two beers, then wandered back into the living room. "How does Jennell feel about him coming home?" He handed Tim a beer and sat down on the couch.

"I don't know. She left when they froze Dad's accounts and news of the side piece came out. She's gone to her mother's."

"So much for standing by her man," Sam quipped. "So is the old bastard sitting at the house alone, or has he moved in with the side piece?"

"He's alone."

Sam bit back the bitter laugh. *Couldn't happen to a more deserving guy.*

Tim nodded and took a healthy swig of his beer. "He's going to prison for what he did, and his property will be sold to make as much restitution as possible."

How many times had his father held the threat of disowning them over their heads to get his way? Although he had disowned Sam long ago, right after the "fuck you" episode. "There goes your inheritance, bro," Sam quipped.

Tim laughed. "I figured he'd go through it long before I ever got it, so I don't really care. Where's Moira?"

"She's run out to help one of the secretaries from school about a school issue."

Tim's gaze fastened on the framed commendations. "I hope you show her the appropriate appreciation. It looks like she's gone way out of her way to make you feel at home around here."

"Yeah, she has."

"While you were gone on your last deployment, she did an-other fundraiser and painted several paintings. Mom and I called to check on her, and Mom got her to come over a couple of times."

"I appreciate that. I worry about her being alone so much. But she's made friends with someone at work, Maggie, and they went shopping together for the wedding. And we had Maggie and her boyfriend over for dinner. You'd like Abe. He's an engineer. Really sharp. Maggie's agreed to be her maid of honor."

"I'm glad to see her coming out of her shell."

"She doesn't trust very easily."

Tim's expression turned grave. "Trevor didn't help."

"No."

"How'd you get her to trust you?"

Sam was silent a moment. She'd been so unbelievably open and sexually needy that first night. She'd been both shy and seductive without even knowing it. "It was just plain blind luck. During and after the dinner at the Del, we talked for hours. When the cops came to interview me the next day and told me someone had been killed at the hotel…it gave me a jolt. I knew she was going for a swim, and I thought something had happened to her. They told me who it was and that she'd found him, so I called her as soon as they left."

"That's some kind of a record. Don't you usually make them wait a week or so before you call? I guess a murder trumped that."

Sam flipped him the bird.

Tim laughed. "She's not the only one who has trust issues."

"Hey, no fair. I trust you and Mom, my team, and Moira."

"That's a short list, bro."

"How long's yours?"

Tim did a one-shouldered shrug. "Not much longer." Tim finished his beer. "Dad really did a number on us all, though you took the hits for us more times than not."

Uncomfortable, Sam glanced away, relieved when he heard the oven timer go off. He hurried to the kitchen, found two potholders, and took out the casserole, leaving it to sit for a moment while he got two more beers out of the fridge.

"You're invited you to stay for dinner if you want to. There's casserole and salad. And I might even be able to scare up some rolls or biscuits if you want them."

"Who fixed the casserole?"

He was tempted to lie, but he didn't think he could pull it off. His brother knew him too well. "Moira did."

"Now I'm certain I won't get poisoned, I'll stay."

MOIRA PULLED IN next to Emily's car, studying the front of the school as she walked toward it. She'd been so excited to be a part of the school when she was first hired. It was her first teaching job after student teaching, and she was so idealistic.

And she managed to maintain that spark for nearly seven years…until recently. She'd taken Mr. Jacobs's words too much to heart, she supposed. Or had she?

Some of the other teachers seemed to believe she played for a living. One male teacher even asked her to do bulletin boards for him. She'd been so taken aback, she walked away without answering. The man had apologized later, but she'd never quite been able to forget. She still avoided him, because every time she saw him, it brought back the hurt and insult.

She had her own curriculum to teach, but she also reinforced the other subjects in the areas she could. Math, history, and some chemistry were built into her curriculum. And now she had introduced graphic design to help her students create websites and set them up to sell their own artwork, she was bringing in computer science and economics as well.

She paused before the main entrance to key in the security code. The shine for teaching had been dulled for her by all the extra duties she took on, too. And even after saying no to this last fundraiser, she wasn't sure she could get any of that shine back, because she'd always have to defend her place here. It would probably be the same at any school.

She pulled open the door. Maybe college would be different. She had her master's. She could get her doctorate. It was just thirty more hours. She could teach college without it, but it would seal her place at the school if she was working on her doctorate while she taught, and most colleges gave a break on tuition to students who were part of the teaching staff.

She reached for the office door and paused to study the shoe lying in the hall just past the door. Someone probably dropped it as they left the building.

She'd put it on Emily's desk. Someone would stop by looking for it. Shoe in hand, she swung the glass door open, passed the reception desk, and strode toward Emily's office.

Her heart skipped a beat when she saw a bare foot just inside the door. She realized in shock that the nails were painted a bright pink.

She eased forward to look inside the room. Emily was lying on her side on the tile floor, her blondish gray hair matted with blood, while a man sat at the computer, his back to her.

Moira gasped as fear shot adrenaline through her system, setting her heart to pounding in her ears. Her first instinct was to go to Emily. With a shudder, she forced herself to ease away, tiptoeing down the hall to Principal Jacobs's office.

Keeping an eye on Emily's door, she turned the knob. The door was locked, so she moved on to the next.

The man stepped out of Emily's office. They both froze.

A black bandana of some kind of mesh cloth covered his nose, mouth and jaw. Dark glasses concealed his eyes, and a black, cable-knit cap hid his hair. He took a step closer.

Blinded by fear, Moira threw the shoe. By sheer luck, it hit him in the face, knocking the glasses askew, and while he grabbed his face, she turned and ran down the narrow hallway, darting through the open door at the end and out into the wide north hallway.

She came to the teacher's lounge and prayed someone had worked this weekend and left it open. She tried the knob, but it was locked.

The man's rubber-soled boots made a distinctive squeaking sound on the highly polished floor behind her.

She flew past the fire alarm on the wall, afraid to pause even long enough to pull the lever. She turned the corner and, midway down the wall, slipped inside the small faculty bathroom and locked the door. She rifled through her purse for her phone and dialed 9-1-1.

She forced her voice down to a whisper when she wanted to scream. Her voice shook as she identified herself and gave the operator the address of the school. "There's a strange man here inside the building. He's wearing black, has his face partially covered by a bandana, and wearing a cap over his hair. He's attacked our secretary, Emily. She's injured, unconscious, and bleeding. He ran after me."

"Where are you right now, Moira?"

The doorknob rattled as it was given a quick twist. She froze and held her breath.

Standing in the dark with only the light of the cell phone, she felt isolated, alone. Though her palms were slick with sweat, she shook with cold.

"Moira?"

She hissed, "He's here," and then went silent and completely still for several moments.

"Where are you?"

She could barely breathe let alone answer.

"You have to tell me where you are."

After several seconds of silence she whispered, "The small restroom just past the teacher's lounge. Around the corner from the office."

"I want you to stay on the phone with me, okay? I've got police units and an ambulance on their way to your location."

"Please hurry."

When she found Mark Travis dead, she'd been shocked and nearly vomited, but she knew Emily. She worked with her. She saw her every day, and they were moving toward a solid friendship.

Tears of fear for herself and grief for Emily ran down her face. Emily had looked out for her. She looked out for all the students. If she was dead, her loss would cut deep with them all. She tore toilet paper off the roll to mop her face and blow her nose.

She remembered when Sam's teammates came to the school to help her set up for her end-of-the-year-art show. Emily had been so funny with the SEALs. Moira's tears flowed faster.

The doorknob turned again.

"He's back and trying to get in." Her voice shook and went up in pitch, though she was trying to keep it to a whisper. He threw himself against the door and the knob rattled. Moira scrambled away to the far wall and shone the light from her cell phone around the small space, looking for something to use as a weapon.

She'd never get the toilet seat off in time. She rummaged around in her purse for something she could use as a weapon and took out her keys and an ink pen. Not much help.

Then she noticed the small desk with a hollow cubby shoved in the corner. The female staff used it to store sanitary napkins and extra rolls of toilet paper. Moira dragged the desk forward and pushed it against the bathroom door as a barrier in case it gave way.

Then she adjusted the cell phone to speaker and set it down next to the sink.

For a brief moment thoughts of Sam flashed through her mind. He'd want her to fight. To never give up. So be it. Gripping the keys between her fingers on one hand and the ink pen with the other, she braced herself.

"Stay with me, Moira. The police are pulling up outside right now."

The door shook as the masked man lunged against it again.

"Tell them to hurry. Oh, and they need to use the code to get in. It's 48795."

The man outside the door suddenly stopped...and silence stretched. Then the dull pounding of his boots grew distant as he ran down the hall.

"Oh, God! I think he's gone away." Tears flowed again.

A few seconds later the operator said, "The police have entered the building and are heading your way. I'll stay on the line until they're with you."

When someone knocked, she caught her breath and her heart drummed so hard in her ears she could barely hear the voice outside the door.

"It's okay, Moira. You can open the door. Officer Walsh is standing right outside to protect you."

Setting aside the ink pen but maintaining her grip on the keys, she unlocked the door and was blinded by his flashlight as the officer swung it up into her face and then away to search the dark space around her. "I'm Officer Walsh from the SFPD, Moira. I'm going to take you out of the building. Okay?" He pushed the desk aside.

Shaking with relief, she dropped to one knee. It took her a moment to collect herself enough to toss the keys and pen into her purse and get her phone. She thanked the 9-1-1 operator for staying with her and ended the call.

"Emily's in the office on the floor bleeding. She needs help."

The officer gripped her arm to steady her. "The EMTs will be with her as soon as we've cleared the building, and in the meantime she has officers guarding her. She'll be transported to the hospital. What were you two doing here alone on a Sunday?"

"There was some money stolen from our school account recently. Because Emily is in charge of it, she's been worried everyone will think she took it. She thought she'd figured out who might have done it and wanted a witness while she searched the files on her computer. She called me earlier and asked me to come. When I got here…"

She struggled to maintain her composure. "I found one of her shoes on the floor out in the hall and picked it up. When I peeked into the office, she was lying on the floor, her head bleeding, and there was a man at her computer. I tried to get into one of the other offices to hide and call for help, but they were locked. That's when he came out and saw me."

The high school halls, with their metal lockers and nooks and crannies, seemed like a perfect hiding place for a million threats. She scanned the area, her entire body hyper-alert. She gripped the officer's shirtsleeve.

"I threw the shoe at him and hit him in the face, then I ran."

Tears streamed down her cheeks again. "He tried to get into the bathroom, but then he must have heard you coming into the building and he ran. He had on rubber-soled boots. They made a squeaky sound on the floor."

The officer pushed open the glass door and guided her outside. She crumpled on the steps and sucked in several deep breaths. She reached for her phone and tapped Sam's number. At the sound of his voice, she teared up again. "I need you to come to the school. Someone broke in and hurt Emily."

"Jesus! Are you okay?"

"Yes, but I need you."

"I'm on my way."

CHAPTER 17

"WHAT TIME DID you get to the school, Moira?"

She studied the detective's face. If Detective Sherman smiled, he might be considered handsome. But as it was, he remained completely deadpan. What were the odds that she'd be sitting in yet another room with yet another detective? At this rate she was going to be on a first-name basis with every detective on the SDPD.

Sam leaned back in his chair and stretched his long legs out beneath the table.

She opened her phone and scrolled through the calls. "Emily called at ten minutes after six. I left about five minutes after she called. It usually takes me forty minutes to drive from home to the school. So I probably got there close to seven."

"Is it common for teachers to work on the weekends?"

"Not every weekend, but yes, it's commonplace, depending on what's going on. The sports teams go in and practice on the weekends. I've gone in on the weekend and prepared materials for my classes when I have a special project planned. The teachers' lounge is usually left open to give us access to the copy machine and laminator, because there's usually someone working. But the door was locked this time." *Why was that?*

"What did Emily say when she called?"

"She thought she'd discovered a way to find out who stole the money from the bank account. She wanted a witness so no one could say she'd done it."

"Did you steal the money?"

Shocked by his question she stared at him. "No. I didn't have access to the account or any passwords."

"But you've worked with Emily while she did the deposits for two different fundraisers."

"Not all the deposits. And I've never been in the room when she accessed the bank account information, and I'm not privy to any of her passwords."

"Tell me how you deal with the money for the charity fund-raisers."

"Each teacher turns his or her money in to the office, and Emily and Cheryl, the other secretary, count the money together. Cheryl's been out sick for a few days, so when I brought the money in for my home room and two other teachers', Emily asked me to stay and help her count.

"The teachers count their own, but we always have two people do it when it's turned in to the office, so everything is aboveboard. So, we sat down together and counted it so we'd get a correct count. We both signed the paperwork for the count. Emily wrote up the deposit slip, filed the receipts, put the money in the deposit bag with the slip, and printed out the check to the company who supplied the materials for the fundraiser. Mr. Jacobs deposited the money that afternoon when he left, and the check to the company went out that afternoon when the mail carrier came by. By the next day, someone had accessed the account and transferred the money to another account. Emily's been upset all week because she was convinced everyone thought she did it."

"But you don't think she did?"

"No. She's an honest person. She's dealt with thousands of dollars before and never taken a dime, and she's been doing this job for ten years. There's no way she's involved in any kind of theft."

"Would you be willing to grant us access to your bank account?"

Sam's hand tightened over hers. "Not without a warrant," Sam spoke for the first time. "You have no cause to even ask for access to her bank account when there's no tie between her and access to the school account. You're fishing."

"You're here as a courtesy, Lieutenant Harding." Detective Sherman warned.

"I also have a law degree and have passed the bar, though I've never practiced. The bank is tracing the money to find out where it went. It may take some time, but they'll find it. You're looking for a reason for Moira to want to hurt Emily, and there is no reason. There are cameras all over the school. Look at the video footage and you'll see everything she's told you about the man who entered the building is true. You'll also see when Emily entered the building, and when Moira did."

The detective flipped the pages of his notes. "Six foot, a hundred and ninety pounds dressed all in black. Sounds a little bit like a Navy SEAL."

Sam flashed a dismissive smirk. "Sounds like a SWAT officer, a security guard, a prison guard, and a bouncer too."

"We're not even sure there was a man."

Moira's lips parted in surprise. "Of course there was a man. I hit him in the face with Emily's shoe. He lunged against the bathroom door to try and get to me."

"Why would he do that?" Detective Sherman asked.

"To keep me from calling the police, maybe. He's broken into a school, assaulted a woman and accessed computer files."

Sherman's brows rose. "Accessed computer files?"

"He was sitting at the computer in Emily's office, and he was accessing files."

"What kind of files?"

For a moment she thought her brain might explode. Moira drew a deep breath. "Really? Emily's lying on the floor inside the door, her head bleeding, and there's a strange man sitting at the computer keying something in, and you think I could just wander in and say, 'hey, mister, what are you doing on that computer?'"

Sherman's cheeks flushed.

"Look at the camera footage, look at the computer, look at the shoe. There has to be proof he was there. He wasn't a figment of my imagination. Plus, the 9-1-1 operator had to hear him trying to break down the door."

She rose to her feet and gathered her purse. Sam followed. "I'm done. And I'm leaving."

THOUGH SHE WAS shaking, she strode out of the room like a badass.

Sam had fought the urge to punch the snide, arrogant detective on the way out, and they were nearly to the elevator before he said, "Breathe, baby. Otherwise you'll pass out in the elevator."

She shook her head and sucked in a quick breath as he suggested. "Why do they keep going over and over the same ground so many times?"

"To try and catch you in a lie. But you never changed your story an inch. And you finally gave him something to work with. Which was what he was working to get at to begin with."

Her outraged expression made him smile. "No one ever asked me about what I saw in Emily's office, just the rest."

They stepped into the elevator and, ignoring the rest of the people, Sam tucked her in close enough to rest his chin atop her head.

"Do you think Emily's okay?"

"I don't know, but we'll call around and try to find out."

"We could go to the hospital if we knew which one."

That wasn't a good idea. They would still be looking at Moira as a suspect, and if she showed up at the hospital…

"I couldn't do anything to help her. He was right there at her desk."

"You called 9-1-1 and got her help." If Moira had tried to face the guy down… The idea twisted his gut into mush.

Why hadn't she told him about the situation at school?

Because it smacked too much of what was happening with his

dad. She was trying to protect him at her own expense. Again.

Once in the car, he realized they were going to have to retrieve her vehicle. "Do you feel up to driving? If you don't, I can take you school in the morning."

"I can drive. But I'm calling in sick for tomorrow. Everyone is sure to ask about what happened, and I don't think I can deal with it."

"I think that's an excellent call."

They drove to the school, but were stopped at the parking lot entrance by a police officer. "Moira wants to pick up her car, Officer."

He keyed his radio and spoke into it for a moment. "Okay."

"You're sure you're okay to drive?" Sam asked.

"Yes, I'm fine."

He studied her expression. She'd cried her makeup off and looked drained, but she was calm now.

The officer waved them forward, and Sam parked next to Moira's vehicle. "Give me your keys."

She pulled them out of her purse. He got out of the car and pushed the button to open the trunk and unlock the doors. She stood back while he searched the vehicle, then handed her the keys.

"Thanks."

"You're precious cargo, Moira. I'm not taking any chances."

She dragged in a shaky, tearful breath that gave him another pinch of guilt. He hadn't been able to protect her. This was the second time she'd been in danger and he wasn't there.

She hugged him and gave him a quick kiss.

His mind raced while he followed her home. They had both been so excited about finally, permanently sharing a home. And now it was ruined by some asshole after...

What *had* he been after? Not the money. The money was already gone. Was he trying to cover his tracks? Or was he looking for something else?

The police were focused on the money, like it was the only thing worth looking for. But what if it was something else? What if it had something to do with a student or a staff member?

He understood the need for secrecy sometimes. His whole career was based on secrecy. But if the guy had been searching personnel files…

He put on the blinker to make the turn into the apartment complex. The two parking spaces designated for Moira's apartment were side by side, and he pulled in next to her. They both got out and hit their key fobs to lock their cars.

He looped an arm around her as they walked to the entrance, and kept it there until they got off the elevator and walked to their door.

"How about I run you a bath and you soak and relax for a little while? In the meantime, I'll heat up the food."

"I couldn't eat, but I'd love the soak and a glass of wine." She opened the screen on her phone. "I'm going to call Mr. Jacobs and see if he's heard anything. And I'll call the sub coordinator to get someone to handle my classes tomorrow."

"All right."

He ran the bath and sprinkled in bath salts while she made the calls. Jasmine-scented steam filled the bathroom by the time she came in.

"I was able to get through to Mr. Jacobs. He said the police contacted him and told him Emily has regained consciousness. She's going to be okay."

The relief in her expression eased some of his tension. "That's great." He turned off the water. "Why don't you climb in and relax while I go pour that glass of wine."

"Thanks."

When he returned with the glass of wine, she had removed her clothes, twisted up her hair to keep it out of the water and settled back in the tub. Her pale skin looked petal soft. Color tinted her cheeks as he set the glass on the edge of the tub and knelt beside it.

"I know why you didn't mention what was going on at school. It was just too close to what was going on with my father. But don't ever try to protect me from anything again, Moira. I can handle anything that's thrown at me, as long as I'm prepared. Okay?"

She bit her lip. "Okay."

He stood and turned to leave.

"You couldn't have protected me from what happened even if you'd known about the money, Sam. There was no way we could have known what would happen at the school. So neither of us could have prepared."

She was right. But it still weighed on him that she was in the thick of things again and there hadn't been a damn thing he could do about it. Worry nibbled at the edge of his mind.

The police didn't believe there was a break-in. And because they already thought they knew what happened, they wouldn't spend any time at all pursuing the person responsible, and Moira would have to get a lawyer to fight this when they fixated on her. Unless Emily remembered who forced her into the office and knocked her out.

They'd been dismissive of the video evidence, which led him to believe the cameras might have been disabled. Something Moira would have been able to do if she had access to the computer setup that ran them. Either that, or she'd have to disable their ability to record, which would only require detaching the main lines from the storage device or hard drive.

There was nothing he could do about any of that, but he could do something for her. "I moved in today, and we're not going to let one asshole ruin our first official day of cohabitation. I'm going to fix you something to eat when you're done soaking."

"Thank you. Something really light will do."

He left the door cracked in case she needed him and went into the kitchen to search for something to fix.

Half an hour later she shuffled down the hallway in her fuzzy bedroom slippers, sleep pants, and a tank top. He stirred the soup he was heating and turned the heat on under the skillet ready to cook a grilled cheese sandwich.

She sat down at the small table and poured a little more wine into her glass before pushing the stopper in.

Sam set her soup and sandwich before her and took the seat across from her.

"Would you like some of my sandwich?" she asked.

"No. I'm good. I ate with Tim earlier." He got her a napkin, then sat back down.

As she sipped the soup and nibbled at the sandwich, he wondered how to approach her about getting an attorney.

"Can you call Tim for me?" she asked.

"Sure. What do you need?"

"A lawyer." She set aside her spoon and took another sip of wine. "Just to be prepared. I don't think the police believe me. And I'm not sure Emily was conscious when she went into the building."

He had never seen her look so fragile.

"I didn't hurt her, and I didn't take any money. There really was a man."

Sam rushed to leave his chair and kneel beside her. "I know you, Moira. I know you didn't do anything wrong. And that you'd never hurt anyone. And I believe there was someone else in the building. But getting a lawyer is a smart thing to do."

"Will you call Tim for me?"

"Of course, if you'll try to finish your sandwich."

"I can't. I think I might throw up. I just want to sip my wine and be."

"Okay."

He whipped his phone out of his back pocket and keyed in the password as he walked down the hallway to the bedroom.

At Tim's brief, hello, he said, "Moira's in trouble. She needs a lawyer. Who would you suggest?"

"What kind of lawyer?"

"A criminal attorney."

"Jesus Christ! What the hell happened?"

Sam stayed in the bedroom to explain so she wouldn't have to hear their conversation.

"Once they get through investigating, she may not need representation."

"It's just a feeling, but I got the idea that they were through investigating and thought they had their woman."

"Shit."

"We can hire our own investigative team and have them go

back over all the police findings, but we'll have to do it before the crime scene has been compromised."

"How can we keep that from happening?"

"I'm going to give you the name and number of a lawyer. The number I'll text you is his home phone. He'll take care of everything. He's a pit bull. But he's expensive."

"You guys always are."

"Hey, you're talking to a state employee. I'll never be rich. But Anthony Reeves already is, and he's good."

"How good?"

"Good enough that everyone here in our office groans every time his name is mentioned."

"And how do you know him?"

"He was three years ahead of me in college, but I like to play basketball, and every Tuesday night we had a game. We shared a beer now and then."

"I'll mention your name when I call."

"Don't expect him to give you a break because he won't. The problem with being good is demand, and you're paying for being pushed ahead of the line."

"How much?"

"Five thousand for the retainer. Then you'll go up from there."

"If Moira is convicted of a crime, she'll lose her job, and she'll never be able to teach again. Not even college. I'm not standing by while they railroad her into jail because they've got tunnel vision."

"And if they don't try that?"

"Then I've bought five thousand dollars' worth of peace of mind for us both."

"There's no way she did this." Tim said. "Not a doubt in my mind."

"I'll tell Moira you said that. It will mean a lot to her."

"If you need anything else, call me."

"Thanks, bro."

He'd hung up only a few seconds before when his phone dinged and a message appeared.

He dialed the number.

CHAPTER 18

THE MAN HAD on a baseball cap, the bill pulled down low. She caught glimpses of his eyes as he looked up. The lower half of his face was dark with a beard, the scraggly growth uneven.

His body was distorted in a strange way, wavering and then getting huge, then small, like she was seeing him from inside a carnival house of mirrors. Her heart thundered in her ears and her breathing hitched. She tried to run faster, but her leg slowed her down. The harder she tried to hurry, the closer he got, though all he did was continue to walk.

The next second a huge truck's grill came barreling toward the side window, filling her vision, and she gripped the steering wheel so hard her hands cramped while she stomped on the gas pedal. The car lunged forward. *Not again.*

Zoe jerked awake, her heart in her throat, and she staggered out of the bed, dragging the sheets with her. Her foot tangled in the cloth and she tripped, instinctively twisting to protect her broken arm, and fell, landing on her hip. She lay back and stared at the ceiling. *Shit!*

Seconds later Hawk appeared in the doorway, a towel wrapped around his hips and the rest of him wet and gleaming with water. She was thrown from confused fear into lust in a whiplash-inducing nanosecond.

"Jesus, Zoe. Are you okay? Did you get dizzy? Did you hit

your head?"

Frustrated with it all, she snapped. "No. I'm just freaking clumsy." She jerked the sheet free and rolled to her knees. She looked up to find Hawk standing over her. Her attention immediately fastened on the towel and the one bare, wet thigh it didn't cover. He gripped her arm and urged her to her feet.

With her eyes level with his chest her voice sounded husky. "You're getting the rug wet."

"How can you tell? Your eyes aren't on the rug."

His masculine amusement made embarrassed heat burn her cheeks. She tilted her head back to look up at him—just to prove she could.

His mouth swooped down on hers, and he kissed her, his mouth hot and urgent. "Come join me in the shower."

For several nights she'd agonized over her feelings for him, both physical and emotional, and decided she had to be certain that the sexual feelings were backed up with others just as strong, no matter how long it took. "I can't. Not yet."

His mouth latched onto hers with a hunger that stole her breath. With his hand cupping her ass and urging her tightly against him, her defenses crumbled. When he cupped her breast and kneaded it, she groaned beneath the lava-hot rush of need that arrowed down between her thighs.

He raised his head slowly, his cheekbones flushed and his gray eyes dark, the pupils swallowing the irises. He brushed her forehead with a kiss. "Let me know when you're ready."

He pulled away and went back into the bathroom so suddenly she just stood there, unable to process that all that sensual heat had been withdrawn. Her tank top, now damp, clung to her skin and she pulled it away. "Damn him."

She was too tempted to follow him into the bathroom, strip off the damp clothes and let nature take its course. Instead, she slipped on a robe and went into the kitchen to make breakfast.

"You didn't used to fix bacon all the time, Mom," A. J. said as he placed six slices on his plate along with the orange she'd peeled and broken into segments.

"You don't seem to think it's a bad idea."

"Nu-uh. Bacon's my favorite," he said around a slice as he chewed.

"Don't eat it all up before your father gets a chance," she warned while she dipped bread to make French toast.

"Is that hard?" A. J. asked.

"No. You want to try cooking a slice?"

"Yeah."

He hopped up from the table and came to stand at the stove with her.

"How do you know when it's done?"

"I let it fry until it stops sizzling, then flip it. If it's sizzling, that means the moisture in the bread hasn't cooked enough. You can lift the edge of the bread and look, and if it's browned just a little…" She demonstrated. "It's ready to flip." After a few minutes, she slid the piece onto a plate and let A. J. do the next one. He was sliding the last piece onto a plate when Hawk came into the kitchen.

"The chef is in the house," Hawk commented. "We'll have to buy you an apron."

"Like the one you wear when you barbecue?" A. J. asked.

Hawk grinned as he poured a cup of coffee. "Mine says 'kiss the cook and bring him a beer.' Think you can handle that?"

A. J. grimaced. "Yuck!"

Zoe laughed. "How about 'chef in training?'"

"Okay."

Hawk grinned. "When do we eat?"

"Now," A. J. said, and carried the French toast to the table.

Sitting at the table with the two of them, Zoe had a sudden déjà vu feeling of family that seemed more genuine than she'd experienced since coming home from the hospital. Conversation between father and son narrowed down to baseball while they ate. When Hawk rose to rinse his plate and put it in the dishwasher, A. J. followed suit.

Zoe lingered over her coffee and nibbled on a half slice of bacon.

A. J. hugged her from behind and pressed his cheek to hers. "Thanks for showing me how to cook the toast, Mom."

She pressed a hand to his cheek. "You're welcome. You did really well."

"I'll practice cracking the eggs next time."

"I'll let you."

He thundered down the hall toward his room.

Hawk bent to brush a kiss against her cheek. "He's thrilled about being so successful with the toast. More than the scrambled eggs I tried to teach him how to make."

"When was that?"

"The morning of the accident."

By unspoken agreement, they called it "the accident," because to acknowledge what it truly was might make what happened more terrifying. She refused to allow it to get into her head. She already had enough to deal with.

"You were leaving for the grocery, and he'd said something...taking you for granted. So I told him he was going to take on the jobs you always do for him so he'd learn to appreciate you more."

Wow.

"He fixed you breakfast but..." He shifted. Though his expression remained neutral, his body language was tense.

"I got to eat the one he fixed for me today. And he even asked to cook it. So he learned a lesson. And we got to build a memory that I missed out on before."

Hawk's smile set her heart fluttering.

A. J. ran down the hall with his backpack "You have everything?" Hawk asked.

"Lunch money?"

Hawk handed it off, then turned his attention to her. "If you need me any time today, just call."

"I will." She walked them to the door and watched while they got in the car and drove away.

Zoe closed the door, locked it, and leaned back against it. He made it so hard to resist him.

She pushed off and limped through the kitchen and down the hall to the master bedroom. She retrieved her purse from the dresser and poured everything out on the bed. She studied everything in her billfold, then moved on to the rest of her purse clutter. There were several practical things, but nothing other than her driver's license told her anything about herself.

She opened her phone. Hawk worked with her one afternoon and showed her how to open it and find her contacts. She looked for Tank. Hawk had mentioned Tank was her stanch friend and ally. Her hand trembled as her finger hovered over the small phone icon. She didn't remember him. How was she supposed to ask him to help her? She dragged in a deep breath and pushed the icon.

"Zoe, how are you?" His deep voice struck a chord, and she got a brief picture of a very large man with a broad face. Her heartbeat thudded at the base of her throat. Was it a memory, or was she just imagining a who would fit that voice?

"I'm doing okay. I want to come in and talk to you. Is there a time today when you'll have a few minutes free?"

"I have a break around one o'clock. If you come then, we can talk."

"I appreciate it. I'll be there. Thanks, Tank."

"See you then."

She ended the call and struggled with her emotions. A life she didn't know she even had had been blown apart. With every new person she met, it was both a wonder that she had been so blessed and painful to realize that she was going to have to earn their love and respect all over again as a different person. If she could just get back one small corner of that life....

She went back to the bedroom for the notebook she was using as a journal and spent an hour writing everything down that had happened this morning, much as she had done since waking in the hospital. Writing about her observations, her feelings, helped hold the anxiety over meeting Tank at bay for a time. And it reassured her to know if she forgot again, it might help her remember.

An hour later nerves drove her to her feet and she went into the kitchen. Cleaning and doing laundry kept her hands busy, but not her mind, so she was able to plan everything she wanted to talk to Tank about while wondering if he really could help her with any of it.

She put a roast and vegetables in the crockpot for dinner and turned it on, then tried to settle on the glider in the sunroom, but was too anxious to relax. She returned to her bedroom to make the bed and choose what she would wear. She picked casual linen slacks, silk blouse, and a sweater, and hung them in the bathroom.

When her cell phone rang and it was her mother, she was grateful for the interruption and thought if she was calling now to check on her, she wouldn't call later. She settled in to talk to Clara and hoped it would distract her enough to calm down.

HE NEEDED THIS run after a sedentary morning of paperwork and phone calls. And it helped him burn off the sexual frustration that lingered after Zoe's rejection.

Well, not quite a rejection. She'd responded like the old Zoe, as if she wanted to drink him down. The thought had him putting on some speed and hoofing it up the incline of sand and sparse seagrass to the sidewalk. His leg muscles burned.

The rubber soles of Langley's shoes slapped the concrete behind him, and Hawk kicked it up another notch. He could feel Langley practically breathing down his neck as they hit the straight stretch leading to his office. The back door of the building came into sight, and he dug for more and crept farther ahead. He whipped past the back door and out onto a grassy area behind the building, his chest heaving like a bellows. Langley blew past him, then circled back.

"If I could catch my breath…I'd kick your ass for…talking me into…this," he wheezed.

Hawk laughed. "Trish will thank me for keeping you in shape. You want to still be ready to chase her around the house when you've finally launched all the kids and have the place to your-selves, don't you?"

Langley shot him a narrow-eyed look. "I have to stay alive until then."

Hawk laughed.

Ryan, Hawk's admin, appeared with towels and drinks while they walked the run off to keep from cramping up.

"Thanks, Ryan."

"You have an appointment at one thirty, sir."

"Thanks for keeping me on schedule."

"You're welcome, sir." Ryan went back inside the building.

Hawk sighed with regret. "He's put in for a transfer to active duty. Best admin I've ever had, but I understand wanting to be in the thick of things."

"We both do." Langley wiped his face with the towel, then slung it over his shoulder. "I sometimes miss the action."

"I do too."

"I don't miss carrying seventy pounds of equipment, or wearing a vest and sweating like a pig at a barbecue."

Hawk laughed again. "That was good." He took a deep swallow of water. "Do you regret being away from the kids so much while they were little?"

"Of course I do. But at the time we had just been attacked, and I believed my duty was to keep our country safe and them as well."

"Before Zoe's accident, she came to me and said she wants to have another baby."

Lang's bushy brows shot upward. "Wow." After a pause he said, "And?"

"I wasn't too crazy about the idea. A. J. is ten, and he's getting more and more independent. I didn't want to start all over again when things are so..."

"Comfortable?" Langley provided.

"But I couldn't bring myself to disappoint her either. I mean she took on every parental detail while I was away and...even though I'm here, most of them still fall on her."

"And you feel guilty."

"Yeah. Damn it. Now it seems it was a really small thing to ask compared to all the crap she's put up with over the past ten years, and even smaller compared to what we've lost now."

Langley drank deep from the bottle. "How would planning another baby have changed things, Hawk?"

"Maybe we'd have been up earlier or later. Maybe we'd have stayed home. Maybe I'd have gone to the store. Who the fuck knows? One small change could have changed everything."

"Or not. Just like any op."

Hawk ran a hand over his jaw. Langley was right. What happened, happened. And wishing he could change it didn't help a damn thing.

Langley wiped his chin with the end of the towel. "If you two get past all this, what are you going to do?"

He thought about it for a nanosecond. "Any damn thing she wants."

Langley grinned. "Good luck."

ZOE STUDIED THE big man who lumbered across the therapy suite toward her. All she could think of was wide. His face was wide, his shoulders, his chest, even his legs seemed wide. He called himself Tank for a reason. He looked like he could bench press a car with one hand.

But the best part was, she was close to tears of surprise and relief, because he was exactly as she imagined him. *Remembered him.* She *remembered* him.

His easy smile inspired one in return. His nationality was a mystery...maybe Hawaiian and something else tossed in for good measure. When he reached her, he offered a hand and tucked her into an all-encompassing embrace that had quick tears pricking her eyes.

"It's good to see you mobile. The last time I saw you was in the neurology wing at Scribe Mercy."

When had she last seen him? Probably the day before the accident. More than two weeks ago. "Thank you for coming to see me."

"When are you coming back?"

"I'd come back tomorrow in a heartbeat. Sitting at home is driving me crazy."

"But?" he supplied for her.

"But... I'm having some memory issues that haven't resolved themselves yet, and headaches, and dizziness sometimes. Is there somewhere we can talk?"

"Sure, we can go into your office. Elizabeth has been filling in for you since you've been out. She's taking your patients, double-checking the patient schedules, and getting everyone to file their therapy notes. But she hasn't been staying in here much. She'll be glad when you're back."

Zoe settled on the small sofa against the wall rather than sitting behind the desk and patted the cushion next to her.

"I'm not allowed to drive for four more weeks." And even if she could, she'd have to use a GPS to find her way here. "I took an Uber from home to get here today."

Hawk told her Tank was her most trusted friend at work. She hoped she could trust him now.

Tank focused on her.

She drew a deep breath. "I remembered you, Tank. The moment I heard your voice, I knew what you look like. But I don't remember even working here, or living here in San Diego. I don't remember being married, or even giving birth to A. J. Ten years of my life have been wiped away."

His usually expressive face froze. He leaned forward to rest his elbows on his knees and hung his huge head as he studied the floor. "Shit!"

"I thought maybe if I looked around the hospital, the therapy unit, it might trigger some memories. But I don't want to run into people I'm supposed to know and have to explain everything to them. I remember my training before I came to San Diego. I still know the job. But all the experiences I've had here are gone. I was hoping you could show me around in a little while. If you have time."

"I'll make time."

"That's…" She was so damn emotional, and she wished she wasn't. "Thank you." She folded her hands to keep them still. "I have to be sure I can still do the job. If I can't, I'll have to resign."

"It would be a huge loss for the unit, Zoe."

"Thanks for saying that, but that was the Zoe you've worked with for ten years. I have to know if I can do the job now.

"I'd like to look through my computer here and see if the information on it triggers any thoughts or memories. I hope I can guess my password or reset it. And just look at some of the work I've done."

"You know you'll have to tell Dr. French about this."

"I knew I'd have to notify someone. I wasn't sure who."

They fell silent for a moment.

"I'm hoping to recover what I've lost, Tank."

"I'll do whatever I can to help."

She started to tear up again and beat it back. "I appreciate it."

"Your computer password is A.J., both lowercase, with periods, his birthday without slash marks, and a hashtag."

"A hashtag?"

"The pound sign."

"Okay. I thought I'd look through some old cases and see if they might shake something loose."

"That sounds like the thing to do."

"I appreciate you letting me do this."

"They're your files and notes. Pull the shades and spend as much time as you need. Everyone will be too busy to notice you're here for the next couple of hours."

"Thanks, Tank."

Once he left, Zoe followed his suggestion. She went through her desk and found nothing but office supplies. On floating shelves above the desk were several pictures of her, her workmates, and patients, along with her license and degrees. Books on physical therapy techniques lined the shelves of a narrow bookcase next to the desk.

Once she opened the computer, she found what she was looking for. Patient files for the past four years. The earlier ones would have been archived. Each file had a photo ID, the patient's medical information, their diagnosis, and the treatment plan. She read through several, wishing she could have copies of the files so she could study them. She wondered if she could access them from home. Probably not. But she could come in on Sundays and go over them. She went into the scheduling area of the software and looked over how to do it. It didn't seem to be too difficult a skill to master.

She could do this. Even if they demoted her from head of the department, she could still do the work…if they'd let her.

Her phone rang, and she scrambled to answer it. It was her mother. Jesus. "Hello."

"Where are you? You're supposed to be here at the house."

"No one told me I was on house arrest, Mom."

"A. J. will be coming home soon."

"He's going over to a friend's house for a couple of hours and won't be home until five."

"Where are you?"

"I'm at the hospital in my office at the therapy unit."

Clara's tone was so strident, and Zoe had to hold the phone away from her ear. "The doctor said no work for at least a month."

"I have to know whether or not I can still do the job, Mom. Otherwise I'll have to resign. And they'll need to have time to find my replacement."

Silence stretched on the other end of the call. "I know how much you love your job. I know what a blow it would be if you lost it. But you have to promise me you won't overdo it."

"I promise. I'm just reading through old case files. Studying them."

"Okay. But from now on, please call and let me know where you are. I worried that you might have gone out for a walk and gotten lost."

"I have GPS on my phone. Hawk showed me how to program it."

"Good. Have you figured out your debit pin number and all of that?"

"Yes. I've got a handle on that. And I took an Uber here. I'll get another home."

Clara sounded calmer as she said, "Please be careful.

Zoe breathed a sigh of relief. "I will, Mom. And thanks for letting me go. I need to do this."

"I know." Clara's voice broke. "But even though you're a grown woman, you're still my baby, and I have to worry."

"I know." And thinking of babies. "I'll make it home in time to be there when A. J. gets home."

"Okay. We'll talk later."

Zoe worked for another half hour, then shut down the computer. Tank came to the door and poked his head in. "How's it going?"

"Good. I know how to do the schedule, and I remember working with the software. I looked through some of my past cases and studied them. A few faces even look familiar." At least she thought they did. "But I couldn't remember their names or any particulars."

"Want a short tour?"

"Yes."

He offered his arm, and she looped a hand in the bend of his elbow, though she hadn't a prayer of reaching entirely around it.

He paused before going into the room. "Elizabeth, she's the blonde, just got back from maternity leave, and all you have to do is ask her how the baby is and you're good to go. The dark-headed fellow on the right side is Josh, and he's not usually very chatty, so if you just wave it will be fine. The man Elizabeth is working with is...."

"Kevin," she supplied. She didn't know how she knew, she just did. "Broken pelvis. He's a SEAL."

Tank moved forward and turned to the farthest point from the rest of the occupants to circle the room. "Do you remember him?"

She remembered laughing with him, and Tank wheeling him out of the unit. "I do. But why him and not my family? It's like something in my brain was shattered, and all I get are disjointed flashes of memory. I don't remember how to get out of my neighborhood, but I remember driving to certain stores. I don't remember having A. J., but I remember how much I love him. I remembered you when I heard your voice, and had the feeling you were my friend, but I don't remember how we worked together.

"Everything else I remember has an emotional component to it. So why Kevin?"

"Seaman Chalmers was funny, and he flirted with you just before you left to go upstairs to the nursery."

"The nursery?"

"On the maternity wing. You've been bottle-feeding some of the babies."

"Hawk said we were talking about having another baby."

Tanks thick brows rose. "Wow. You hadn't mentioned that."

Her face heated. Would she have mentioned it to Tank? "He said I'd just broached the subject with him the night before the accident."

"We deal with traumatic brain injuries all the time here in the unit, Zoe. The patients have a hard time showing up on time because they can't remember their appointments. They'll remember your face but not your name some of the time. But the memory lapses you're describing don't sound like your typical TBI. Have you consulted a psychologist? This sounds more like PTSD."

"The only event in my life that has ever affected me in a traumatic way, other than losing my father, was when I was hit by the truck that damaged my leg."

"And you nearly had a repeat performance with the truck that crushed your car, broke your arm and fractured your skull."

"But I don't remember the accident..." But she dreamed about it just this morning.

If her problem was more psychological than physical, could

she get back to normal more quickly. Could they use hypnotism or something to get her memory back?

When Tank took her around the therapy room, it all seemed so familiar. But then she also worked on much the same equipment in Kentucky.

Elizabeth pushed the wheelchair with Seaman Chalmers in it toward them. "Zoe, it's so good to see you. How are you feeling?"

"I'm doing well."

"How much longer will you be out?"

"I have four more weeks of forced medical leave. And another four with the cast." She raised her left arm.

"Bummer. You know Seaman Chalmers?"

"Yes." Zoe offered her hand and Kevin shook it. "It's good to see you again, Kevin."

"I'm glad to see you're up and moving around. We got word of the accident on the base. Some of the guys went down to get a look at the car. You were lucky to walk away."

"Yes, I was. I can tell your therapy is going well, because you look like you're moving better already."

"I'm doing what you told me to do. Follow every direction to the letter and don't overdo it."

She smiled. "Good."

Remembering what Tank had said about Kevin, and to lead the conversation away from that, she looked at Elizabeth. "How's the baby?"

"She's great."

"Email me some pictures. I have to go and take care of my own not-so-little baby. A. J. will be home in a little while."

"Take care of yourself," Elizabeth said with a quick hug.

"I will." She turned to touch Tank's arm. "Thanks, Tank. I'm going to call my ride."

"Call us if you need anything," he said.

"Will do." She returned to the office, retrieved her purse and phone, and called her Uber.

A headache had been building while she was talking to Elizabeth, until now it was pounding behind her eyes. Nausea rolled through, and she swallowed against it. She caught the elevator and stepped to one side to allow a large man to get on. The door closed.

He glanced at her. "Aren't you Lieutenant Commander Yazzie's wife?"

She looked up. He had a square jaw, and strong features. The cleft in his chin looked like it had been hewn with an ax. His brown eyes were laser-focused on her. A dark bruise marred one cheek. His hair was neatly trimmed and lay close against his head.

"Yes, he's my husband."

"I'm Seaman Owen Morgan, ma'am." He offered his hand, and she shook it. "We heard about your accident on post. Glad to see you're okay."

"Thank you." She leaned against the railing inside the elevator as it stopped on a floor. She swayed with the movement.

Morgan gripped her elbow to steady her. "Is someone coming to pick you up?" he asked.

"Yes."

The elevator door opened to the lobby. "You look a little pale. How 'bout I wait with you until they come?"

"You don't have to do that. I can just sit close to the door and watch for my ride."

"I don't mind. I don't have to report back to duty until tomorrow. What kind of car do they drive?"

"A goldish-colored Chevy Equinox."

He guided her to a row of seats along one wall. "I'll keep a lookout for the car. Why don't you just close your eyes and take it easy until it gets here?"

"Are you here visiting someone?"

"I strained my shoulder and had some inflammation. I was here getting it checked out."

"You need to put some ice on that cheek too," she suggested. She barely registered his comment about a minor accident during training, and it looked worse than it was.

If only these headaches would stop. Even moving her head made the pounding worse. If her mother found out she overdid it, she'd never hear the end of it. At least she'd have some time to rest so she'd be up when A. J. and Hawk came home.

A touch on her shoulder woke her, and Seaman Morgan stood over her. "Your ride's here, Mrs. Yazzie."

Zoe eyes were drawn to the cleft in his chin again. A feeling of Déjà vu struck her. Something about his broad shoulders and chin looked familiar.

Morgan helped her out of the chair, walked with her to the door, and opened it for her. He kept his hand on her arm as he walked with her to the Uber.

"I'm sorry you were hurt in the wreck, Mrs. Yazzie. I hope you feel better."

She'd have to mention Seaman Morgan's kindness to Hawk. But then she'd have to admit she had another headache because she'd overdone it.

"Thanks for your help." Her Uber driver was standing by the open back door smiling at her. Eager to get home, she limped forward.

CHAPTER 19

For the first time since being hired, Moira didn't want to go to school. Despite the lawyer's reassurances the day before, she was nervous about walking in and facing all the other teachers after the police treated her like a suspect.

Had they called people at school and interviewed them? She'd never know who they spoke to and what they said. She'd never know who thought she was guilty and who didn't. And the not knowing was harder than facing down the doubters.

She already felt isolated from the rest of the teaching staff because of the discipline she taught. To be further isolated right when she was coming out of her shell… And what would Maggie think?

That last thought nearly sent her into a tailspin.

She parked the car in her normal spot and gathered her bag. She'd planned special lessons that would keep her and her students especially busy to help the day pass more quickly.

As she walked into the main hall, a couple of students greeted her. She smiled at them and breathed a small sigh of relief. Maybe what happened hadn't spread through the building yet.

She went into the office to get her mail and paperwork.

Maggie appeared at her side. "How are you doing?"

"I just needed a day to regroup."

"That's understandable."

She asked the one thing that had been tormenting her. "Have you heard how Emily's doing?"

"She's going to be fine, but she has a concussion." Maggie gripped her arm. "Are you okay?"

"I've been better."

"Have you got your things?" Maggie asked.

"Yes."

"Let's go to my room so we can talk."

They wove their way through the crowd of students and down the hall toward Maggie's room. When they passed the small bathroom just past the teacher's lounge, Moira looked away.

"They had a locksmith replace the bathroom knob and lock yesterday. The mechanism was bent."

From the man lunging against the door.

They entered Maggie's room, and she closed the door. "The police I.T. guys have been here going over Emily's files and trying to trace the missing money."

Moira nodded. "Good. I hope they find it."

"Everyone is speculating how the money disappeared. Neither of you are computer wizards, and it took someone who knew really his or her stuff to hack one bank account and transfer the money to another. If they find out who it is, they're going away for a long time. It's a federal crime. Like robbing a bank."

"Doing graphic arts and building websites is the limit of my skill."

"That's what I told the officer who called me," Maggie said.

Moira's throat went dry. "How many other teachers have they talked to?"

"Pretty much all of them. Even the lunchroom ladies."

"They didn't believe me when I told them about the man in the office."

"What man?"

"There was a man in Emily's office on her computer. He had on a knit cap, and some kind of bandana over the lower part of his face, and dark glasses." She went through everything that had happened. Just as she had with the police.

"So that's why they had to repair the bathroom doorknob."

"Yes."

Maggie didn't question it. "You must have been terrified."

"I was. I don't know why he came after me. Unless it was to keep me from calling the police."

"Or he wanted something from you."

"Or he was enraged when I hit him in the face with Emily's shoe." Moira shivered.

"You were actually close enough to hit him?"

"No, I threw Emily's shoe at him, and I must have had all this adrenaline going and just some blind, stupid luck, because I hit him in the face."

"Who in our building has killer computer skills? Or an I.T. degree?" Maggie asked.

"The computer programing teacher. But for him to be involved would be too cliché. Besides, I'm sure the police have already questioned him and looked into his background."

"I hate to even say this, but we have some really gifted students."

"All it would take would be access to Emily's passwords and opening an account under an assumed name at the same bank. Emily was authorized to transfer funds from one account to another. They would have to write a check to withdraw the money before the bank was alerted to the funds being gone."

"You've given this a lot of thought."

"When you've been accused of hurting someone you care about, and told to your face they don't believe you were terrorized…"

"No way would you ever hurt Emily, Moira. No way. And if you say there was a man here, there was a man here."

She closed her eyes against the quick rush of tears. "You don't know how much I appreciate your loyalty." She cleared her throat. "I spent all of yesterday trying to figure out who the man could be. His hair, face, and eyes were covered, but I've been thinking about body type. We have several men in this building who are close in height, but none who were in as good shape as this man was, and none of them would have had access to Emily's passwords."

"It has to be someone who works in the office. But the only man in the office is Mr. Jacobs."

"I can't even begin to imagine Mr. Jacobs dressed like a SWAT officer."

"What if this man wasn't here about the money and was after something else? You said he was in the office on the computer."

"The police will be able to follow his keystrokes and figure out what he was looking for." Moira ran her hands over her hair and twisted it at the back of her neck. "I'm sick of trying to figure this out."

"You need to be careful until they catch this guy, Moira."

The bell rang, and she gathered the paperwork she'd picked up in the office. "I will."

The students were curious about what was going on, but she told them they'd all know once the police finished their investigation. She tried to keep the rest of her day normal and busy by challenging the students.

She'd just gathered her lunch when someone knocked on the door. She opened it to find Detective Sherman. Her heart fell. "What do you want?"

"I just need to ask you a few more questions, Ms. McKee."

"You can wait until the end of the school day. I need to eat my lunch."

"You can eat while I ask my questions."

Moira went to her desk and withdrew her purse and the card Anthony Reeves gave her. He'd taken a retainer of two hundred fifty dollars, because he hadn't believed they'd be pursuing her as a suspect, and called it a friend's discount. Having his business cards gave her some confidence.

She handed the card to Detective Sherman. "Anthony Reeves. Have you got a guilty conscience, Ms. McKee?"

"No, I just believe in being prepared. And he's a family friend. Make an appointment with him, and I'll answer your questions in his office."

"We don't need to go down this route, Ms. McKee."

"After what I experienced on Sunday, I think we do. I told you everything I know and everything that happened on Sunday. You accused me of hurting my friend, stealing money I had actually reported to you as being missing, and inventing the man who attacked Emily." She walked past him to the door and opened it. "Goodbye."

"We know there was a man in the building. We've watched the security footage, and the truth is, he deleted it all, but our tech department was able to recover it."

"You should have done that before you accused me of lying." She moved to her desk and retrieved her lunch, walked past him and through the open door, and strode down the hall.

In the main hall, she passed sporadic groups of students going back to class from lunch.

"Don't you want to help get the guy who hurt Emily?" Sherman asked when he caught up with her.

"I did help you, and you treated me like a criminal. I told you *everything* that happened, and you wanted to make me out to be the bad guy. Go do your job and leave me alone."

"Detective Hart and Buckler said you were a stand-up person."

This guy was a real asshole. "Be sure to tell them I said hello." She turned down the hallway to Maggie's room.

"We got a court order to go through your bank records. You have quite a nest egg started."

She stopped. Rage crept up her throat and threatened to escape on a scream. "I *earned* that money. I have a paper trail for every single piece of artwork I've sold in the past three years."

"We know that. We checked you out with the gallery owner who's selling your work."

She thought her head might explode. "If you have damaged my professional standing with Valerie, I will sue you. I'm calling my lawyer now and getting a restraining order for harassment."

She jerked her phone out of her pocket. "Wait." He covered the screen with his hand. "I explained to her that we were just doing background on you as a witness. Your professional standing with her is fine. Did you ever hear his voice? Did he speak?"

God, why wouldn't he just go away? "No."

"Was there any kind of insignia on his clothing?"

"No."

"What kind of boots did he wear?"

"Black, Rubber-soled. They laced up."

"Did he wear gloves?"

She closed her eyes and went back to the office when he stepped out of the office. "Yes. They were black, too. They weren't leather, either. They looked like sports gloves." She opened her eyes to find him studying her.

"Do you have a photographic memory?"

"No. But I notice details."

"Did he remind you of anyone you know? The way he moved? His physical presence?"

"No. He was very fit. Very aggressive. His shoulders were very broad."

"You threw a shoe at him?"

"Emily's shoe. When he came out of the office, he took a step toward me and I just threw it. It hit the glasses he was wearing, and he grabbed his face."

"The cop who escorted you out of the building said you had your keys locked between your fingers and you were prepared to fight."

"I'm getting married in five weeks. I wasn't going to let some asshole cheat me and my fiancé out of that."

He smiled and it changed his entire persona. "I'll leave you alone now so you can eat your lunch."

Moira glanced at her watch. "I only have ten minutes now. We only get twenty minutes." *Asshole.* She trudged back to her room the way she had come, tossed her lunch on her desk and locked the door behind her.

Then she went into her art storage closet and shut the door. She brushed her finger over the screen and searched for her gallery's number. She took several deep breaths and brushed away the tears that suddenly trickled down her face. "May I speak with

Valerie, please? This is Moira McKee."

The bell rang just as she was ending the call, and she went to her classroom door and unlocked it. Mr. Jacobs stood out in the hall. Moira studied the red scratch that ran the width of his cheekbone. Her tongue was numb. "Did you need to speak to me, Mr. Jacobs? I was making a personal call."

"I just wanted to check and make sure you're okay. I didn't see you come in this morning."

"I'm fine. Just very busy, since I missed yesterday." Students walked between them to enter the room.

He frowned. "I'm glad you're back, Moira. I'm glad you're safe."

"Thanks." She was grateful for her students' interruption. All she could see was the scratch across Mr. Jacobs' cheek where a pair of glasses would have fallen when she threw the shoe.

SAM SLAMMED THE gate to his weapons cage. "Listen up." He turned to face his team. "I have an announcement to make."

They all locked up at once. "Squirrel will be transferring back into our team."

"Great!" Swan said.

The other remarks were positive but restrained. After all, Rosenburg would be stepping back into the slot left by their fallen brother, Seaman Marsh. The loss was still new to them all.

"When?" Swan asked.

"Next week. He has some things to finish up this week before he can come in."

He ran his thumb over the edge of the short stack of envelopes in his hand. Swan, with his bad attitude toward women, gave him pause. No matter how hard he tried, Sam had never gotten him to open up about the divorce that caused it. If any of them declined the invite, it would be Swan.

Bullet, their sniper, wasn't the newest member of their team, but one who had only met Moira a handful of times. He might decline as well.

"I've got something for each of you. Gather 'round."

"I hope it's a fucking lottery ticket. I could use some spare cash," Arrow said.

"Maybe you should try out for the Padres, Arrow. You have the arm for it." Denotti quipped. "I want one of those paintings Moira does. I could use something to hang on my bedroom wall."

"Yeah, a nude. And we all know what you'd be doing with that." Beckham said in a dry tone. The whole team roared with laughter.

Sam waited until things calmed down to pull out the wedding invitations. "This is going to be insignificant after that, but what the hell. I'd like to see your ugly mugs at the wedding. So, I'm making it official." He passed the cards out. "Book has promised to come."

"No shit!" Swan brows rose. "You'll be a miracle worker if he makes it, LT."

It had taken some arm twisting, but he'd wrung a promise from Book. It would do him good to get out of the house and be a part of the team again. Even though he was in a wheelchair.

Sam tried to block out how thin and frail the man looked. Now he'd managed to run off his girlfriend after putting her through a year of hell, he was alone and wallowing in the circle-jerk his life had become since his accident.

"I may have to depend on some of you to go by and load him up. Think you can handle that, Swan?"

"Yeah, I can do it."

"I also need you to bring a date. This is going to be me and Moira and our closest relatives and you guys. If you don't bring a date, you won't dance.

"And another heads-up. We're playing poker for my bachelor party. No strippers, just us, a few other friends, my brothers, several cases of beer, plenty of food, and the cards."

"That sounds a little…dull, LT," Gilly said.

"I want dull. The last bachelor party I attended damn near killed me."

The guys all laughed.

"I'm serious. It took me a week to remember what the hell had gone on, and even then I wasn't sure about all of it."

"Damn, LT." Bullet's grin was wide and very white against his dark skin. "That's…hard to imagine."

"It was the last time I got drunk, last time I drank scotch," He suppressed a shudder. "And the last time I went to a bachelor party, too."

Arrow shoved dishwater blond hair out of his face. "Don't trust yourself, huh?"

Sam laughed. "I have a perfectly healthy bachelor party phobia."

Gilly snorted in disbelief. "This coming from a guy who runs into buildings infested with armed terrorists or cartel assassins."

"Hey, I can take the armed assholes out, but I don't want to face Moira knowing some stripper rubbed herself all over me two nights before we got married."

"Is she having a bachelorette party?" Swan asked.

"I think she and some of her school friends are going out to dinner and then going back to one of their homes for a wedding shower. So, no bachelorette party."

"Where are they going out to eat?"

"I don't know. It's her maid of honor's choice."

"How much trouble could a group of schoolteachers get up to, Swan?" Gilly shook his sun-streaked head and shot him a warning look. They'd all heard Swan's tirades against women plenty of times.

"I don't know. LT lives with one, he ought to have a good idea."

Sam shook his head. "Nothing nearly as wild as SEALs can. And nothing that I'm worried about."

"I had that attitude too, until I saw the photos on my ex's phone."

Sam held onto his patience by a thread. "I've seen all the pictures on Moira's phone, Swan. She's forever showing them to me because she uses them for paintings. She's digging deep into her painting career and selling her artwork at a gallery. That's what she was busy doing the whole time I was deployed. And she's got the house fund to prove it."

"House fund?" Beck asked, his interest piqued.

"She puts some of each sale she makes into a savings account for a future house. And uses a small percentage for materials and shipping."

Beck turned his attention on Swan. "When would she have time for what you're suggesting?"

Swan looked away. "I wasn't suggesting anything. I just want LT to be careful. She might be a good woman. Or she could just be better at hiding things than most of them."

The whole group groaned.

"Jesus, Swan. You need to get over it and move on," Denotti snapped. "LT should kick your ass. You just insulted his lady."

"I didn't insult anyone. I just told him to be careful."

Sam drew a deep breath. "I trust Moira, Swan, because I love her, and I know what kind of person she is. And I know she loves me. Let me show you the painting she just finished for our bedroom." He took out his phone and flipped to the photo he'd taken of the portrait.

He handed the phone off to Swan, though the others huddled up to share the screen.

"She hung it over our bed. She said it was so she'd feel like I was watching over her when I'm deployed."

Denotti relieved Swan of the phone. Then, after studying the photo, punched him in the shoulder. "You're a fucking asshole, Duck."

Before things could escalate, Sam said, "We're moving on. I've reserved laptops in one of the classrooms. We have some new navigational software we need to check out since we may be using it during our next deployment."

"Think we'll be deployed before the wedding, LT?" Gilly asked.

"I don't know. I hope not. Moira already bought her wedding dress. And she hates shopping. She may kill me if we are." Gilly's laughter didn't assuage his worry. He'd feel guilty as shit for disappointing her if the whole thing had to be postponed at the last minute.

The team settled into one of the classrooms and was working on the software when Swan wandered over. "LT... I'm sorry. Your lady didn't deserve what I said."

"No, she didn't, and neither did I, Swan." He was silent for a moment. "That hatred of your ex you carry around will turn on you one day." He studied Swan's face. He seemed too young to harbor such raw, bitter emotions. "If you don't want to come to the wedding, I'll understand. But you're part of my team, and I hope you will." And he hoped Swan could put his rage aside for the hour the service would take.

Between Swan and Trevor, they could turn the whole thing into a shitshow. He'd put Denotti and Beck in charge of keeping the two of them apart.

Sam's ass was dragging by the time they called it quits for the day. The sleepless, stressful nights were catching up with him. He took a seat inside his cage and propped his feet on one of the equipment racks. When his phone rang, he glanced at it and studied the name and number. *Who the hell is that?* He was careful about who had access to his number. He hit the button. "Yeah."

"Is that always the way you answer the phone?" Thomas demanded.

"It is when it's a strange number. Whose phone are you using?"

"That's not important. I'd like to meet with you. I hear you're getting married."

He wondered how his father might try to manipulate the wedding to his advantage.

"What do you want to meet about?"

"I was just going to update you about everything that's been happening."

"Tim pretty much keeps me in the loop, Thomas."

"I have a wedding gift for you and your fiancée...Moira, isn't it?"

Sam wanted no part of whatever it was. There were always strings attached to anything and everything Thomas Harding offered you. "We don't really need any wedding gifts. We've both got pretty much everything we need already."

"I think you'd be very interested in what I have for you."

"I don't think so, Thomas."

"Why not, Sam? You weren't averse to taking my money when I paid your college tuition."

"And I've been hearing about it for ten years now. Keep the wedding gift. I wouldn't want to have to hear about that one for the next ten."

He hung up and swung to his feet. The phone rang again, and he started to block the number, but paused. The number had to be a burner phone. He remembered Tim saying the cops had tracked Thomas's cell service to prove he wasn't with Jonathan Walker at the time of his death. But they didn't have this number.

CHAPTER 20

HAD SHE REALLY remembered Kevin Chalmers? Every time she made a connection with someone, she second-guessed herself. Some of what Tank said sounded reasonable. And some of it sounded like wishful thinking. Because if it was PTSD, then she'd need to work with a psychiatrist to find out what had caused her to block out her life.

What could possibly have happened to make her want to escape? She wasn't an abused wife, a neglected wife, or unfulfilled. The life she led didn't read like that. Everyone she spoke to reinforced how great she and Hawk were, how good a physical therapist she was, and how good a mother.

And their sex life must have been... She couldn't allow herself to think about it. It was like being a voyeur observing someone else's intimate moments.

Then what happened to frighten her into this protective shell?

"Will you go to my game this Saturday, Mom?" A. J. asked, bringing her back to the moment.

"Yes, of course I will." She would face the parents and hopefully remember a few of them.

A. J.'s beaming smile was a gift. One she appreciated more each day. But with every new memories she collected, she longed for the old ones to resurface.

As soon as A. J. finished eating, he left the table to put his plate and silverware in the dishwasher.

"Did you get your homework done at Justin's?" Hawk asked.

"I still have some language arts to do." His expression mirrored how he felt about the assignment. Zoe knew it was his least favorite class.

"Get to it and you and I will shoot some hoops before you take your shower."

"Awesome." He trotted out of the room and down the hallway out of sight.

"You're so good with him."

"It's the carrot and the stick. You dangle something as an incentive, and he's eager to get things done so he can get to the carrot."

"I'll check his homework while you two are out playing."

"How do you deal with him when I'm not here?" he asked.

She answered automatically, "I keep him busy." An elusive memory hovered just out of reach. When it wouldn't come, she shook her head and changed the subject. "Tank suggested something to me today, and I think it may be worth pursuing."

"What?"

"We deal with a lot of people who have brain injuries, and most have short-term memory problems. They can't remember appointments, or names. Some have to keep a journal to help them remember what they did the day before.

"But I don't have short-term memory issues. Instead, I get these scattered memories and recognize random people."

Hawk leaned forward and braced his elbows on the table. "You recognize random people?"

"Yes. I went to the hospital today to see Tank." When he started to say something, she held up a hand. "I took an Uber. I didn't drive. As soon as I heard his voice on the phone, I could picture him. And there was a young SEAL I began therapy with the day before the accident. He was in the unit today, and I remembered laughing with him and Tank about something, but I couldn't remember what we were laughing about. It's like remembering a face but having no context to connect it to a situation or event. A photograph or a short piece of film that offers me just enough information to give me hope, then snatches it away."

"Why haven't you been telling me about this?" His features looked wooden with control. "You remember random strangers, but you don't remember us."

The hurt and accusation in his tone nearly broke her heart. "I don't *remember* them, Adam, I just *recognize* them. I don't know how I know them, or where I've met them, or anything about them. I recognized Tank, but I don't remember our history together."

"You recognized Tank, but you still don't remember me."

She just hurt him all over again because she hadn't recognized him at the hospital.

But she'd know him now in the dark. His touch, his scent, the tone of his voice, the way he molded against her even in his sleep. Her mouth went dry as every nerve came alive with a memory of running her fingers through his thick, dark hair while she straddled his lap and he took her distended nipple into his mouth. Her body was suddenly aching and ready for him.

"My body remembers you." Her voice dwindled away to a whisper. And maybe even her heart.

She thought Tank might be right. Maybe there was more than an injured brain keeping her from remembering.

"Dad, I'm finished," A. J. said from the hallway.

"Bring your work in here and leave it on the table for Mom to check while we play. I'll be there right after I change my shoes."

A. J. came back to the kitchen in record time, homework in hand.

"You and Dad are like you used to be."

"Are we?"

"You hug each other a lot. And you kiss." A. J. wrinkled his nose.

Zoe laughed. A memory rose of him in the car in front of an elementary school. "You used to kiss me goodbye when I dropped you off at school."

"That was like in second grade, Mom."

She remembered! She could picture him getting out of the car and going into the building. He always looked over his shoulder before he entered the building to see if she was watching. The tiny ache she experienced when he stopped checking that she was still there rushed through her with the memory.

"Are you okay, Mom?"

"Yes, I'm okay." She went over and put her arms around him, pressing a kiss to his forehead just as Hawk came down the hallway. "Have a good practice."

WHILE SHOOTING HOOPS with A. J., Hawk thought about Langley's complaints about being outgunned by Tad when playing basketball. A. J. was in fifth grade, but already nearing five feet tall. He loved all sports, but his two favorites were baseball and basketball. His coordination was good, he liked to be active, and he, like many boys, wanted to be a professional athlete.

Hawk saw himself in his son, but he also saw Zoe's sensitivity in his temperament. He didn't expect A. J. to follow in his footsteps and become a SEAL, but his current goal of playing ball for a living would probably change to something more realistic.

But damn, it was fun teaching his son how to shoot baskets, guard his opponent, and steal the ball. They were both sweaty by the time they settled on the sunroom steps with bottles of Gatorade and towels draped around their necks like jocks.

"You told me and Justin to keep an eye out for strange cars coming by our house."

A. J.'s comment set off a spike of adrenaline that jolted Hawk's heart until it was drumming in his ears. "Have you seen one?"

"No, but Justin said some guy in an old car asked him if the lady who lived here was okay. Justin said, yeah, so the guy just said 'good' and drove away."

"Did Justin say when this happened?"

"Yesterday."

"Did Justin say what the man looked like?"

"No. He just said some man in a sweatshirt."

Hawk took several breaths to calm himself. He didn't want to scare A. J. or Justin, but he'd call Justin's father as soon as they went in.

"Mom remembered something," A. J. said.

Jesus. He was going to do this father/son bonding every day. His son was proving to be a gold mine of information. "What was it?"

"She said I used to kiss her before I got out of the car to go into the school when I was little. So she must have remembered the elementary school."

She'd mentioned that same thing to him before the accident. What about that made her keep going back to it?

He wondered what else she might have remembered. And why the hell wasn't she telling him about these things?

"I think she's getting better. Don't you?"

She wasn't suffering daily headaches anymore. And her balance was more stable. "Yes, I think she is."

"She tries hard to remember. She writes down things she remembers in her journal and things that are happening now. I asked her why she was doing that. She said in case she forgets again."

Sweet Jesus! His throat closed tight, and he looked away, afraid of what A. J. might read in his expression. His eyes stung, and he quickly blinked the sensation away.

Of course, having treated brain-injured people, even in Lexington, she'd be aware of all the complications she might experience.

"That isn't going to happen, is it, Dad?"

Hawk forced a calm he didn't feel. "No. I'm sure it isn't. She's doing better, and she remembered taking you to school." It was like she was chipping away at the block to her memory a little more every day.

And she called him Adam, just as she used to do when she was trying to make a point about something important. He'd been angry before then, but that small, unconscious tell calmed him.

Her memories were locked up. She just needed one thing that would act as a key. But what the hell could it be?

She'd been about to tell him an idea she and Tank discussed when he interrupted.

"She's still good at checking my homework."

Hawk smiled. "Moms are good at that."

"She doesn't like math as much as you do."

"Everyone has their strengths and their weaknesses."

"But she's really good at geography."

Hawk laughed. "I'm better at playing video games."

A. J. laughed. "And basketball and baseball."

The best part of being a Dad was just hanging out. If they had a girl, would Zoe be hanging out with her, talking clothes, hair, and whatever else girls were interested in, and leaving him out in the cold?

"How 'bout we go in, take a shower, and get Mom to watch a movie with us?"

"Okay." A. J. leaped up, then turned to ask, "We're not going to watch a kissy-face movie, are we?"

Hawk laughed. "It's called a chick flick, and we'll find something we all like."

He popped the popcorn, got the movie started, and left Zoe and A. J. on the couch while he slipped away to make the call.

"Hey, Frank. You know I told the boys to be on the lookout for any unusual cars in the neighborhood. A. J. just told me Justin said some guy in an old car was asking about Zoe yesterday. I don't want to scare either of the kids, but do you think you could ask Justin about it?"

"Jesus! I've told him a million times never to talk to strangers. I'll ask him right now and call you back. And I'll check my security camera footage and see if it picked up anything."

"Thanks."

When the phone rang twenty minutes later, Hawk was already on his feet before Zoe could get up. He took the phone in the kitchen.

"It was a young guy in a gray USD sweatshirt. He had long,

curly hair and a beard and was wearing a baseball cap. I checked the security camera. It caught the car, but the images of the guy aren't clear, and the camera angle was wrong for the plate number."

"I don't want to drag you guys into anything, but I have a number for the detectives who are investigating the accident Would you mind calling them and telling them everything you've told me?"

"Sure. Anything we can do to help catch this bastard. How's Zoe doing?"

"A. J. and I both think she's better, stronger. The cast won't come off for another six weeks, but she's healing." They talked a few more minutes and hung up.

Hawk slipped back into his place on the couch next to Zoe and dug his hand into the popcorn bowl.

A. J. was yawning wide enough to crack a jaw by the time the movie ended, and he headed to bed without being prompted.

When Zoe moved to pick up the popcorn bowl and drinking glasses, Hawk grasped her hand and tugged her back down.

"What were you going to tell me about you and Tank earlier? You said Tank had an idea."

She tucked her hands between her knees. "He thinks I need to see a psychologist. The neurologist I see suggested it, but I wasn't ready. Tank thinks maybe some of the emotional stuff surrounding the accident is affecting my memory."

He thought about that for a moment. "Like PTSD?"

"Yes."

"It was a major traumatic event."

She nodded.

"Have you had any flashbacks?"

"No, but I dreamed about the accident this morning."

The fall she had this morning. "Is that why you fell out of bed?"

"I didn't fall out of bed. I got out of bed and got tangled up in the sheet somehow and tripped. I couldn't catch myself with this damn cast on my arm."

He smiled at her outrage. "What did you dream?"

"It was disjointed and jumped around, but it doesn't take a psychologist to figure out it was about the accident."

"Tell me."

Her body language changed, tensed. "I dreamed about a man following me. He had a baseball cap pulled down low, hiding his eyes, but his lower jaw was shadowed by a beard and he looked...unkept...like he hadn't showered or shaved. I ran as fast as I could, but he just kept walking. He never seemed to walk any faster, but he kept getting closer. The closer he got, the more afraid I was.

"Then the next moment I was in a car and there was a huge truck coming at me. The silver grill shone like it had been polished recently, and I felt like it was going to climb through the window. I gripped the steering wheel and floored the gas pedal, but I couldn't get out of the way. I woke up before it hit me."

"Did you write down the dream in your journal?"

Her head whipped in his direction. "How do you know about the journal?"

"A. J. told me about it."

She drew her long hair over her shoulder and twisted it into a tail. Something she always did when nervous.

"Are you really afraid you'll forget everything again?"

She remained silent for a long moment. "At first I was, but the doctor said it was unlikely, barring any other injuries."

She didn't sound very convinced.

A. J.'s comment about how hard she was trying hit him with a wave of guilt. Hawk grasped her hand and tugged her to her feet. "We've had a long day. Come to bed."

Her cheeks flushed.

She'd said her body remembered him. Was she making an excuse for her response to him?

He wasn't a stranger to her any longer. They'd been sleeping together for three weeks. Three *long* weeks. The first two weeks he'd been careful, but this past week she was more active. And apparently moving back to normal, since she was reaching out to Tank and going to the hospital. She wasn't ready for a full-fledged physical relationship, but there were other things he could do to please her. And if they helped break down some of the distance between them, or possibly triggered a memory, it would be a good thing.

Or was he manipulating the situation to his advantage?

His mission was to win his wife back, and whatever he needed to do... She was worried about being someone different, but she wasn't. She was the same Zoe. And he loved her. He wanted to earn her love all over again.

Once in their room, he went into the bathroom to change into his sleep pants and T-shirt, just as he had since she came home from the hospital. By the time he emerged, she'd slipped into one of the cotton gowns she often wore. He wondered if she gravitated to that particular one because it was her favorite before.

"I remembered something about us." She sat down at the foot of the bed.

She said *us*. She so often referred to thoughts and feelings in a manner that distanced them from the present. Hawk moved to join her. "What was it?"

She plucked at the fabric of her gown with her fingertips. "It was something...intimate."

His heart beat a heavy rhythm against his ribs and in his throat. "Was it earlier, when we were in the kitchen?"

"Yes." Her cheeks flushed.

"Do you want to know about the first time we were together?"

Her eyes looked dark as she glanced up. "Yes."

"While Brett was still in the hospital, your sister Sharon had to have an emergency C-section. Your mother went to help her and left you here to watch over Brett.

"I tried not to step over the boundaries of host and friend, but by then we'd lived together here for a couple of months. I already knew I wanted you, and I wanted more than just a quick roll in the hay. But your mother left me to watch over you, and I really fought those feelings because I thought it was a breach of her trust if I took advantage of us being here alone."

Zoe's mouth curved in a smile.

"There were a couple of my teammates who had a real interest in you, too. It drove me crazy that my hands were tied while they were free to put the moves on you. But you kept turning them down because you didn't think they were serious."

"Because of my leg."

"Yeah. Though I have to tell you, neither of them gave a damn about your scars, Zoe.

"We went to Lang and Trish's for a cookout, and Bowie, one of the guys on my team, put the move on you, and I just couldn't take it anymore. I cornered you against the kitchen counter and kissed you. Your response when you kissed me back... It was a fucking miracle I didn't embarrass myself."

She laughed, the sound triggering his own smile.

"We started dating. And in between going to the hospital to check on Brett, my physical therapy because of my knee, and working on this house, we fell in love. Then one night you walked in here, stretched out on the bed, and told me to turn off the light."

Zoe bit her lip and took a deep breath.

"I think I was more nervous than you when we made love that first time. You'd never been with anyone, and I was damn afraid of hurting you."

"Obviously you didn't."

"But we did have one slight scare."

"Really? What?"

"The condom broke."

Her mouth flew open. "Oh my god! That wasn't when I conceived A. J. was it?'

"No. That was months later."

"Months?"

"Yes. We couldn't keep our hands off each other. So when I was deployed, you didn't know you were pregnant until I was gone, and you didn't want to worry me.

"When I got home, you met me at the airport. I'd already bought a ring to propose, and I'd have done it before I left if I hadn't been deployed without warning. There you were, so beautiful and pregnant. I dropped to one knee and asked you to marry me right on the tarmac."

"So you swept me off my feet."

"And you rolled right over me like a tank. From the moment we met there was no one else."

She rested a hand on his thigh just above his knee. "There's never been anyone else but you."

His heart actually leapt. "I know that, Zoe. But how do you?"

"That memory, flashback, whatever you want to call it…" She shook her head. "There couldn't be."

She slid back on the bed. "Turn out the light and come to bed."

The thought of touching her sent blood rushing south and stole his breath.

AS HAWK CRAWLED up the bed to join her, Zoe found her breathing labored. Was this how it was when they first made love?

Being close to him set every cell of her body alight, her nerves raw with the need to be touched and an aching emptiness just waiting to be filled.

Hawk's gray eyes were dark as he raised himself on an elbow to look down at her. She cupped his cheek and ran her thumb over his cheekbone. As he bent his head to kiss her, she slid her arms around his neck and brought his mouth to hers. Their tongues tangled and parted in heated battle as they pulled at each other's clothes. He had to pull away to bail out of his T-shirt and pajama pants, and when he rolled her gown up, she wiggled free of it. He slid down to take one distended nipple into his mouth and sucked while he kneaded the other breast.

That brief flash of memory she experienced early hadn't prepared her for a single moment of the incredible sensations. Zoe bit back a groan and cupped the back of his head. When his lips came back to hers, she stretched, bowing her body against his instinctively, and the brush of skin against skin lit a fire inside her. Her hands moved over his body in ways she'd wanted to do since the first night they slept together.

He pressed openmouthed kisses down her abs and belly to the curve of her pelvic bone and eased her panties away. When he nibbled at the inside of one thigh, Zoe caught her breath. He parted her with his thumbs and strummed the hypersensitive heart of her with his tongue. The need to feel him inside her quadrupled.

"Adam." The name was torn from her as she clutched and twisted the bedclothes.

He rose up, sliding his body over hers, and entered her with a single thrust.

The sensation of having that emptiness pulsing inside her filled set off a chain reaction of pleasure and release. She'd barely caught her breath when he began to move in long, even strokes, stoking her need all over again, and building the pleasure to a pitch so intense she could barely breathe. Her body strained beneath him, mirroring his movements, reaching for a fulfillment she'd already tasted and wanted again.

"Zoe."

Her name, whispered in a voice strained and husky with passion, tripped her over into orgasm. After one final thrust, his held still, and she felt the powerful pulse of his release deep inside her.

Had it always been this way for them?

Quick tears threatened for all the passionate, precious moments she'd lost. She fought back the need to weep by stroking his back and holding him, giving him all the tenderness she could.

Hawk looked down at her. "I love you, Zoe."

The tears rose up again and spilled down her temples.

"Whatever it takes, we're going to get through this."

"A SEAL never gives up." Emotion kept her voice at a whisper.

"And neither do you."

CHAPTER 21

A HEADACHE POUNDED in Moira's temples. Oversleeping and skipping breakfast because she was running late wasn't the smartest thing to do during an already stressful time.

And to make things worse, things seemed to have intensified for Sam at the base during the past week, and she was getting more and more worried that he and his team might deploy before the wedding.

At school the rumor mill had kicked into second gear, and if one more person stopped to pump her for information under the guise asking her how she was—she might just get arrested for punching them. She finally settled for hiding out in her room to avoid everyone.

But what weighed on her just as much as the dissatisfaction with her job were her suspicions about Mr. Jacobs. She purposely avoided him, and even locked her door during her planning period and hid out in her storage closet.

She couldn't continue to do this the rest of the year. It was time to talk to someone about it. Maggie seemed the one person she could trust, but she'd been afraid of sounding crazy. But Maggie was always a place of calm during the storm, just like her boyfriend, Abe.

As soon as the lunch bell rang, Moira released her students, locked her classroom door, and booked it down to Maggie's room.

Maggie locked her classroom door and beckoned for Moira to move to the back of the room so people couldn't see they were still in the room while they ate. "I know some people have been harassing you."

"Yes, they have been." Moira sighed. Because Maggie had known Mr. Jacobs for several years, Moira couldn't bring herself to voice her thoughts. It would only make Maggie start worrying as much as she was.

She forced herself to take a bite of the grilled chicken she packed for lunch, but there were so many other things bothering her, she just shoved her food away and rested her forehead in one hand. "The police went through my bank records and accounts because they thought I might have stolen the money. I haven't told Sam. He's very protective, and he'd go ballistic."

"Shit! I'm sorry Moira."

When her stomach lurched, she reached for her drink instead. "They didn't find any inconsistencies or anything."

"Of course they didn't," Maggie jumped in.

"There's something I've been holding back from you because it seemed like I'd be gossiping about Sam's family's private business, but you need to know. Sam's father has been arrested for embezzling from his clients."

Maggie covered her mouth with a hand. "Oh, my God!"

"It seems he had a mistress and spread himself and his bank account too thin. He'll probably go to jail, and more than likely his business is gone, and Sam's brother Trevor will lose everything because he works with his dad."

"How's Sam doing?"

"He's stressed, though he tries to act as though he doesn't care. He and his dad haven't been close since he was twelve. But...the man's his father.

"And Sam and his team may deploy right after the wedding, or even possibly before. He and his team train all the time, but all that intensifies just before a deployment. And while he hasn't exactly said anything, he's been asking me to keep the wedding plans in place to please our family and friends, but he wants to slip away and get married just in case. So if he's called up we can go ahead with the reception. And we won't be out all the money it costs for everything."

"How long have you been holding all this in?" Maggie asked.

"Since before we went shopping for our dresses."

Maggie reached out to touch her arm. "I'm sorry, Moira."

She fought hard not to tear up. "You don't want to cancel on being my maid of honor because Sam's dad is a criminal, do you?"

Maggie gave one bark of laughter. "You're not going to go all gangsta on me, are you?"

Moira smiled for the first time. "No. I'm not even sure I even know how to 'go gangsta.'"

Maggie shook her head. "Neither of you have control over his dad's actions or the deployment thing."

"And that's what makes it so hard. We're at the mercy of things out of our control and have no say in them. I've never even met Sam's dad. And I'm glad, because I'd want to punch him for everything he's done to Sam and his family."

"I think I'd help you." Maggie said, finally taking a bite of her sandwich. "I can see the reason Sam and his dad don't get along. The man obviously has no honor. He's been unfaithful to his wife…"

"Two wives." Moira said.

"And he's embezzled money while his son's busy risking his life for his country."

Maggie nailed it on the first try.

A tap came at the door, and Maggie went to answer it. "I invited Tonya Morgan to come down and eat with us. She's stuck in that room next to the office making copies all day, and I feel like we need to be a little more welcoming. She's alone and doesn't have any family here or know many people."

"That's a good idea." Moira needed to get her mind off family stuff, and it would help to focus on someone else's needs instead of her own.

Tonya brought with her a drink and an apple. "I only have a few minutes. If either of you have anything you need copied, I'll take it back to the office when I go."

"I have a few things. I'll get them together while you two talk and eat," Maggie said, taking half a sandwich with her.

"How's it been going, Tonya?" Moira asked.

"Good. I've found a part-time job after school." She sounded excited.

"What will you be doing?"

She chewed a bite of apple. "I'll be working nights and weekends as a server for a catering company. They said I'll be making ten dollars and hour and tips."

"Wow! That sounds great. What company is it?" She tried to eat a bite or two of the food she'd brought.

"R and D Catering." She munched another bite.

"That's the company that's doing the catering for my reception. We were just going to do an outside thing at Sam's mother's house, but we were worried about the damage to her yard and gardens. And we were worried about having room for everyone if it rained. So we've booked a space close to the church and hired the caterer and a DJ so we can dance afterward." Moira popped the cover over the food she had left and opened her bottle of water.

"That sounds like a good plan." Tonya tossed the apple core into the trash can close by and sipped her soft drink.

"I hope it will be. It's not going to be a huge wedding. Just about sixty people. If you're not working, or even if you are, you're welcome to join us. I'll give you all the specifics and add you to the guest list. It's June tenth, if you can come."

"School will be out before then, and I'll be working full time for the caterer. I told them I'd be available full time. I'll ask if I can work the reception and stay afterwards."

"It's a shame that you have to work, but it'll be great if you can stay. The wedding is just before. I'll bring you an invitation. And if you don't have to work, you can still come. Although if you decide to bring a date, let me know."

"No date. I'm separated from my husband, and I'm not interested in dating again."

Her adamant tone of voice put that to rest. "I'm sorry you're going through that."

"Me too."

Maggie rejoined them and left the papers she needed copied on the table. "You'd think since we have workbooks I wouldn't need anything copied, but my students need more practice than the workbooks that go with our texts can provide."

"That's what I'm here for," Tonya said, her tone easy.

"All the teachers are thrilled you're here. We used to have to use part of our planning periods to copy tests and other materials. And if they don't plan ahead and have to do their own, that's on them."

Tonya chuckled. "I can name a few, mostly the men, who forget and come running in at the last minute."

"I bet I could name a few, too," Maggie said.

The bell rang and they all rose to go. "Thanks for inviting me to join you," Tonya said.

"Consider it a standing invitation when you have time." Moira said.

"Thanks." Tonya slipped out of the room, papers in hand.

"Inviting her to the wedding was a nice thing to do, Moira."

"I've been in her shoes, and it doesn't cost me anything to extend the hand of friendship. And besides, Sam's team will be there, and they're all young, single, buff men who will need a dance partner."

"She didn't sound like she was open to romance."

"I got that. But a little fun won't hurt anything."

SAM LEANED BACK into his desk chair. His office space was an afterthought in his weapons cage because he stored his work computer there. Right now he was reading through Seaman Morgan's file for the third time. Morgan had been Brian Marsh's best friend. Master Chief thought Morgan might heal if he was with the guys who carried Marsh home after their last mission.

Sam wasn't so sure. It seemed more likely that Morgan might hold his team responsible for what happened.

The whole thing seemed a bad idea.

On top of that, things weren't working for Morgan at his team.

He picked up the phone and called Master Chief Marks. At Marks's hello, he didn't beat around the bush. "Master Chief, I'm calling about your request."

"What do you think, Lieutenant?"

The word "no" was on the tip of his tongue, but he had to appear to be cooperating. "I'd like to meet with Seaman Morgan before making a firm decision, sir."

"That's a reasonable request. You have a feel for your team's dynamics, so why don't you reach out to Lieutenant Carlson and Morgan?"

"Can you tell me why he wants to transfer out of his current team, sir?"

"He wants a fresh start. He had a bumpy landing here after the last deployment because his wife packed up and left before he made it home. Plus, the loss of his best friend has been hard on him. He thinks a change would put all that behind him and allow him to move on to something new."

"But Seaman Marsh was our teammate, sir. He was Morgan's best friend, and he may think there's some blame to assign there, sir. And because of the sensitivity of the mission, I'm not allowed to fill him in on what happened."

Master Chief Marks remained silent. "I don't believe that's the case. He said Marsh spoke highly of all his teammates, but if you have any reservations after you meet with him, I'll be happy to hear them."

"We thought a lot of Marsh too, sir. My guys are still dealing with his loss." And Morgan might only stir it all up again.

"Maybe that's why Morgan thinks your team would be a good fit. He would have something in common with your guys."

Master Chief had the bit between his teeth.

"What about the legal issues he's dealing with, sir?"

"I think legal is about to get everything pled down to a misdemeanor and community service."

At least Morgan could move on without all that hanging over him.

But a cramped feeling of dread had taken root in Sam's gut. "I already told the men Rosenburg would be returning to his place on our team. He's finished his current training, and I thought he'd easily slide back into the empty slot."

"I'd like to see you give Morgan at least a shot, Lieutenant."

Sam got the message. "Okay, sir." His team deserved better than to take on someone else's problem. Though it had been nearly five weeks since the initial episode of drunk and disorderly, he'd be watching Morgan like a hawk, and the first hint of an issue, he'd be all over it. "I'll reach out to Lieutenant Carlson and set up the meet tomorrow, Master Chief."

"Good. Don't hesitate to contact me if you see any problem at all."

"Thank you, Master Chief."

Closing out the call, he raked his fingers through his hair. "Fuck."

He keyed in Carlson's number and set things up for oh-eight-thirty.

All the way home he stewed about the meet and about Master Chief forcing his hand. Why the hell was he so adamant about giving this guy a place on his team when letting Rosenburg return to the position would make his team deployable more quickly? Rosenburg knew all the guys, had worked with them for two years before, and he had upped his training level to complement their needs.

He was relieved to see Moira's car in the parking lot. Being with her was the highlight of his day. He grabbed his gear out of the back seat of the car and double-timed it into the apartment building.

The scent of cinnamon hit him just inside the door and the timer on the stove beeped a persistent, irritating alarm. He dumped his gear in the floor, went into the kitchen, hit the timer button to shut it off, and opened the oven door.

Ahhhh. Snickerdoodles. His favorite. He removed the cookie sheet and set it on top of the stove. With the cinnamon and vanilla smell of the cookies in his head, he thought of Marsh. Moira had made a huge batch and sent them all off with a dozen cookies to snack on, and they'd shared with the flight crew on the trip. But Marsh had squirreled his away until after their first mission, then brought them out. For Sam the taste had reminded him he had someone special at home waiting for him, and he savored every small bite of his one and a half cookies.

"Sam?"

He looked up and realized he hadn't even noticed when she came into the room.

"What is it?" she asked.

"Nothing. I just got home, and the oven beeper was on. I took the cookies out."

"Thanks. I'll put in another batch."

When she came closer to move around him in the miniscule kitchen, he caught her close. "I need to tell you something. I've been avoiding it since I got back from deployment." His mouth was dry and a dull ache started in his gut. "Because none of us are married, there aren't any wives for you to hang with from our team… so you weren't aware. One of my guys didn't make it back home from our last deployment, Moira. Marsh. Brian Marsh.

"I gave out the wedding announcements today to my guys, and they're all coming, even Book. All but Marsh."

"Sam." She got up on tiptoe to put her arms around his neck and hug him close. "I'm so sorry."

The hitch in her breathing as she cried triggered a flood of emotion for him, too. He closed his eyes against the tears that burned behind his eyelids.

She stroked the back of his head. "I love you. Whatever you need, I'm here."

CHAPTER 22

SITTING INSIDE HER office and staring at the computer seemed natural to Zoe. She had taken over doing the weekly scheduling of patients and other small things, which thrilled Elizabeth, who wanted to be home with her three-month-old baby rather than doing paperwork.

She'd gotten to know the rest of the staff a little in the past two weeks and was beginning to feel confident she could still do the job. But ultimately it would be up to Dr. French.

But Tank was worried because she hadn't spoken to Dr. French yet. In a sense she was lying by doing the work and not admitting to her memory issues. And Tank's disapproval weighed on her in ways she couldn't fight. She might not remember everything they'd been through together, every patient they'd worked with together, but the emotions that ruled their relationship were there. And he was disappointed in her.

Zoe closed the computer and rested a hand on the stack of folders she pulled and set aside for the meeting. She'd already gone through most of her patient files for the past four years, which had been a learning experience, as well as humbling.

She was proud of how much she'd learned and mastered in the past ten years, and the number of people she helped. But she also learned that because of this handicap, she would never be able to bring that experience to the job the way she did before. Not unless she could recover the lost memories. And it might not work even then.

It was time to go to Dr. French and talk to him about it. Her six weeks were almost up, and he would need to put someone else in her place.

She reached for the phone and dialed the extension from the list taped to the desk next to the phone. "Hello, this is Zoe Yazzie. I need to make an appointment to speak with Dr. French."

"How are you, Zoe? It's good to hear from you."

"I'm working my way back."

"That's good. Dr. French can see you this afternoon if you like."

"What time?"

"How soon can you get here?"

"I'm downstairs in the therapy wing right now."

"Give him fifteen minutes and come on up. I'll tell him you're here."

"Thank you."

She hung up the telephone and for just a moment thought she would be okay.

But a wave of grief and loss rolled over her, and for a moment it felt as if the undertow was holding her beneath that wave, unable to breathe.

She didn't remember the job, but reading every note, every plan of treatment for the disabling injuries her patients had experienced, clearly showed how much she loved it—and she still did. If Dr. French let her go, she couldn't imagine how she'd start over.

Would she have to re-take all her classes and be relicensed? Would she have to prove constantly that she was physically and mentally healthy enough to care for someone else? It was all so unfair.

It took every moment of the fifteen minutes for her to recover her composure. When she rose to go to Dr. French's office, she didn't remember where it was. She fought the urge to scream and instead went back to the list on the desk to check the floor and room number.

Then she collected her purse, locked the office door, and walked toward the elevators.

"Zoe," Tank said from behind her.

She turned to face him.

He frowned and his long legs ate up the distance between them. "You okay?"

"I have a meeting with Dr. French."

"You've been doing okay, haven't you?"

"Yes."

He wrapped a big, gentle hand around her arm, and they got into the elevator together. "Don't step down, Zoe. Just tell him you need to take a leave of absence until you've completely healed. You can fight your way back from this. You still have the knowledge base you need for the job. Elizabeth told me this week about how you made a notation on an electronic post-it note about one of her patients. It was some kind of strategy to get him to embrace his therapy. And it worked. That was the kind of thing you always used to do. You still have what it takes! You just need time to break through this memory issue or at least to adjust to it."

After she and Hawk made love, she'd hoped some kind of miracle would happen to restore her memories. But it hadn't. If her husband couldn't break through those barriers, what could? "I may never be able to do it, Tank."

"You have to try. And taking a leave of absence will give you time."

The elevator door opened, and she started to step out. Tank caught the door with a large hand. "Dr. French is about sixty, white hair, and tanned skin. He likes to play golf. His secretary Donna Woods is about the same age but dyes her hair blond to cover the gray. She's got several grandchildren. She keeps a secret stash of candy in her desk drawer for when they come to eat lunch with her."

"How do you remember all this?" Zoe asked.

"I've been here a while now. You're the one who told me about the stash. She mentioned it to you one time."

He was trying to protect her. A flood of emotions rose again, and she swallowed back the tears as she stepped out of the elevator. "Thanks, Tank."

He nodded and released the door, and it closed between them.

She followed the numbers on the doors until she found Dr. French's office.

The woman sitting behind the desk was exactly as Tank described her. "Zoe, so good to see you. He's waiting for you. Go straight in."

"Thank you." She crossed to the door, tapped lightly, then opened it.

Dr. French reminded her a little of her mother's husband, Russell. He had the same stature and build, but his hair was silver-gray instead of white, and his features were much sharper. Sharp chin, nose, and a gleam in his eyes. His suit jacket was draped over the back of his desk chair.

He was stooped over a golf club and swung it in a practice putt, then realigned to hit the ball. The ball hit the putting machine in just the right spot and shot back to him. He looped it with the putter and placed it back on the spot where he wanted it. "I hear you've been coming in and doing paperwork."

She wondered who told him. "Yes, sir."

"You're supposed to be recovering."

"I'm trying."

Her answer seemed to pique his interest, and he straightened away from the long runner of artificial turf and placed the putter in a stand. His brows were darker than the gray of his hair and hugged his nose in a frown. "Have a seat." He gestured toward one of the chairs in front of his desk. As soon as she was seated, he took the other. "Tell me what's going on."

"I've been out for five weeks, but I'm still having some issues."

"Such as?"

"Some memory lapses and headaches."

"Short-term memory or long-term?"

She couldn't lie. "Long-term."

"How much have you forgotten?"

"When I first came out of the coma, I didn't remember my husband or my son."

"But you do now."

"Yes, but it's taken some time." She still didn't have her earlier memories back. Simply knowing who they were now left out everything that made them who they were.

"You don't remember me, do you?"

"No."

"What about your training?"

"I'm good there. I know you can't take my word for it, that you may want to test me in some way."

"We'll get to that. I'd want our own neurologist to check you out, Zoe. Our people have more experience with head trauma and brain injury than any other doctors. Would you be open to that?"

She was close to tearing up again. "Yes. Of course."

"When would you be ready to start?"

She looked at her watch. She had to be home for A. J. "Tomorrow."

"I'll call and have things scheduled. And I'll call you later and let you know where and when."

She was shaky as she rose from her seat and put a hand on the desk for support. "Thank you, Dr. French."

"You've always gone above and beyond for us here, Zoe. And you've been with us for ten years. We're going to give you all the help you need to get past this."

"Thanks, Dr. French."

She'd come expecting to have to resign. But instead of writing her off, he offered help instead.

HAWK READ OVER Langley's report about Seaman Morgan.

The man was making strides to recover the ground he lost immediately after returning from deployment but had requested a change in assignment. Langley was pushing for a meeting between

Morgan and Sam Harding. Hawk knew Sam liked to choose his own guys, and there was a careful balance of personalities that went into forging a strong team. It only took one asshole to cause an issue.

It was Langley's job to oversee all personnel on post, a huge job, and one he was doing well. And they needed to fill spots as they became available. He also trusted that Langley was looking out for all the guys. But he needed to put his own concerns to rest.

He closed out the report and pulled up the next, the paperwork on Morgan's wife Tonya. Law enforcement had found her and notified NCIS that she was safe, alive, and well. That at least put his mind at ease.

It was amazing how one experience in life could color other situations. He'd run several speculative scenarios about her disappearance through his mind, all leading with Morgan having done something to her.

And every one of the scenarios was based on Derrick Armstrong's treatment of his ex-girlfriend and the hostage situation that followed. He could have lost Zoe back then, and had come dangerously close.

With the renewal of their physical relationship, things seemed more normal between them. She still had moments when he could practically see her struggling to pull the memories up and out of limbo, which seldom worked. But they were building something new between them.

The ding of a text on his cell phone interrupted his thoughts and he glanced at it. It was Zoe texting him. She'd spoken to Dr. French, and he wanted her to have a complete workup at the hospital in the next few days.

He texted her back that it sounded like a good idea and it didn't hurt to have a second opinion. Though they were intimate again, and she was more relaxed with him, there was still a distance between them. She was holding things back. What she wrote in her journal was one of them. He wanted to read it, but knew she'd feel it was a breach of her privacy.

He answered the phone when it buzzed. "Master Chief Marks

is here, sir, and Lieutenant Harding left something for you," Ryan said.

"I'm coming."

He closed the reports out and tucked his phone into his hip pocket.

Langley bobbed his head and lowered his voice. "We're running late."

Ryan held up the envelope from Lieutenant Harding. "I'll put this in your office on the desk, sir. It could be time sensitive."

"I'll open it as soon as I get back."

They left the building and got into Langley's SUV.

"I lost track of time. SDPD did a wellness check on Morgan's wife. She's alive and well. Lives in a small two-bedroom with a female roommate and is working at a high school as office staff."

Lang whipped around and wove his way through the base traffic. "Good. I had some weird shit going through my head about him possibly storing her belongings and her body somewhere, and but telling everyone she moved out and took everything with her."

"I had the same idea. That's why I called in a favor with one of the men on the force who used to be in the teams." Hawk took a beat then said. "If you thought he was capable of it, why do you want to transfer him to Bravo team?"

"I've come to the conclusion that three quarters of the world is capable of shit like that if they get angry or obsessed enough, Hawk. You have to give everyone the benefit of the doubt until you know for sure."

"I made the mistake of doing that once before, and we both know, up close and personal, how that turned out."

After a lull, Langley asked, "How's Zoe doing?"

"She went in today to tell the head man about her memory issues. Instead of firing her or laying her off, he wants the neurologist there to do a workup for a second opinion."

"That sounds like a good idea."

"I hope so."

"Your SEAL impersonation needs some work, man."

Hawk laughed half-heartedly.

"What the hell is wrong?"

"I guess I just didn't realize how hard it is to sit behind the desk every day and do *for* the teams instead of doing things *with* them. I miss being active."

"I do too." The reluctant note in Langley's voice had Hawk glancing at him.

"If you tell Trish I even came close to saying that, you're a dead man. She's floating around the house like she's on cloud nine. Her man is home at six every night for the first time in twenty-two years, and I'm doing the Dad thing on a consistent basis. And I'm getting rewarded for all of it in ways I'm not going to mention."

Hawk chuckled. "Thanks for sparing me."

"But it's still...killing me."

Hawk rubbed the back of his neck. "I keep reminding myself about all the shit details Zoe has had to deal with over the past ten years while I've been gone. And all the parenting she's had to do without backup."

"Roger that."

"They've had to make their own happiness, while we've been cowboying all over the world. Doing what we loved."

"Yeah."

They fell silent, each dwelling on his own thoughts.

He used to believe he had a handle on how to make Zoe and himself happy until this fucking accident torpedoed the whole thing. But he hadn't factored in his own dissatisfaction with this new assignment.

But at home their lovemaking was new and different, just as it had been when they first started out. It was hard for him to keep his hands off her. She was both the same and different. Different enough that sometimes he had the wild, guilty feeling that he was cheating on the old Zoe.

She'd been trying to explain to him that very same thing, but he hadn't understood until they made love again for the first time.

They pulled up to the parking area. Langley got binoculars out of the trunk and handed him one, and they walked the rest of the way to the shooting range. The team was working through a long series of precision firing drills, and though they never needed an audience, he and Lang just wanted to watch from a distance and see how the team worked together.

"Too bad we didn't bring our Sigs. We could have gotten in some target practice," Langley said.

"We can do it some other time. I've been coming out and keeping sharp."

Langley glanced his way.

Hawk looked through the binoculars, watching the first two teammates work through the course. Every team got the same training, but through working and training together, teammates learned to read each other's body language. Swan and Gilly moved toward the targets, their M4s tucked in against their shoulders. Swan took the first two targets, double-tapping the wooden forms twice in the chest and once in the head. Gilly tapped his shoulder and moved ahead and double-tapped the next two. It was like watching a very carefully choreographed ballet. Not that he'd watched much dance. Every two targets they switched out, tapping each other's shoulders to change position. Smooth as silk.

Sam partnered himself with Morgan. Hawk watched their movements together, and could find nothing wrong with their performance. Morgan worked as though he'd always been a member of the team.

They left without approaching Sam or his team. "What are we doing here, Langley?" Hawk asked.

"Figuring out ways to get the hell out of the office."

Hawk laughed. "Why do you think I run every day?"

"Fuck!"

Langley's sudden exclamation brought him to a stop.

"If it's this bad and I'm still on the base, dealing with things important to the guys and to their survival, how bad is it going to be when I retire?"

"You don't have to retire. You can reenlist until you drop in your tracks."

"Is that really any better?"

No, it wasn't. After their last deployment, they both realized the toll it was taking on their wives and made decisions for their families' benefit instead of their own.

"Make a plan, Langley. You have two years to put one in place. I'm already trying to figure things out. In a year I'll be closing in on my twenty, and by then I'll have a plan to move on to something else or I'll re-up.

"We're fucking SEALS, man. We haven't given up when we've been pinned down and gotten within a gnat's eyebrow of getting our asses shot off. Hell, I've almost been blown up three times that I can think of. There's life after this. We just have to figure out what we want to do afterward, and we both have to figure out how to leave this behind."

Langley rubbed his forehead as though he was in pain. "There's the rub. Can you think of one single thing we can do that can take its place?"

No, he couldn't, but he was going to have to. "Maybe we can figure out something we can do together. If we can come up with a plan, I'll hold off re-enlisting and throw in with you when you retire."

"You'd do that?"

"Yeah. We've had each other's backs for years now. Why would that ever change?"

That seemed to calm Langley. "All right. I've already ruled out the private contractor thing. I'd just as soon stay in as go that route."

"Roger that."

You couldn't trust the kind of backup you got with private military contracts. Couldn't trust how well their training stood up when shit hit the fan. "We'll come up with something. And we'll make it happen."

CHAPTER 23

MOIRA WATCHED WHILE one student removed the tables' heavy vinyl coverings while another swept the clay dust off the floor. Without the students' help, there was no way the janitorial staff could keep the dust from creeping out into the hallway. Also, the floors in her room were slick, and needed to be mopped to prevent accidents. So she'd do it herself, then go home.

When the bell rang, she shooed the kids out and went to the janitorial closet to get a mop and fill the bucket. While she mopped, her thoughts wandered.

Three more weeks until school ended, and these were the last of the clay projects to be fired. They worked with underglazes this time, and she would fire the pieces today before going home. Next they'd apply the final glaze, and she'd fire them again. She'd have to rush, but they'd be ready for the end of the year art show next week.

She thought about the one last year, when Sam and two of his men helped her get things organized. Emily was so funny that day. She even flirted with the guys a little. The office wasn't the same without her there.

She still hadn't returned to work. Moira didn't blame her. If she'd been attacked by someone in the building, she wasn't sure she'd feel comfortable returning either. She was attacked, but he was never able to get his hands her. She was lucky.

She pretended not to be worried when Maggie asked, but it still weighed on her mind. And weeks had gone by since the police started their investigation, and neither she nor Sam had heard a word.

What if Sam was deployed before they found the man and arrested him?

Four more weeks until the wedding. She was getting a bit nervous now—not about the wedding, never about marrying Sam, but because he might be deployed before they got to say their vows.

It hadn't been that long since his last deployment, so why couldn't they choose another team to send? Just this once. All she wanted was a few more months before having to tell him goodbye again.

Maggie appeared at her door just as she finished up the floor. "We do have janitorial staff who do that."

"I know, but it's a kind of therapy. Plus I feel guilty because they have to mop every day when I'm doing clay. It makes such a mess, even when the students are throwing on the wheel.

"But luckily we're just under-glazing and I'll only have to fire these. They'll put clear glaze on them tomorrow, and I'll fire them once more. Two days' work should finish all this off, and then we'll start setting up the panels for the exhibits."

Maggie stepped farther into the room. "Some really beautiful pieces come out of all of this work. But it *is* a lot of work on your part. I don't think anyone in the building realizes how much you do."

Maggie set her bag down on a table at the door and tiptoed over the freshly-scrubbed floor to Moira's desk chair and sat down. "Did you hear that the Board voted to cover the expense of the fundraiser?"

Moira breathed a sigh of relief. She'd been worried the staff might have to kick in some of the money.

"But they've put in a directive…no more fundraisers for at least three years."

"That sounds good to me. I was really burned out after this last one and didn't want to do it any more."

"What is it, Moira? You've been really down for the past few weeks."

"I've been thinking... I might not come back next year."

Maggie's jaw dropped. It took a moment, but she managed to pull herself together. "What would you do?"

"I could go back to school and get my doctorate and teach college. Or I might take a stab at an in-house residency program at one of the galleries here."

"There's not a doubt in my mind that you'll get one if you apply."

Moira looked up at Maggie.

"I don't want you to quit. You are so good at what you do, Moira. The students here would take a huge hit if you left. You bring out their creative spirit, and they thrive under your instruction. And...it's selfish of me, but even though we don't get to hang out much during the school day, I still like having a friend here to sit with at assembly and at lunch and after school, like now. Please think about it some more before you do anything."

Moira rinsed the mop in the huge metal bucket and put it through the wringer. "I haven't talked to Sam about it yet. He's been distracted with his father's situation and some kind of restructuring going on with his team."

She started to tear up and looked away. "One of the members of his team was killed during the last deployment, and he's been dealing with that on top of everything else."

"God." Maggie brushed her hair back with both hands. "I don't know how you do it. And I certainly don't know how he does."

Moira set aside the mop and dragged a chair over to the desk. "We have separate lives, just like other couples. My life is school, my art, and Sam. Sam's life is his team, his job, and me. When he's deployed, we FaceTime every other day, and he emails me if he's in a place where we can't do that. When he's home, we spend as much time as we can together." She leaned forward and focused on Maggie. "Tell me how your and Abe's lives are any different."

Maggie paused a beat. "Abe's life is in an office with a computer. There's no danger for him to face. But he does have to travel some, and then we basically do exactly what you do."

"Sam would go crazy sitting in an office. He has to be moving, challenging himself. Even when he's doing things for pleasure."

Maggie laughed.

Realizing what Maggie was imagining, Moira laughed. "I was talking about sailing. Which can be a challenge, depending on the weather."

"You're not so different, you know. Always pushing yourself, striving for more."

Maggie was probably right.

"Are you through here?" Maggie asked.

"Yes. I'll just roll the mop bucket back to the janitor's closet." She went over and grabbed the heavy mop, guiding the bucket out the door and down the hall. She didn't have the strength to lift the bucket and empty it, though, so she'd have to ask one of the janitors to do it.

On her way back to her room, she heard her name being yelled in the hallway and paused at her classroom door to see what was happening. Mr. Jacobs appeared around the corner, running down the hallway toward her. In pursuit were two men in police uniforms.

Jacobs's expression was frantic and his cheeks bright red. Though he was wearing rubber-soled shoes, his movements were lumbering and clumsy. Moira reached for her door and started to close it.

"Moira, wait," Jacobs yelled.

He was upon her before she could slam the door. He pushed her back in, shut the door, and locked it. The two police officers hit the door with enough force to shake it while Jacobs just stood there, gulping air and trembling.

Moira backed away toward Maggie, who was huddled against the smart board.

One police officer's voice came through the six-inch-wide strip of glass set in the door, demanding he come out.

"It wasn't me, Moira. It wasn't me. I'd never hurt Emily. Never. I'd never hurt you either. I'd never hurt anyone. You have to believe me. You have to tell Emily. She's worked with me since I was hired. I could never raise a hand against her."

Tears streamed down his face, and his cheeks and ears were such a bright red, she wondered if he might have some kind of medical issue.

"Why don't you sit down, Mr. Jacobs?"

"I took the money. I admit I took the money. I was going to lose my house. I was behind on the payments, and I just needed enough to hold off the bank until I could figure out…what to do. But I didn't hurt Emily. I swear it."

"I know you didn't." Just seeing him running down the hall toward her confirmed that beyond a doubt… "I'll tell them that. Please sit down, Mr. Jacobs."

The police officers had stopped pounding on the door, though one was watching Jacobs, gun drawn.

She pulled a chair out for Jacobs, and he collapsed into the seat. She rushed to one of the sinks, jerked open the cabinet, and filled a plastic cup with water, then wet a paper towel. She handed him the towel and set the cup of water on the table next to him. "Put the towel on the back of your neck and sip the water. You need to calm down."

He gulped air as though he couldn't get enough. "You'll tell her it wasn't me."

Tears of sympathy blurred her vision. "I'll tell her. But she already knows you'd never hurt her."

Jacobs reached for the cup of water, but his hand hit it instead. It tipped over, spreading water across the table and rolling off the other side and into the floor. He looked up at her, and for a moment she could see real, raw panic in his eyes.

His skin suddenly went from red to pasty. "Mo…." He grabbed at his tie and tugged, clawing at the fabric over his shoulder. His teeth were gritted, and he grimaced, then tumbled out of the chair and landed with a thud, his head hitting the floor with a whack.

"Get the door, Maggie! He's having a heart attack." Moira knelt and eased him onto his side. Saliva rolled out of the side of Jacobs's mouth, and she grabbed the damp towel to wipe it away before she turned him on his back. She jerked his tie loose and pulled it away, then unbuttoned the top buttons of his shirt. She felt for a pulse, but there wasn't one. For a moment her mind went blank. "He's not breathing, and he doesn't have a pulse." She positioned her hands and started compressions.

One of the officers touched her shoulder. "I'll do CPR if you can do the breathing." The other officer called in for an ambulance.

"Maggie." Moira looked up, searching for her in the room, and was vaguely aware of Detective Sherman standing over her. "Go to the office and get the defibrillator."

While the officer changed places with her and did CPR, Moira rolled to her feet, went to her desk, and got the emergency kit, removing the rubber emergency barrier and returning to place it over Jacobs's mouth. She and the officer worked together to get a rhythm going—two breaths, then thirty compressions. Time seemed to stretch as they waited for the device.

The other officer returned with the AED with Maggie running in behind him.

The officer checked for Jacobs's pulse and breathing and shook his head. "Nothing."

"Someone get the scissors on my desk." She opened the machine and set it up, quickly cutting Jacobs's T-shirt away to place the pads on his torso as she'd been taught, and waited for it to charge. As soon as it was fully charged, she hit the button, sending a shock of electricity through Jacobs's chest. The line on the machine's screen remained flat.

It seemed to take forever for the machine to calibrate again. She pushed the button again. A slow, erratic rhythm showed on the screen, then slowly picked up speed to a normal beat.

Moira leaned back against the heavy table leg closest to her, every muscle twitching with reaction. She hugged her knees and rested her head on them while tears streamed down her face.

Maggie knelt next to her and tucked some tissues in her hand before rested a hand on her shoulder. After several moments, Moira was able to beat back the emotions enough to dry her eyes and blow her nose.

A male hand appeared within her line of sight, and she reached for it and for the first time she looked at Detective Sherman.

"You're cool under fire, Ms. McKee," he commented. He pulled a chair out so she could sit down.

"No I'm not."

Maggie came to sit with her and brought her a drink of water. "You're awfully pale. Just relax for a minute. The EMTs are almost here." She looped her arm through Moira's in a show of comfort.

Fifteen minutes later the EMTs arrived. They removed the pads and set up their own system, assessed Jacobs, pronounced him stable enough to move, and loaded him onto a gurney to be transported to the hospital.

Sherman sent the two officers to accompany him to the hospital and report back if there was any change.

He came back to where they sat and pulled out a chair to sit across from them. "When he wakes up, your principal will be arrested for embezzling money from the school's accounts. And for attacking you and Mrs. Browning."

The clumsy, choppy way Mr. Jacobs had run down the hall… "He may have stolen the money, but he isn't the man who chased me down the hall. And he certainly didn't attack me or Emily."

Detective Sherman features hardened into a scowl. "What do you mean?"

"The man who ran after me was in better shape, his shoulders were wider, and he could run. He moved fast, and with grace, like an athlete."

Sherman rested his elbows on the table between them. "Think of this, Ms. McKee. What are the chances of two different men perpetrating crimes in your school?"

"I don't care about the odds, Detective. It wasn't Principal Jacobs who chased me. I just now watched him run toward me..." she shook her head. "I'm certain of it."

Sherman's jaw tightened. "What kind of relationship do you have with him?"

The insult was like a slap, and she felt the heat rise in her face along with her anger. "I have a professional relationship with Mr. Jacobs and that's all. He's my principal. I rarely even speak to him. You can ask everyone here in our building."

"I may just do that."

Maggie spoke for the first time. "That sounds very close to a threat, Detective. Moira's telling you the truth. Outside of school business, she and principal Jacobs only speak in passing. And if she says he isn't the man who chased her down the hall, he isn't. She's a trained observer. You may see her as just a high school art teacher, but she's an artist above everything else. She can capture a movement with a single line."

"Who are you?" Sherman's tone was more a demand than a question.

"I'm Margaret Jenson. I teach math here. And I'm Moira's friend. If there was anything at all going on between them, I'd know it."

Sherman eyed them both with disgust, rose from his seat and stalked out of the room.

"He's pissed because you just made his job harder," Maggie said.

Still riding a wave anger and very close to tears again, Moira said, "Fuck him."

Maggie's brows shot up, and then she laughed.

On impulse, Moira hugged her.

"I could have never been as calm as you were through all this, Moira. You weren't even scared."

"Yes, I was. But Mr. Jacobs looked and acted so desperate. And I was more afraid the police would shoot him if I didn't get him calmed down. Then I was afraid he might die right here in my classroom."

Maggie brushed a hand over her brow. "He's been my principal since I first started teaching. I can't believe he's being arrested." The shock and disappointment in Maggie's expression gave Moira a twinge.

Maggie glanced at her. "You're not even surprised."

Moira shook her head.

"Why?"

"Remember how he pressured me to do another fundraiser? There was just something desperate about the way he pushed for it. The project would have brought in a large grant, but it wasn't really feasible. Then when the money in the account disappeared… He's the only one who's in and out of Emily's office often enough to have figured out what her password might be."

"But you didn't say anything."

"I wanted to but… What if I said something and I was wrong? It only takes a single person saying something—something that gets the gossip mill going—to destroy a someone's reputation. I knew if I said it to you, it wouldn't go any further, but your feelings toward Mr. Jacobs would change, and then you'd have worried about it as much as I have."

She looked up to see Maggie studying her.

"What is it?"

"You just notice so many things about people, Moira."

The last time she hadn't paid close enough attention almost cost her her life.

"It makes me wonder what you've noticed about me," Maggie said.

"I've noticed that I can trust you to have my back. I thought you were going to kick Sherman's ass." She forced herself to her feet, and even though her legs still wobbled like rubber, started to pick up the debris left behind by EMS. Maggie quickly got up and helped her.

Once everything was back in its place, Moira gathered her things and Maggie did the same.

"That detective was a dumbass. And if he could even imagine

you'd have an affair with a forty-five-year-old, married principal while you have a sexy, gorgeous fiancé you're crazy about to go home to every night, he needs to hand in his shield."

Moira laughed and shut the door behind them. But just in case Sherman returned, it was time to program Anthony Reeves's phone number into her cell phone.

They came out into the main hall to find a cluster of twenty or so teachers talking softly. They turned toward the two of them expectantly. Moira's heart fell.

"You did the hard work, I got this," Maggie said. "Go home."

They shared a look, and Moira rested a hand on Maggie's shoulder. "Thanks, Maggie." Moira continued on to the glass doors.

Maggie turned to the group. "Mr. Jacobs had a medical emergency and was transported to the—"

The door shut behind her. How she wished it was for the last time.

SAM FELL IN behind a string of cars leaving the base. Moira once teased him that the mass exodus of SUVs looked like a CIA motorcade. He smiled at the memory.

Having someone to go home to was the best. She tried to make their home a stress-free zone for his benefit, and he realized he hadn't done much lately to return the favor. Maybe tonight they could veg out in front of the television, make slow, easy love, and go to sleep early.

Which meant he needed to get all the shit out of his system before he reached home. Dammit, there was really no good reason to reject Morgan. He'd been focused and ready to take on anything they threw at him. He'd be the fucking new guy (FNG) for six months or longer, which would be a pain in the ass for him. But he'd probably do okay.

But that meant Rosenburg was shit out of luck with the transfer. After he already told him there wouldn't be a problem. Fuck!

And now he had to take backwater on the whole thing with his team *and* Rosenburg and it sucked. Fuck!

But they all knew that the Head Shed got the last say, and Sam had no say in it at all this time. They'd gotten lucky with the last two guys, who transferred in because Lieutenant Commander Yazzie gave them a list of candidates and allowed him to choose after interviewing them. Which almost never happened. Book's accident was a special circumstance, and now Sam wondered why Marsh's death wasn't.

Because Master Chief Marks was calling the shots now when it came to personnel. Dammit.

While he was in the elevator going up to Moira's apartment/their apartment, Sam wondered if he should have stopped and picked something up for dinner. He hadn't even called. He was going to have to get better about all this couple stuff.

He let himself in and stopped when he saw Moira sitting on the couch, her feet propped on the coffee table, her head tilted back and her eyes closed. Her skin glowed so pale and soft, and her red hair fell in a curly mass around her face. He loved the different textures and colors of…her. "Hey, babe." He sat down beside her.

"Hey." She turned her head, and her blue eyes looked like a winter sky, but there was nothing cold about them. "Mr. Jacobs had a heart attack in my classroom today because the police had come to arrest him for stealing the fundraiser money."

"Jesus." It took him a second to process that. "Is he still alive?"

"Yes. One of the cops did CPR while I did the artificial respiration. He'll be arrested as soon as he's out of the hospital—if he makes it.

"Detective Sherman is angry because I told him I didn't think it was Jacobs who chased me. They were going to charge him with the assault on Emily, too, but I know it wasn't him."

Moira had too much empathy for people. Was she protecting Jacobs out of pity? "How do you know?"

"The guy who chased me was a natural athlete. He moved like

he was used to running. Mr. Jacobs runs like an uncoordinated fifth grader. And the other guy had an aggression in the way he attacked the bathroom door that I've never seen in Mr. Jacobs."

"How did Jacobs steal the money?"

"I don't know. But the cops had a warrant to arrest him. Jacobs told me and Maggie that he stole the money, but he didn't hurt Emily."

"Told you?"

"Yeah. He came running down the hallway and locked himself in my classroom with me and Maggie. The police officers were beating on the door at first, but I got him to sit down and tried to calm him. Then he had the heart attack, and we unlocked the door and let the officers in."

"Jesus, Moira! Was he holding you hostage?"

"No, nothing like that. He wasn't aggressive at all. He was just crying and begging me to tell Emily he wasn't the one who hurt her."

"Shit." He shook his head. "Come here." He stretched out an arm to urge her to curl in against him, resting his lips against her forehead and breathing in the scent of apple shampoo that lingered in her hair.

"God, I can't wait for this school year to be over."

He tightened his arm around her. His phone rang with the theme song of *The Exorcist* and he jerked it free from his shirt pocket, declined the call, and placed it on the seat cushion.

It rang again and he declined again.

"Maybe you need to answer it."

"No."

"Who is it?"

"My father."

Moira burst out laughing, and he laughed with her. "You are so bad. Your father isn't a demon, or possessed by one."

"You've never met him."

The phone rang again, playing the same song.

Moira's arm tightened around him. "Answer it and see what he wants."

"Money. It's the only thing he ever wants or needs." With a sigh he pushed the accept button. "What is it, Thomas?"

"I'd like to see you."

Wasn't happening. "What for?"

"You're my son, I want to talk to you."

"Then talk."

"I'd like to talk face-to-face."

Of course he would. He thought he'd be able to manipulate Sam more easily face-to-face. It's harder to say no when looking into someone's eyes. "Moira and I have both had a long day, and we haven't eaten yet. I'd just as soon deal with this over the phone."

Thomas sucked in an audible breath. "I'm not going to be able to afford an effective defense. They've frozen my accounts, and I'm not allowed to borrow money against the property I own. I know you have a piece of property worth a lot of money, and you could borrow money against it."

Caught between the urge to either explode with fury or laugh hysterically, Sam withdrew from Moira.

He wasn't surprised by the request. In fact, he'd half expected it. And as he expected, Thomas went straight for the one personal possession Sam loved the most, and the one thing Thomas was most jealous of because Sam had loved and respected his grandfather so much more than he ever had his father. "No."

"I paid for your college education. You owe me."

"I don't owe you shit. You and the bank aren't getting your paws on my boat. So you just have your wife hock all the jewelry you bought her, and the side piece can do the same. And each can sell her new car. And anything else worth anything, since it all came from money you stole from your clients. And if you were really smart, you'd try to make as much restitution as you can and accept the punishment you deserve for stealing from people who trusted you." He hung up. When the phone rang again, he blocked the number. The same burner number he'd saved before.

Moira's arm tightened around him again. "I'm sorry, Sam."

"He won't be calling again. I've blocked him."

"I should have never told you to answer his call. I'm sorry."

He sucked in several breaths, trying to rein in his temper. "It's okay. I didn't answer because you told me to. I answered because I knew he wouldn't stop calling until I did."

Every interaction he had with his father was always a disappointment, because he was a narcissistic asshole who only thought of himself.

He turned his attention back to Moira. The concern and compassion he read in her expression eased his temper. "I'm truly finished with him, Moira. I've waited since I was twelve for him to grow a heart and a conscience. I've known for a long time it was never going to happen, but I thought, just maybe, this episode would create enough of a chink in his armor that he'd act like a flesh and blood human being."

He shook his head. "I'm done. I'm not giving him anything more. I'm finished."

Just saying the words released the enormous pressure he'd struggled with for decades. Pressure to care about the man who gave him life when he'd known all along their relationship was damaged beyond repair. Pressure to help, even when he felt Thomas had finally gotten what he deserved. Pressure he realized he'd been putting on himself, because it certainly hadn't been coming from Tim or Trevor.

He turned his attention back to Moira. "I need a shower and some food, in that order. What about you?"

"I could use both, too."

He rose and offered her a hand. When she took it and stood, he scooped her up. "We'll rinse the day off and move on to better and more important things," he said with a smile as he carried her down the hall.

"Sounds perfect to me."

CHAPTER 24

ZOE FOLDED HER hands as she faced the two detectives across the dining room table. She checked her watch to make sure she still had a couple of hours till her therapy appointment.

Detective Crider smiled at her as though to reassure her. Her partner, Detective Wilson, seemed all business.

"We appreciate you taking the time to look at some of the images we've managed to find of the man driving the truck involved in your accident." Detective Crider seemed to be choosing her words carefully. "Are you sure you're okay to do this?"

Zoe appreciated her asking, even though she already assured her over the phone that she was fine. "Yes, I'm fine."

"It's taken several weeks, but we've been able to lift these from security cameras in a couple of locations near where the truck was stolen."

"Okay."

She laid one of the photos in front of her. It was a side view of a man in the driver's seat, the lower half of his face darkened with a beard, and his hair covered by a baseball cap. A streetlight was behind him, so he was more a silhouette with tiny details than a complete image. Zoe studied it for a long moment. She shook her head.

Crider placed another photo on the table, this one taken from the front from a traffic camera. His baseball cap was pulled down low enough that it covered his eyes. A deep cleft in his chin was partially obscured by the scruff covering the lower part of his face.

She'd seen someone with a deep cleft recently. Oh, yes. The SEAL who helped her at the hospital. But he was clean-shaven.

A lot of men in the San Diego area probably had a cleft like him.

"This one was taken from the parking lot where the truck was stolen."

The man wore no cap, but his hair lay in thick curls over his forehead and ears, and his beard darkened his jaw. Even though the photo was blurry, or maybe because it was, the man in her dream came to mind. And his unrelenting pursuit of her.

And once again she was reminded of the SEAL who'd been so kind to her and helped her. But he had short hair and no beard. It was probably someone who resembled him slightly.

She tried to imagine the man without the shaggy hair and beard, but it was difficult.

An unrelated memory came to her of Hawk walking down an aircraft platform, his expression intent as he searched the crowd. Her heart thrilled at the sight of him.

"Ms. Yazzie. Do you recognize him?" Detective Crider asked.

"I'm sorry, but no. I can't be certain it's the same man. He was behind me, and I was fighting the wheel. I just kept catching glimpses of his chin." She drew a deep breath. "If I don't know this man, why would he attack me? And I'm certain I don't know him."

What was the name of the young man she met at work? Her head had hurt so badly when they met, she'd been feeling nauseous, and her vision was a little blurred. Seaman Owens. Wasn't that it? She'd meant to mention his kindness to Hawk.

"Maybe the attack on you was as random as the attack on the owner of the truck. This guy has an anger management issue. So if you see him again, call us right away."

"I will."

Crider gathered the photos. "We'll showing these to your

husband."

"Good. He may know him. I'm sorry I couldn't be more help."

The defense would point out her brain injury and call her memory into issue anyway.

She walked them to the door and was surprised when Detective Wilson turned to face her. "You remembered something else while you were looking at the photo." His tone sounded like he was accusing her of something.

The man was large, imposing, and looked like a boxer. If he was trying to intimidate her, he'd picked the wrong woman. She was too used to being around lots of alpha males, both on the job and off. She was beginning to remember some of them and their posturing.

"Yes, I did."

Her smile seemed to puzzle him, so she decided to explain. "I get these random, unrelated memories out of the blue. I got a flash of my husband walking down the ramp of a plane, his hair long enough to hang along both sides of his face and his beard scruffy. His background is Navaho, I guess you've noticed. He was tanned from being in the sandbox, his skin dark." He'd looked like a true warrior. "It was the day he asked me to marry him."

"And you just remembered it?" he asked.

"Yes."

"What correlation would that memory have with this suspect?" His brown eyes were piercing.

"The man's hair is long and untrimmed and his beard scruffy and unkept. He hasn't seen a barber in a while."

"Like someone just home from deployment," Crider said.

The two detectives looked at each other, then back at her.

"Or it could be someone just too lazy to get a haircut, or someone homeless," Zoe said.

"We're going to check all that out. I hope those memories just keep coming, Mrs. Yazzie," Wilson said.

"I hope so too."

Zoe was still mulling over the memories when she settled in a chair in the psychologist's office. It was her third appointment since seeing Dr. French, and she was getting impatient with the process.

She wanted her life back. All of it, not just the stingy bits and pieces her brain doled out according to its whim.

Dr. Sullivan had asked tough questions and was thrilled when she told him she was already writing her thoughts and feelings down in a journal. The doctor pushed her to write more.

Dr. Sullivan had an abundant bob of thick, caramel-toned blonde hair, and looked younger than early fifties. She'd worked with numerous military patients, and she treated Zoe as one. Zoe's early injuries were as horrific as some of the others Dr. Sullivan counseled, and with her brain injury, Zoe supposed she somehow qualified.

She told Sullivan during their first meeting that she didn't want to be handled with kid gloves. The doctor took her at her word.

As soon as they settled, Sullivan's opening volley to their meeting was, "What was your first thought every time you came out from under anesthesia after surgery, Zoe?"

She spoke without thinking. "Not again."

"Why?"

She'd talked about this several times with other doctors, and her feelings hadn't changed. "Before every surgery, the doctors always promised that my leg would feel better, that my scars would look better, but they never did. I was already disfigured, and they were disfiguring me even more by trying to put me back together."

"If you could have one more surgery and it would wipe away all the scars, would you have it?"

"No."

"Why not?"

"Because no doctor would ever be able to convince me they could erase them. There have been too many broken promises.

"My surgeries were torture. There came a time when they

were worse than the pain my leg caused me." And still did "Worse than the stares and comments people made. There came a time when I had to say enough, no more, never again, and leave behind the thing that was hurting me and focus on what was left."

"How old were you then?"

"Ten."

"And your parents went along with it?"

"They didn't really have a choice. I refused to allow the doctors to touch me. I'd had enough."

Her mom had wanted to keep trying because she knew what a disfigurement like hers would mean later in her life. Her father had seen the emotional toll every surgery was taking. Finally they decided to wait and let Zoe decide if she wanted plastic surgery later.

"What's the last thing you remember thinking when that truck was coming at you?"

The grill of the truck was right there, smashing its way into the car, she threw up her arm to protect her face. She'd dreamed about those moments countless times. Then she realized she'd actually raised her arm, and lowered it.

"Not again," she said.

A beat of silence trickled by…then another.

"How similar was the experience to your first accident?"

Zoe's mouth and throat were so dry she couldn't speak. She reached for the bottle of water on the table next to her, twisted off the top and took a drink. "I—wasn't rolled under the bumper and dragged beneath this time."

"No, but your car was rolled."

And that grill coming at her….

"Following the first accident, what was the time you were the most at ease, felt the safest and most secure?"

"When I was working my first full-time position as a physical therapist at Courtland and McCabe Physical Therapy."

The pieces clicked into place. "What can we do about this?" she asked Dr. Sullivan.

"I believe once you're over the trauma of the accident, you'll continue to regain memories, but there's never any guarantee. You may have to decide to move on without them."

"That's what I'm already doing."

"How is your relationship with your husband?"

She thought about the question for a moment. "He still loves me. I'm afraid to believe completely in my feelings for him."

"Why?"

"He was a stranger to me five weeks ago."

"How long do you think it takes to fall in love?"

She thought about Hawk teasing her, protecting her, holding her, making love to her.

"As long as it takes to say the words."

HAWK RAISED HIS face to the sun's warmth. The weather had stretched from moderate temperatures to hot, spring sliding right into summer without him even noticing.

Once inside the house, Hawk started taking things out of the manila envelope his admin handed him when he left the office.

He found Harding's card, tore open the heavy envelope, and opened it. The front had magnolias painted against a background of blue and purple, and he recognized Moira's style. He opened the card and smiled. A wedding announcement. He hadn't gotten a wedding announcement in several years. The higher his rank, the more segregated his acquaintances got. There was also a note inside urging them to come. It promised to be a small gathering with food and dancing. And Moira was eager to meet Zoe.

He wandered down the hall to the kitchen and out the open door to the sunroom. Zoe looked up as he sat down beside her. "When did you get home? I didn't hear you come in."

The thud-thud-thud of A. J. and his friend, Justin, shooting hoops carried easily to where they sat.

"Just now. I stepped out of the office for an hour or so this afternoon and had to finish up some things. It put me behind."

"I went ahead and fed the two bottomless pits, aka A. J. and

Justin, but I have a plate in the microwave for you. You're lucky there was anything left."

Hawk chuckled. "I'll eat in a few minutes. I got a wedding invitation today." He placed the card in her lap.

Zoe studied it for a moment. "That's a beautiful illustration. Pretty enough to frame."

"Moira's very talented. She's the one who did the painting in our bedroom. Sam is a member of Bravo."

"Do you want to go?" She looked up.

"It's unusual to be invited. Once you get a certain rank, a certain position, the guys start backing off. Sam hasn't done that. But the administration doesn't encourage mixing either."

"But you don't want to dismiss him."

"No, I don't. I thought it would give us a chance to get out of the house, and for you to meet a very talented young woman I think you'll like, and we could dance a little."

A grin lit her face. "I hadn't remembered yet that you like to dance."

"I do with you."

"Do I like to dance?"

"You do with me."

She laughed, then fell somber. "What were we fighting about before the accident?"

Her memories were coming back, but in bits and pieces, and they rarely provided a complete picture. "We weren't fighting. We were debating about whether or not to have another child."

"You didn't want to, did you?"

"I was thinking that I'd be close to fifty by the time he/she was A. J.'s age. And sixty by the time she/he left the nest."

"You don't have to worry. I've been back on my birth control for several weeks."

"I've decided I want to make a baby with you if that's what you want."

She turned her face away to hide her blush.

Amused at her embarrassment, he grinned. "Does that idea excite you as much as it does me?" He whispered against her ear, his lips skimming her cheek.

"It's gotten quiet outside. I better go see what the boys are up to."

She went to the exterior door, and he thought he might have misread her reaction.

She glanced over her shoulder. "We'll talk about this later…in private."

He knew he was grinning like a fool as she went out the door.

CHAPTER 25

S CHOOL WAS OUT! The last two weeks had been so close to unbearable, now she felt like a bird let out of her cage. She actually slept late this morning, for the first time in months.

As long as no one canceled at the last minute, the wedding arrangements were finished, and she had two whole days to relax.

Moira read through her database of wedding arrangements and the contact information that went along with them. Flowers, check. String quartet for the wedding, check. The high school band director had whipped his top students into shape for the wedding for a donation to the music department and fifty dollars apiece for the kids. And the kids were thrilled to be playing for her. She couldn't wait to hear them. So, music, check.

She read Sam's arrangements for the rehearsal dinner to him and put a check mark beside each one. Venue, check. Buffet, check. Flower arrangements, check. Wine, check. Flowers for the reception after the wedding, check. Bouquet for Maggie and boutonnieres for himself and Tim, his best man, and Trevor, and her brothers, who would be acting as ushers. Her own bouquet was being designed by her mother.

For such a small wedding, it was turning into more work than she'd thought possible. But it was all done.

All she needed to do was make a few phone calls to double-check everything was a go. Her mother had helped as much as she could from Berkley, but the bulk of it fell on Moira. Though her parents pitched in to pay for church decorations, and the cost of the reception, she still ended up making all the arrangements. Food for sixty people, mostly family and friends, as well as Sam's teammates and their dates, hadn't come cheap, but it could have very easily stretched into thousands more if they hadn't limited the number of attendees. And Sam was taking care of all the wine, beer, mixers and booze, and paying the bartender.

"Should we have eloped?" she asked as she tossed the paperwork on the coffee table in disgust.

Sam draped an arm over her shoulders. "You're your mother's only daughter. I'm my mother's oldest son, and the apple of her eye." He grinned as he said it. "They'd have disowned us both. Mothers live for this stuff. Besides, who doesn't like a party?"

She hated to think it, but it was a very expensive party. Was she being a cheapskate?

Probably. But she'd been scrimping and saving since before college, and it was hard to break free of that behavior, even for this.

Sam's phone rang and he grinned. "I'll be right down." He tapped out of the call and rose to pull her to her feet. "My guys are here to get me. If I win at poker, we'll be able to get out of hock."

Moira laughed. "Just have a good time." She smoothed the front of his shirt.

"You too." He cuddled her close and suddenly dipped her, giving her an extravagant kiss, then setting her back up. "That's for luck."

A little woozy, she asked, "For you or me?"

"Both."

"I need it more than you do. You've never been in a room full of wine-crazed schoolteachers. We don't get out very much. We stay home and grade papers."

He laughed. "I love you, and I promise I won't pay any attention at all to the stripper."

"Tim already called me and told me he would keep a very

strict eye on you. I told him I wasn't worried at all." She smoothed the rich brown hair at his temple. "I love you. Have you got your money?"

He patted his shirt pocket then kissed her again.

"Play good and clean them out," she said as he reached the door.

He was still laughing as the door closed behind him.

She put away all the paperwork and went to check how she looked one last time. Her hair was out of control, but she'd long since given up on taming it. Her colorful, painterly top and black leggings were comfortable and reflected her style. Her phone rang and she reached for it. Maggie's voice came over the line, "I'm downstairs."

"I'm on my way."

Once Moira was in the car, Maggie turned to her before starting the engine. "What happens at the hotel stays at the hotel."

Moira laughed. "What's going on?"

"We're going to have dinner at the hotel. Then we have one of the larger conference rooms reserved for the shower. We couldn't, for obvious reasons, have this event at school since alcohol will be involved."

Moira laughed harder.

Maggie pulled out of the parking lot and turned west. "I can't promise you that all the gifts will be tame. Some of our staff members are a little more sexually liberated than most people realize. And there was a rumor going around that a few of them wanted to make sure you could take care of yourself when Sam is deployed. If you know what I mean."

Moira laughed and covered her face with her hands. "Don't tell me anything more. I'll get nervous and be waiting to uncover something embarrassing in every box or bag."

"I'm just going to ask this one question, and then neither of us are going to think about this anymore, since everyone at school has gossiped the subject to death."

Moira knew what she was going to ask before she said it.

"Have you heard anything about Mr. Jacobs?"

"He's been released from the hospital and charges have been filed. But the assault charges have been dropped for now. He got bail."

"How do you know?"

"Sam has a friend who's a lawyer and has his ear to the ground." God bless Tim. "He's not supposed to tell us anything, but he kind of gives me updates in a roundabout way."

"I wonder what he'll do now he's been fired?"

Moira shook her head. "He'll never be able to work as a teacher or principal again."

"He was a good principal until..." Maggie stopped, took a deep breath, and changed the subject. "This is a BYOB thing, and I've brought us each a bottle of wine. The hotel is furnishing soft drinks, water, and juice. Everyone is sneaking in their drink of choice. We weren't really supposed to do that, but the manager is a student's father. He said he's taking the night off, so he won't be on duty. What he doesn't know, he can't talk about."

"You're making me more nervous by the moment."

"Good. You're entirely too calm for a woman who's getting married in two days."

Moira smiled. "When you're sure of something, there's nothing to be worried about."

At the hotel, Maggie left the keys to the car with the valet, and they walked through the huge lobby and down a side hallway to the restaurant. The hostess guided them down the center aisle of the restaurant to a back room lined with tables, where Moira was stunned to see at least twenty teachers sitting at the tables, and a few more trickled in while she stood there gaping.

When Emily rose and started toward her, Moira hurried over to greet her, and the two of them hugged. "I'm so glad you're here. I've missed you, Emily."

"After everything, I needed a break. But I wanted to be here for this. You may have saved my life, Moira. There's no telling what could have happened if you hadn't walked in and drawn him out of the office until you could call the police."

"It wasn't Mr. Jacobs."

"No, it wasn't. It's taken me a long time to convince that young detective of that."

"Sherman?"

"Yeah."

Moira nodded. "He's an asshole."

Emily laughed. "Yes, he is, but now he's convinced we're both telling the truth, he's on the hunt again."

"I'm glad to hear it."

Emily smiled. "I'm so happy for you and your Sam."

"Thanks." Moira suddenly felt close to tears and hugged her again. "I guess I should walk around and thank everyone for coming."

"It's going to be fun tonight. I'm eager to see what Maggie and some of the others have in store for you."

Moira was saved from saying anything to that when Maggie asked her what she wanted to drink. "A Shirley Temple. I have a hunch I may need to stay sober."

IT DIDN'T GET much better than a cold beer, a plate full of chicken wings, a made hand, and a stack of chips. And even if the porn flick playing on the huge flat screen television at the end of the room had enough moaning going on to rate a 9-1-1 call, he was having a good time sharing some down time with his team.

"Jesus Christ!" Gilly's voice came from down the room from the third table. "That guy's a freak of nature."

"Is that jealousy or admiration we're hearing in your voice, Gilly?" Denotti asked, his back to the screen. He tossed down two cards and asked for two more.

"That guy could be an MP," Gilly said.

"What do you mean, Gill?" Swan asked.

"He's already carrying a billy club."

The guys laughed.

Denotti turned to look over his shoulder. "Whoa."

His reaction earned another round of laughter.

"Why isn't she screaming?" Swan asked. "In most horror flicks they scream and run."

"It's not supposed to be a horror flick," Arrow commented before throwing a chip into the pot.

"She has that deer-in-the-headlights look like it is one," Bullet commented. "They freeze first, then they always jump the wrong direction."

"She's jumping, all right." Swan said.

Sitting next to Sam, Morgan laughed and nearly snorted his beer.

"I don't think I've watched a porn flick since high school," Sam said.

"I didn't know they made them that far back," Tim retorted.

Sam narrowed his eyes. "Just for that, I'll raise you ten."

Tim studied his hand. "Crap. I fold."

Morgan shook his head and folded.

Trevor laid down a flush.

"Sorry Trev." Sam spread out his full house.

His "Shit!" held no heat. "Your deal, Sam," Trevor said and shoved his seat back. He drained the last sip of beer from the bottle, then said. "I'll be back."

"I'm getting some more of that bean dip and chips." Tim said and slipped away to the overloaded food table.

"God help us," Sam murmured.

Morgan grinned. "You three seem to get along okay."

"We have our moments." He hoped the truce would last until after the wedding.

"I have two brothers, too. We can't be in the same room for five minutes."

Morgan was so quiet, it was hard to get a bead on him. "Is that why you left home and joined the Navy?"

"I joined the Navy because it's what I've always wanted to do."

"Were you already enlisted when you got married?"

"Yeah. I thought Tonya was on board, but she wasn't prepared for the long separations. We argued about it before I left for deployment, but I never expected her to just walk out with everything and disappear. The way she just vanished…" His jaw worked, and he reached for his beer and drained it. "Everyone looks at me like I abused her. It never happened. Never. Everyone hears the word SEAL and they automatically assume things that aren't true."

Sam had wondered about Morgan's wife's sudden disappearance. But the wellness check Master Chief Marks mentioned had put some of that to bed. He'd like to be able to tell Morgan what Marks shared, but he'd been ordered to leave it alone. One word could put all of Morgan's anger and frustration to rest. But it might set off a whole other set of issues, too. Would he go off trying to find her? *Damn it!*

Sam picked up the cards and began shuffling them. "I get what you're saying. I recently had some of the same prejudice directed at me. Shake it off and move on, Morgan. Ultimately the only people's respect you have to maintain is your team's and your fellow SEALs'." He looked up. "We've got your six."

Trevor came back to the table, set a fresh brew in front of each one of them, collected the empties, and tossed them in the trash.

Tim slid into his seat with a bowl of dip and chips and set it between him and Morgan.

A sudden crescendo of moans from the television filled a lull in the conversation as everyone concentrated on their cards.

"Glad somebody got off," Denotti commented. "Swan, you've been studying those cards for ten minutes. Make a bet."

The entire room exploded in laughter.

MAGGIE REFILLED MOIRA'S wineglass.

They'd eaten dinner, played hilarious games, consumed more candy than she'd allowed herself to even taste in two years. And opened the shower gifts.

"How are we supposed to get home tonight?" Moira asked.

She'd only been this drunk once before.

"When I call him, Abe is going to get an Uber to drop him off here, and then he'll drive us both home in my car."

"Good." The paper plate Maggie held was completely covered with the bows from her gifts. She couldn't believe thirty-five people had shown up for the party, and some of them never even spoke to her once in the six years she'd been teaching with them. Why now? Unless Maggie said something.

There was just one more gift. For the most part they'd been thoughtful, sweet, and lovely. And there'd been several gag gifts like edible underwear and one very large eraser shaped like a penis. She'd laughed harder tonight than she had in the past six months, and enjoyed every minute of it.

She hoped Sam was having as good a time.

She turned to the last gift, about the size of a shoebox, and detached the bow and card and handed them to Maggie. She broke the tape on the wrapping paper and peeled it off. It was a plain green box with nothing printed on it. She opened the end of the box and took a peek. The pink tip of something was obscured by a plastic form and her stomach dropped. Maggie hadn't been teasing. She shot Maggie a look, and Maggie grinned.

Biting the bullet, Moira reached in and freed the dildo. The toy was large, a natural shape, and looked almost real, which was creepy. And battery-operated.

"Does it stand up to what you're used to?" the health teacher Mrs. Curtis yelled from the back.

All the ladies laughed.

She purposely turned it from side to side and grinned. "It may be a little on the short side. Sam has nothing to worry about."

Everyone howled.

She stood up and extended the toy to the first woman, Marsha Gambrel, the chemistry teacher. She looked like she'd been poked with a cattle prod.

"If I have to have my picture taken with this, you gals are going to, too. I'm not going to be blackmailed for the next ten years."

Everyone laughed again.

"What about a group photo?" Marsha suggested.

Her reluctance to touch the gift had Moira laughing. "I'll settle for that."

It took a few minutes to get everyone arranged behind the long tables, some sitting, others staggered behind, and Moira sitting on the table and holding the gift high.

Maggie took the photo, and Moira slipped off the table to turn to the group. "I know we're all stuck in our classrooms most every day, and we don't get to see each other often. But I've loved spending time with you all. I appreciate you coming tonight, and thank you so much for all the lovely gifts you've given to me and Sam. Although I'm not sure my fiancé will feel quite the same after he sees his replacement." She held up the dildo and they all laughed again. "But thank you."

Things started breaking up, and the ladies gathered their things, some pausing to hug her or Maggie. When the last had left, Emily stayed behind to help them clean up.

"I think we're going to need a moving van for all the gifts," Moira said.

"I think we'll be able to get them all in the trunk and back seat," Maggie said. "We may have to put you on the hood."

Emily said. "I can transport some of them too. Whatever you need me to do."

Moira shared a surreptitious look with Maggie. Obviously Emily wanted to talk to her. "Thank you, Emily. I appreciate it. It isn't too much out of your way?"

"No, it's not."

They organized the gifts, and Maggie went to get a luggage cart.

"You're sure you're okay?" Moira asked.

Emily nodded. "Yes, I'm fine. I knew it had to be Mr. Jacobs who stole the money, but I didn't want to say anything. I really liked him." Her eyes shimmered with tears.

Everyone on staff was grieving over his betrayal.

"I also knew it wasn't Mr. Jacobs who forced me into the

school. I was standing at the door keying in the code when this man ran up and shoved me through the door and followed me in. He was too muscular, too strong to be Mr. Jacobs."

"The police will figure it out."

"Are you really going to leave the school?" she asked.

"I don't know. I haven't made up my mind."

"Mr. Jacobs would be upset if what he said to you had anything to do with your decision. For what it's worth, he was upset when you left that day."

Moira remained silent. She was burned out. She should never have taken on all the extra projects, and should have just spent time on her art outside of school.

Emily's continued. "This get-together with the staff wasn't just because you're getting married. It was a show of support to let you know they don't want you to leave."

"I suspected as much. And I appreciate it."

"You'll think about it some more?"

She nodded. "I will."

Maggie returned with the luggage cart and they started loading the gifts.

CHAPTER 26

NSTEAD OF THE classical tunes they normally heard at weddings, this string quartet played popular romantic tunes. The four young adults' faces were so serious and focused, Zoe touched Hawk's thigh and leaned closer. "They must be some of the students from her school. They're really good."

"Yes, they are."

"What kind of music did we have at our wedding?"

"One of the guys from another team who'd been deployed with mine played guitar and sang. I asked him to take it on. And when he got out of the teams, he went into music production. He's with one of the recording studios in Los Angeles now."

She refused to push herself to remember. It was getting her nowhere and just added to her helplessness and frustration. Asking seemed to make it easier on Hawk, because it also gave him an opportunity to be proactive.

Realizing it was the accident that caused the memory loss and not something about her marriage had relieved her stress as well.

The music slid into more upbeat tune.

"You wore your hair at our wedding just like you have it to-day, but with flowers woven through the braids."

She raised a hand to touch the braid looped into a figure eight at the base of her head. Had she done it subconsciously?

A man walked past their pew, his profile catching her attention. Zoe squeezed Hawk's arm. "I met that man at the hospital the first day I went to see Tank. I had a headache when I went down to catch my UBER. He sat with me and watched for the car until it came."

"That's Seaman Morgan. He's been transferred to Sam's team. You didn't mention meeting him."

"I couldn't remember his name."

Hawk looked toward the man as he slid into the pew with the rest of his team and their dates. "I'll have to thank him."

MOIRA GRIPPED HER father's arm and closed her eyes to listen and feel it while the music resonated in the church vestibule. She was glad she and Sam had decided on unconventional music instead of classical. The students had been more eager to learn those songs.

"It's beautiful, isn't it?" she said, and opened her eyes to look up at him. Bryan McKee's dark hair had gone silver at the temples and was beginning to thin on top, but it didn't detract from his pleasant, manly face. His blue eyes, so similar to hers, held a hint of humor much of the time. Today they showed pride and just a touch of sadness.

"You are, too. You're glowing, sweetheart."

"He loves me. No matter how hard it is when he's gone, he shows me he loves me every day he's here to make up for it."

"Hush, Moira." Maggie sniffled and fanned her face. "You're going to make me cry and ruin my makeup before I ever make it down the aisle."

Moira chuckled. The last strains of one song ended and the beginning notes of *You and Me* reached them through the door. Maggie opened it.

The nerves fluttering beneath Moira's ribs smoothed out as soon as she saw Sam, Tim standing by his side. Sam smiled, and the bubble of joy inside her expanded until she teared up. He looked so masculine and handsome in his dress white uniform with all the ribbons and medals displayed on his chest.

Her father kissed her cheek and handed her off to Sam, and he helped her up the stairs to stand before the minister.

"You're so beautiful," Sam whispered, and kissed her.

"That's supposed to be at the end," the minister admonished.

They laughed, and everyone joined in.

Moira handed Maggie her bouquet. She and Sam clasped hands and turned toward the minister.

THE SCENT OF flowers and food wafted to them while they stood at the head table at the reception. It looked very much like every other formal dinner he'd attended in the past, but for the flower arrangements on each table and the tiny bottles of champagne with their names on them at each place seating. Where the hell had Moira found those?

Sam slipped up close behind her and tucked his cheek against hers. "We've said our vows, the marriage license is signed and tucked away in the minister's pocket, Gypsy is stocked and ready to go. We could just slip away now, leave them to party, and sail on down the coast."

"We can't just leave all our guests here," Moira said. "My parents would kill me. They're paying for all of this."

"I have more important things on my mind. I'm ready to get you out of that dress and consummate the marriage."

Moira laughed and reached up to caress his cheek. "Are you still worried that they might call you in before we have a chance to leave for the honeymoon?"

"No. Lieutenant Commander Yazzie would have given me a heads-up if that was going to happen."

"Is that why you invited him?" she asked.

"No. He's supportive of all the men. He's been through multiple deployments and pretty much done it all as a SEAL. Or almost all. I just feel like he's been so supportive of us both and…" He couldn't really put it into words.

"I understand. Before they start serving the food, we should say hello to them, but let's start with your father and get it behind us," Moira suggested.

He hoped it wasn't going to be a shitshow. One negative word toward Moira and he'd bodily throw Thomas Harding out of the building. "Okay."

Thomas was seated at the end of the table, as far away from Sam's mother as Sam could get him. As they approached, Thomas got to his feet. There was a sag to his jaw, and deep groves marred both sides of his mouth. He'd obviously lost weight since being hauled into court two months before.

"Moira wants to meet you, Thomas."

She extended a hand, and Thomas accepted it and shook it. "Thank you for including me in the wedding party, Moira."

"You're Sam's father, and I thought it was important for you to be here."

"This means a lot to me. This will probably be the last family function I'll be a part of for a while. I've decided to do as you suggested, Sam. Make as much restitution as I can and accept the prosecutor's deal."

Sam was too surprised to speak for a moment. "Do Tim and Trevor know?"

"No, not yet. I'll call them tomorrow. My lawyer and I will be going to the DA's office together in the morning."

Sam nodded. "Good." He'd hoped for this, but he didn't fully believe it. Thomas had something up his sleeve.

"I wish you the best, Sam, and you too, Moira."

"Thank you," Moira replied for both of them.

As they walked away, Sam said, "There's something more going on. He's way too humble. If he's accepting the deal and going to jail, there's something else we don't know about going on in the background."

"He could be worried about all the publicity."

"Publicity or not, he's finished. He's a lawyer, and he'll be convicted of stealing from his clients."

They moved on to Lieutenant. Commander Yazzie and his

wife. The Commander's wife was as small and slender as the commander was large and muscular. The scars on her legs were covered by hose, but the stockings weren't heavy enough to cover the fact that she was missing part of her calf muscle. He'd noticed earlier that her walk was more of a sway than a limp, as though she was compensating with every step.

When the caterers announced the food would be served when everyone was seated, they were talking about the painting Moira did for the Yazzies, and the possibility of Moira meeting with Zoe to go swimming one morning. They exchanged numbers before they walked away.

HAWK ESCORTED ZOE back to the table and looked across the reception hall to where Seaman Morgan sat with his team. "I'll be right back. I want to speak to Morgan before he leaves. Since he's here without a date, he may take off as soon as the meal is over."

"Go ahead, I'm fine here."

The men and their dates took up two tables. As soon as he appeared at the table where Morgan was sitting, the whole table of SEALs got to their feet. Decked out in their dress whites, they made an impressive bunch.

"At ease, men. I'm only here to speak with Seaman Morgan for a moment."

The young SEAL stepped away from the table with him.

"My wife told me earlier that you ran into her at the hospital one afternoon and how you waited with her until her UBER arrived to take her home. I want to thank you for seeing she got to the car safely."

"No problem, sir. I hope she's doing better now."

"Yes, she is. I appreciate what you did." Hawk extended his hand.

"You're welcome, sir." Morgan said as he shook it. "Could you tell me who that older man is at the end of the main table?"

"That's the groom's father, Thomas Harding."

Morgan sighed. "Shit."

"Is there a problem, Morgan?"

Morgan moistened his lips. "Maybe, sir. Probably. Yes, there's a problem." He glanced in Sam's direction. "Nothing that can't wait until after the wedding, sir."

Hawk wanted to pursue the meaning behind the comment, but the doors to the kitchen area opened, and the staff began to serve the meal.

He started to turn away when his attention was snagged by Book in his wheelchair sitting next to Swan one table over. Hawk moved around the table to Book. "Seaman Ashe."

Book looked up. His sun-streaked brown hair had dulled to light brown, and he had the hollow-eyed look of someone who had been ill, though Hawk knew it wasn't illness riding him into the ground, but the injury to his spine that kept him tied to his wheelchair and the subsequent depression he struggled with constantly.

Hawk knelt next to the wheelchair. "I'm glad you're here to help Sam and Moira celebrate."

"Sam and Swan came by to pick me up, so I didn't really have a choice." Although Book's complaint lacked any true heat.

"If that's what it takes, Book. There are some wheelchair basketball games that go on at my son's school on the weekends. I heard you played basketball in high school."

"Yeah, I did."

"I'll check into the schedule for their games and come pick you up. My son A. J. would enjoy watching them play. You might want to look into joining one of the teams."

"I don't know."

At the sound of a chair scraping against the floor, Hawk's head jerked toward the other table. Morgan had leapt to his feet, shoving his chair back away from the table. He moved like a bullet to intercept one of the servers. He grabbed her arm so hard one of the plates of food she carried to hit the floor and shattered, splattering food across the tile.

"Let go of me," a woman's voice cut across the distance. She shoved the other three plates onto a serving tray.

"Jesus Christ, Tonya. Why the fuck did you run off and just disappear? Do you know what you did to me? My teammates thought I was an abuser. They thought I'd killed you."

Hawk was on his feet in a second and rushed to reach the two.

"Do you know how much shit I had to take because you were too much of a coward to stand your ground and tell me you wanted a divorce? Damn you. Damn you to hell." Morgan clinched his fists, and for a moment Hawk thought he might hit her.

Sam broke into a run from the front table and reached them at the same time Hawk grabbed Morgan's arm. "Morgan, you need to take this somewhere else."

Tonya took a step toward Morgan. "I'm not going anywhere with him. I'm not coming back either, Owen. I sat at home for eight long months waiting for you. I was ready to climb the walls by the time I moved out. Even working two jobs didn't help.

"We were so happy when you first enlisted. Even with the trainings and everything. But when you became a SEAL... I can't sit at home for three quarters of the year and be satisfied with a quarter of your time. There's more to life than that. I need someone who'll be an equal partner, not just a visitor passing through.

"Every time I told you how unhappy I was, you'd say 'we'll work it out when I get home.' But you never *came home*." Her voice rose and her composure cracked. "And then when Bryan was killed..." A sob escaped. "I can't sit at home and wait for that knock on the door. I'm just not brave enough. I'm just not." With a sob, Tonya broke and ran back toward the kitchen.

Several moments passed before Hawk said, "Sam, you have a wedding reception to take care of. Seaman Morgan and I can take a seat with my wife and talk some things out."

"Morgan?" Sam waited for the man to acknowledge his agreement.

Morgan's throat worked as he swallowed. "I'm sorry for all

this, sir."

"Not a problem." Sam waited again.

"I'm okay, sir."

Sam's eyes met Hawk's before he turned away to return to the head table.

"Come with me, Morgan." Hawk ordered.

"Sir," Morgan seemed to have to push every word out. "There's another problem."

"Does this problem have anything to do with Thomas Harding?"

"Yes, sir. It has everything to do with him."

"Can this problem wait until Sam and Moira have left for their honeymoon?"

"As long as the police are here to make certain Thomas Harding doesn't skip town as soon as they're gone."

"We'll deal with it, Morgan. Let's go have something to eat. Plus, I promised my wife at least one dance, and I mean to keep that promise."

When Morgan smiled, Hawk was glad to see him rallying.

"I understand, sir."

CHAPTER 27

ZOE WATCHED THE two men cross the hall to the table. The rest of their tablemates were members of Moira's family, an aunt and uncle and their two sons. She introduced them to Hawk, and Hawk in turn introduced Seaman Morgan.

"It's nice to see you again, Seaman Morgan." He seemed younger than when she saw him at the hospital and carried with him a slightly wounded and vulnerable air.

"You can call me Owen, ma'am."

"Owen."

The conversation that circled the table was cordial and mostly consisted of questions about the Navy, since none of Moira's family had ever enlisted, and they discovered a wealth of information in Hawk and Seaman Morgan.

The tension Zoe sensed riding both Hawk and Seaman Morgan distracted her from her meal. She noticed the number of times the young SEAL glanced at the head table, as though keeping watch, or waiting for something to happen.

When Moira left the table and headed to the restroom, Zoe excused herself and did the same.

She quickly took care of business, but took her time washing her hands and waited for Moira to come out of the stall.

"I never realized how much effort it would take to pee and try and keep the train of my dress out of the toilet," Moira complained as she joined her.

Zoe chuckled. Too curious to resist, she tried to formulate a question about what occurred just before the meal, and was relieved when Moira saved her the effort.

"We appreciate Lieutenant Commander Yazzie taking care of Seaman Morgan."

"He's one of his men. Hawk tries to look out for them all."

They walked out of the bathroom together.

"One of the servers is a coworker from school. We don't know each other well enough to be friends."

From Moira's tone, Zoe doubted they ever would be.

"She recently got a job as a server with the catering company we hired to provide the food tonight. It turns out she's Seaman Morgan's wife, and before he returned from deployment, she moved out of their apartment with most of their furniture, without notifying him, and just disappeared. She didn't even call to let him know she was all right." Moira's outrage showed in her voice and body language.

"So, it seems he's been catching flak from some of his former teammates. They've been suspicious that he might have abused her or worse. He asked for a transfer, and ended up on Sam's team. And Sam invited him to the wedding."

"Which created the perfect storm."

"Something like that. I'm not upset that there was a scene. I'm upset because she was such a coward and left him hanging in limbo, and put him in a position that compromised his bond with his teammates and…"

"Left him without support when he needed it most."

"Exactly."

Zoe placed a hand on Moira's shoulder. "You're going the be the perfect SEAL wife. And don't worry about Seaman Morgan. Hawk will see he gets whatever he needs."

Moira's shoulders relaxed, shedding the tension Zoe had sensed since they started talking. "I may be calling you for advice."

Zoe didn't know how much help she'd be at the moment, but said, "Anytime."

"Thank you, and now I need to get back and cut the cake." Moira rushed off.

Zoe froze as the word cake triggered a kaleidoscope of unexpected memories and emotions. She made her way back to the table slowly, trying to adjust.

Rested a hand on Hawk's sleeve as she sat down, she said. "We had a small four-tiered cake with buttercream icing. The bottom tier was vanilla, the one above chocolate, and the other red velvet. We saved the small top tier in the freezer. You were deployed during our anniversary, and we forgot the cake until the next year. It had fallen apart, so we threw it out and went for ice cream instead."

"You remembered the wedding?" He looked so hopeful, she hated to disappoint him.

"Only parts. I remember you shooting my garter off your finger and hitting one of the guys in the eye."

Hawk laughed. "It was Bowie I hit in the eye. Served him right for trying to steal you away from me early on."

"He was sweet and funny, but I was never interested in him."

"Good."

She laughed at his aggressive tone.

Moira's aunt and uncle and their sons moved to the head table where they could talk with Moira's mother and father and watch the dancers.

She could tell she'd interrupted Hawk and Morgan's conversation. "I'm not leaving, so you might as well talk. If it's not about government secrets, my clearance is high enough. I keep enough medical secrets that it should count."

The two looked at each other. "Everyone will know by tomorrow," Morgan said with a shrug. "I'd been drinking nearly every day, but I still needed to see a lawyer about divorce and who I could hire to track Tonya down. So I called and made an appointment. It was dusk by the time I got out of the meeting. The first thing I noticed was my car was gone. I hunted for it for about thirty minutes, but it was gone. Later I found out it had been towed because I parked in the wrong damn spot. And like a fucking fool I'd left my cell phone in the cup holder. Sorry, Mrs. Yazzie."

"No problem." She heard worse in the physical therapy wing. How did she know that?

"I went back to the office, but it was locked up tight. When I walked back out, I saw two guys standing at the back of one of the lots and was about to go up to them and ask for either a ride or to see if one of them would call me a cab. One was driving a blue Mercedes and the other a silver truck.

"One of the guys was huge. Six-four easy, two-fifty. He could have stomped the other guy into the ground. He's reaming the smaller guy out and sounds like he wants to get physical. He starts to walk off, and the smaller guy takes out a metal pipe from behind the car. He must have had it leaning against the side of the tire or something.

"He whaled on the back of the big guy's head like he was trying to knock it off his shoulders. The guy went down, but he kept hitting him, his whole body into it.

"When he straightened up, I ducked behind one of the cars in the lot, but he must have seen movement because he went back to the car and pulled out a gun.

While he was working his way around the cars toward me. I was working my way back to the vehicles he left unprotected and found the keys to the truck lying on the street next to the dead guy." He shook his head. "I picked up the keys and got into the truck. Thank God he couldn't shoot for shit, because he never hit glass, but he hit the tailgate a couple of times as I pulled out.

"I booked it to McP's to see if any of the guys were there and left the truck parked on the street with the keys in the cupholder in case someone put out an alert. I called Franco from there, hoping he'd come pick me up, but he said it would be a couple of hours. They were all tired of my behavior and had pretty much dumped me by then. Though LT did try to get them to babysit."

"Why didn't you call the police?" Zoe asked.

"At the time my teammates thought I'd probably done something to my wife. She disappeared. I'm a Navy SEAL, I've been drinking, and I'm driving a dead man's truck. What do you think the police would think?"

Zoe's heart ached for him and his lack of choices.

"Franco comes to pick me up, and I've had more than a few, and we get into it for fuck knows what. Probably because I'm drunk again. Someone calls the cops, and I'm worried about getting arrested, and that's exactly what happens. When the cops drag me out to their car, the truck is gone. Someone's stolen it."

"The only proof I have of all this is the two bullet holes in the tailgate of the truck. And the people at McP's who served me. Because I didn't have any blood or anything on me when I got there, but the guy who used that pipe was covered with gore, and some of it has to be in the Mercedes he drove away in."

HIS WIFE. HIS wife. Just those two words gave him a sense of belonging he was careful not to tip over into ownership. Moira would nip that shit in the bud.

Moira belonged to him as he did to her. It made him feel possessive and a little scared. What if he fucked up like Morgan? Morgan's wife had fucked up, too, but it sounded like Morgan had dropped the ball big time.

Sam led Moira out onto the floor for their first dance as husband and wife and drew her in close.

"I haven't told you how handsome you look in your uniform." She ran her fingertips over the ribbons and medals on the left side of his jacket. "You'll have to teach me what each of these means."

"We'll have plenty of time for that." They danced in silence for a moment.

"They say you learn from your mistakes, but I've learned from others'." He rested his chin against her hair. "I will find a way to call you as often as humanly possible whenever I'm deployed."

"I know you will. You always have."

He wanted to maintain the focus on them, but Morgan's situation kept popping back up in his thoughts. "When did your friend

Tonya start working at the school?"

"About six weeks ago, and she's an acquaintance, not a friend."

"Okay." And three weeks after she started work at the school, someone broke in and tried to access employee files. Someone strong, fit, six foot, dressed all in black. Someone who could have been looking for a home address of a wife who'd gone AWOL.

"I promise if ever I get pissed off enough to want to leave, I'll wait until you're home, and feed you something that will give you Montezuma's revenge so bad you'll be unable to leave for like a week while I bitched at you, and *then* I'll set fire to all your possessions out on the lawn and serve you papers."

He laughed. "Thanks for the warning. I'll do all I can to avoid that. I promise."

When the music ended. Sam handed Moira off to her father and went to ask his mother to dance. Then he danced with his new mother-in-law and former college professor. He laughed at her wit, something she'd never exhibited in class when he was in college. Next was Moira's maid of honor, Maggie. She was high on excitement and a little too much wine and nearly talked his leg off, so he was glad to pass her on to her boyfriend, Abe.

He noted his father was no longer seated at the table and had slipped away without dancing with his new daughter-in-law. Sam was relieved. As polite as he'd been, the man could turn on a dime, and Moira had already experienced enough crap behavior from his family.

Moira was dancing with Trevor when he made his way over to the Yazzies while keeping an eagle eye on his brother. Though he'd been on his best behavior the last few times they'd seen each other. He hoped it was a serious start to a change.

He dragged a chair over and joined the Yazzies and Morgan. "So, what's the plan?" he asked.

"Plan?" Hawk asked.

Sam turned to Morgan. "Six weeks ago Tonya, your wife went to work at Moira's school. Three weeks ago, there was a break-in, and one of the secretaries was forced into the building and somehow knocked out so the man could access their computer system. When he left the office, he saw Moira and chased her down the hall, and she hid in a small faculty bathroom while he pounded on the door trying to get in."

To Morgan's credit, he maintained eye contact and never flinched. "Tonight was the first time I've seen Tonya in eleven months. Tonight was also the first time I've spoken to her, and I still have no idea where she's been working or where she lives. Otherwise I'd have shown up at her home or place of employment to demand we meet about the divorce instead of hiring a PI to find her."

Sam looked away. The man seemed sincere.

"I know I was a major fuckup for the first month we were back from deployment. My head was messed up and I was angry...about everything. And I had a whole month off base to gnaw on everything and make it worse. But I'm not the answer to this. It wasn't me."

"Then what the hell's going on here?"

Morgan raked his fingers through his hair. "Nothing. I thought changing teams would be the answer, but it's not." He glanced at Yazzie. "Especially now. I'll apply for a transfer to the east coast. I don't have anything to keep me here now." He rose. "I'll call the number you gave me first thing in the morning, Lieutenant Commander. I'm going home."

"Call tonight and tell Detective Crider of the SDPD everything. They'll need to take steps."

"Roger that, sir." He walked away.

Moira wandered over to sit beside Sam.

A familiar sharp pop-pop-pop sound came from the front of the building. Sam lunged to his feet at the same time Hawk did. The tile was slick as they both raced toward the entrance of the building.

Sam reached the door first and peered through the thick glass, searching for any danger.

"I'm calling 9-1-1," Hawk said from beside him.

A trail of blood smeared the sidewalk and disappeared over

the side of the steps. It had to be Morgan's. Sam cursed, shoved open the door, and, keeping as low as possible, looked over the side of the steps. Hawk was right behind him.

Morgan lay on his side behind the shrubbery planted at interval across the front of the building.

Sam jumped down over the side of the steps and placed a hand on his chest. "Where are you hit, Morgan?"

"I don't know. My shoulder." He seemed rattled.

Morgan's uniform jumper prevented Sam from being able to see the injury. He untied his tie and raised the V-shaped edge of the jumper to see beneath. The hole where the bullet entered his shoulder was bleeding sluggishly. He folded the tie and tucked it under the fabric and pressed down on the injury.

Morgan caught his breath but didn't cry out.

Hawk stood above them with the cell phone to his ear talking to the 9-1-1 operator.

The rest of the team spilled out of the building onto the sidewalk.

"I need something to put pressure on his wounds, and we need an ambulance."

"Ambulance is on its way," Hawk answered. He barked orders over his shoulder and Denotti rushed back inside to get something to help stem the bleeding.

Morgan's eyes opened and his voice was a pain-filled groan laced with rage. "I was wrong, he can shoot. The fucker."

"Who?" Sam asked. "Who shot you?"

"Your father."

CHAPTER 28

ZOE POURED COFFEE into the mug sitting in front of Detective Crider, then took a seat across from her. "Are you sure I can't get you anything to eat?"

"This is all I need," Detective Crider said, adding milk and raising her mug for a sip. "I'm sorry I'm disturbing your weekend, but I thought the two of you would like to know that we've made an arrest. The young man who hit you lives in a neighborhood not too far from here. His name is Cody Ward. I'm not at liberty to give you any information about his background, but he's twenty-two and an adult."

"He was at the bar and saw the stolen truck parked on the street outside with the keys inside and decided to take it. The day he hit you... The gas pedal stuck, and he panicked. He'd been driving around the neighborhood trying to figure out a way to stop the vehicle, but was too high to figure out that all he had to do was to put the truck into neutral or just turn off the ignition. He saw your SUV, big, sturdy, and kept hitting you, trying to keep his speed down." She shook her head and leaned forward to add more milk to her coffee before taking another sip.

"He's been charged with DUI, possession, assault with a deadly weapon, reckless driving, theft of a motor vehicle, and a few other things. He will go to trial and, even though what happened to you caused by a mechanical failure, he will serve time.

He's responsible for a lot of property damage and physical injury. Had he not been impaired, he could have stopped the truck fairly easily."

Zoe reached out to fold her fingers over Hawk's clenched fist. "We got lucky. It could have been even worse than it was. I'll never call your vehicle a tank again."

His expression relaxed somewhat from the taut control he imposed on them when he was angry and said, "At least he'll be in jail where he won't be stealing anymore cars or hurting anyone else." He left it at that, though he looked like there was a lot more he wanted to say.

"He was the man who drove by and asked your neighbor's boy about you, Mrs. Yazzie. And he confessed to everything as soon as we picked him up. So perhaps he does have a conscience."

"Maybe there's hope he'll be able to turn his life around, then," Zoe said.

"I know you're aware that this case overlaps with another." Crider took another sip of coffee and set the mug down. "We spoke at length with Seaman Morgan at the hospital about the truck this morning. Since he's one of your men, I know you're concerned about the ramifications of what he did, Lieutenant Commander. We know he was fleeing for his life and took the truck to escape. The two bullet holes in the tailgate corroborate his statement.

"The fact that he didn't report the murder is a sticky point, but since he'll be the state's key witness in the murder trial, and was the victim of an attempted murder by the same perpetrator, the DA won't be pursuing charges of any kind against him."

"Good," Zoe and Hawk said together. Hawk squeezed her hand.

"Is he going to be all right?" Zoe asked.

"He was hit once in the shoulder and once in the hip, but he'll make a full recovery."

"There were three shots," Hawk said.

"The other bullet ricocheted, and we believe it may have hit the shooter since there was blood at the scene. We haven't been able to locate Thomas Harding yet, but we have a citywide BOLO out on him. If he's injured, he'll have to seek medical attention sooner or later."

The detective rose to leave. "You seem to be doing much better, Mrs. Yazzie."

"I am. I'm slowly recovering bits and pieces of my memory, and I'm stronger now."

"Good. Hopefully that will continue."

The detective collected her things, paused, and set them down again. "By the way, the suggestion you gave us when we came by with the still shots was right on the money. We searched for traffic tickets on the street where the murder took place and discovered where Seaman Morgan's car had been towed. We pulled his booking photo from the disturbing the peace charges and matched it with the photo of him driving the truck.

"We were going to follow it up, and pick him up, but then the traffic cam photos we were looking at from the accident were of a different man. Both had longer hair and a beard, and the two looked so similar, we weren't sure which was which. You said it could be someone just home from deployment or possibly someone who was just too lazy to cut their hair or shave. You were right on both counts."

"The perfect storm," Zoe said. "We've been having quite a few of those lately."

"The stars sure had some kind of wicked alignment going on. We rarely have cases dovetail like this. Let's hope this doesn't happen again."

When Detective Crider left, Zoe turned to Hawk and squeezed his hand. "Poor Sam. Is there anything we can do for him and Moira?"

"I don't know, but I'll reach out and see if there's anything he or his family needs."

"They'll postpone their honeymoon. Which will be a real shame."

Hawk slipped an arm around her waist, and they walked back

to the kitchen and out into the sunroom. "Hopefully not. If I were him, I'd leave today and not look back. Whatever happens will happen whether he and Moira are here or not."

They settled in the glider. Zoe rested a hand on his thigh. "I know you haven't been as satisfied with the job you have now and that you'd rather be in the thick of the action like you were before."

He was silent a moment. "I haven't said I was dissatisfied."

"You don't have to. I saw the light in your eyes when you raced off to face the threat last night. Your current position doesn't offer you anything close. I know you love it. The action. The brotherhood. Even the danger.

"I know you took the promotion and the job so you could be home more. I know you made that sacrifice for A. J. and me. But if you're not happy doing what you're doing, you can walk it back, can't you?"

He frowned and studied her face. "I don't know. What's all this about, Zoe?"

"It's the carrot doubled." She started to tear up but pushed back her emotions.

He laughed. "I'm not sure you can do a double carrot unless you have a double problem you have to work through to get to the carrot."

"Well, I'm doing it." She jerked her chin up. "Because we've already worked through one of the problems."

"What's the other part?"

"I need to say something before I tell you that."

"Okay." His pale eyes held a hint of humor.

She knew he'd been waiting for her to say the words. Hoping for them. The memory of his proposal had been her talisman against uncertainty. The splotchy memories of their wedding, the cake, his team and how they were together, had only been the icing.

"I love you. Not because of any memory, but because of the way you look at me, touch me, care for me. Because I just do."

He probed her expression. "Thank God." He held her tightly

against him and when he kissed her it with such tenderness the tears she'd stifled came rushing forward.

He brushed them away. "What's the other carrot?" he asked his voice gruff with emotion.

"I want the baby you said you'd make with me. We have A. J. He's my boy, and I love him. And I want another one."

A smile quirked his lips. "I can help you make that happen. In fact, we could start right now. A. J.'s over at Justin's playing video games."

She felt the heat rush to her face. She hoped she'd never get past that first blush of desperate need every time he provoked it. "We could do that."

Hawk chuckled, offered his hand, and tugged her to her feet, then swung her up into his arms and carried her to their room. "I believe this might be a triple carrot," he said as he shut the door with the side of his foot.

"Enough with the carrots," Zoe said and kissed him.

"DON'T YOU THINK we might need to wait, just in case your mother or brothers need us?" Moira asked.

Sam sucked in a deep breath. They were already getting a late start because they ate breakfast with her family and saw them on their way. Sometimes her need to take care of everyone at her own expense was frustrating.

He lined up their bags next to the door. "I talked to Mom earlier this morning. Tim's staying with her, just in case Thomas might be stupid enough to go by her house. Trevor's still working at the office calling clients. He's groveling to try and salvage some kind of business once everything is settled. Dad won't be going by there.

"And he knows there's nothing for him here. If the cops or anyone else need to get in touch with us we have the sat phone on board."

Moira smiled. "Okay." As soon as she picked up her purse,

her phone rang, and she frowned while digging down in a side pocket to take it out. Her expression changed instantly. "It's the asshole."

Sam laughed. So Detective Sherman was still on her shit list.

She opened the phone and put it on speaker. "Yes, Detective Sherman."

"Good morning, Ms. McKee."

"It's Mrs. Harding as of yesterday, Detective."

"Congratulations."

"Thank you."

Sam chuckled at her icy politeness.

Detective Sherman cleared his throat. "I'm calling to notify you that we've made an arrest in the school break-in."

Moira leaned back against the back of the couch. "Good."

"You may recognize his name. You have him in one of your classes. His name is Tyler Hanson."

Her expression shifted to disappointment. "Oh." Sam moved to stand next to her. "He's a good student. He's a star on the track team, and he's quarterback on the football team."

"So, I've heard. He's also an expert hacker. Jacobs paid Tyler five thousand dollars to find the passwords, withdraw the money, and transfer it to a number of accounts, where Jacobs withdrew it as cash."

Moira leaned her head against Sam's shoulder, and he cradled her there.

"Why would Tyler come back to the school to hack the computers again?"

"He felt things closing in and was trying to leave a bogus trail with another hack. His girlfriend was going to alibi him after he transferred more money from the account, but he didn't count on you and Emily going into the office. He wasn't able to finish."

Sam ran his fingers through his hair. He owed Morgan a major apology. But what were the odds that his ex-wife would go to work at Moira's school? There were too many interlocking pieces, and they were all coincidences. What were the odds?

Moira shifted and straightened. "Thank you for calling to tell me who was responsible, Detective."

"You're welcome. Congratulations again."

"Thank you."

Moira closed out the call. "Why? Why would Tyler do it?"

Sam thought about it for a moment. "He had the skills. A person in authority was buttering him up, encouraging him, paying him. This was a challenge, and imagine the high he must have experienced after being successful."

"And now he's changed his future forever. This is like bank robbery."

"And assault because of his attack on Emily."

"Shit. He's only seventeen."

Moira rarely swore, and only when she was really upset. In an effort to soothe her disappointment Sam said, "Maybe they'll take that into account and charge him as a minor."

"I hope so." She sighed.

Sam brushed her temple with a kiss. "Come on. Let's get out on the water so you can leave all these crazy coincidences on land."

"Is that why you like being out there so much?"

"Yeah, it's the one place I go where I can leave everything behind."

"Everything but me."

He smiled. "Never you." Which sounded corny as hell, but it was true.

She reached for her purse and bag. "Let's go before someone else calls."

He could call the hospital about Morgan from the marina.

Since it was a weekend, the marina was busy, with several boats waiting to put out to sea. The breeze carried a hint of salt, sea, and fish. Sam gripped Moira's hand to help balance her as she stepped up on the wooden rail and then stepped aboard. He handed her the bags one at a time and followed.

"You haven't told me where we're going," she reminded him.

"North. We'll go to Newport Beach, then Marina del Rey, and on to San Francisco. It's a more challenging sail, but you'll love it.

And San Francisco is fantastic."

He unlocked the hatch going down in the cabin and pulled it open. "Go ahead and go down. I'll bring the bags in a second. I want to make a quick call, and the reception sucks inside."

"Okay. I'll take one of the bags." She picked up hers and went on downstairs.

He scrolled through his contacts until he found Morgan's number and tapped it.

"Hey, LT." Morgan sounded okay. A little like he'd been asleep. "I thought you'd be long gone on your honeymoon."

"We're on the yacht. How are you?"

"High."

Sam laughed. "Good stuff?"

"It's keeping me happy. No pain."

"Good. And to make your day even better, I got some news today you'll want to hear. They've arrested the guy who broke into the school. He was a high school student. One of Moira's students, in fact. He hacked the computer system to transfer money from the school account to several other accounts for the principal."

He prepared to eat crow. "I'm sorry I shot my mouth off last night. I was wrong. Two teams of us have been wrong. I think we all owe you and apology. When I get back, I'll deal with this."

"Forget it, LT. It isn't worth the hassle. And I won't be around for much longer anyway."

Morgan's comment piled on the guilt. Because Sam knew the man was serious made it that much worse. "I think you should reconsider. It's going to take some time for you to heal. Wait until you're back in fighting shape before you make a firm decision."

There was a long pause, and Sam waited without breaking it. "I'll think about it."

"Good. I'm going to get underway. I'd like to get out of the Marina before noon."

"Safe travels, LT."

"Thanks."

He closed out the call, stuffed the phone in his back pocket, and picked up his bag. He went down the steps and froze. Moira was sitting on one of the bench seats at the galley table, her back to him…

…and across from her sat his father. His skin was pasty, his hair in disarray and glued to his head with sweat. And his Glock 19 was aimed at Moira.

Sam had had many guns pointed at him. His mind always shut off the fear until the danger passed. But seeing a gun pointed at Moira was a different experience. Adrenaline shot his heartrate up, and it took all his control not to charge the bastard just to draw the gun away from her.

"You okay, Moira?" he asked.

"Yes," she breathed softly.

He set his bag down and started toward the table.

"Don't, Sam. I will shoot her."

Sam believed him. The man had already killed once, and very recently. "What do you want, Thomas?"

"I want you to go topside and get underway. You're going to sail out of the marina just like you planned. Then you're going to take me to Mexico and drop me off. You can go on your way after that."

"You need medical attention, Mr. Harding," Moira said. "That bullet hole in your stomach may already be septic."

"I'll get it taken care of when I'm across the border."

The thought of her staying in the cabin with Thomas was unbearable. One wrong word, and Thomas wouldn't hesitate to slap her around. "I'll have to have Moira's help raising sail once we get out into the bay."

"Once we're out on the water, I'll let her come up to help."

He turned to go back upstairs. "Leave your cell phone, Sam."

Shit! He'd hoped the man would forget it. He took it out and set it on the galley counter.

With one foot on the stairs to the deck, Sam turned to face Thomas again. "I never believed you capable of murder. I've always known you're a bastard. Hard. Demanding Uncompromising. Selfish. Egotistical. But I never dreamed you'd kill someone.

And *why*? You've lost everything because of it."

"I haven't lost it all. There's three hundred thousand dollars on board in a backpack. That will be enough to give me a start somewhere else."

Thomas swiped the sweat off his forehead and dried his hand on his pants. "It's a real shame you weren't the one who came to work with me. Trevor's weak and easily manipulated. He's good at following orders, but little else. Tim was too smart for his own good, and it was fortunate he left the firm. Otherwise, I'd have eventually had to get rid of him."

Moira jerked in response to that. Thomas smiled, obviously amused. "I meant fire him, not kill him. He is after all *my* son."

He transferred his attention back to Sam. "If you had come to work for me, we'd have been unstoppable. You have the brains, the drive, and you're as hard as I am. But you have one weakness."

Sam raised one brow. "What's that?"

"Morals. A conscience, if you want to call it that."

Sam had no idea how to reply. He shook his head. He couldn't understand why his mother had ever married this empty, soulless human being.

Whatever Thomas saw in Sam's expression shifted his mood. "Get on deck and get us underway."

He had no choice, but he'd get Thomas up on deck some way, somehow, and take him out if he had to. Moira turned to look over her shoulder, and he met her gaze. If he said anything to her, his father might hurt her just to get even with him for all their past disagreements.

He turned and went up the stairs to get underway.

MOIRA LET THE silence stretch. Though Thomas had stopped pointing the gun at her, he still had it in his hand.

"Get me a drink of water."

His voice was weaker now Sam was gone.

Grateful for an opportunity to move away from him, Moira

slid out of the booth.

"Try anything and I'll shoot you in the back."

She didn't reply, just went to the small fridge on the left of the galley and pulled out a tray of ice cubes and a bottle of water. Sam's phone lay on the counter just begging to be picked up, but since Thomas was bound to notice its absence, she left it where it was.

The boat's engine started, and she grabbed the edge of the counter to steady herself as they got underway. Sam must be backing out of the slip.

She placed an ice-filled glass and a bottle of water in front of Thomas, he gestured for her to return to the booth.

"Open the bottle."

She twisted it open and set it in front of him again.

"Thank you," he said as he poured the liquid into the glass and drank thirstily. Sweat ran down his cheek, and though he looked pale, two spots of color stained his cheeks.

"You're not at all the kind I expected Sam to marry."

"What kind am I?"

"A doormat."

She smiled. She used to be, and she still struggled with confrontations, but she'd learned to stand her ground. "Think what you like."

His eyes narrowed. He moved gingerly to pull his shirt up. The bandage covering his abdomen was brownish with dried blood. "I need fresh bandages. They're in the cabin."

"You need a hospital. If the bullet has nicked your intestines, it could lead to peritonitis, and you could die of the infection."

His face turned to stone. "Get the fucking bandages."

She went to the back of the boat to the cabin and found the bed she made with fresh sheets stained and the room trashed Bandages and other items lay on the wall-mounted nightstand. A large backpack lay beneath the nightstand, and she unzipped it and peeked in to see bundles of money stacked inside. She gathered all the medical supplies and a small pair of scissors and returned to the main cabin.

She dumped the bandages on the table and went into the galley to get a container and fill it with warm water. When she returned to the table with it, Thomas had already cut away the bandages, torn open a gauze pad, and coated it with antibacterial ointment. He squeezed the water out of the cloth, and lifting his shirt, wiped away the dried blood and what already looked like infection seeping from a wound just above his waistband.

She waited for him to finish, then offered him a paper towel to dry the area. He pressed the gauze pad to the wound and held it while she wound the gauze tightly around his body and taped it in place.

She cleaned up the mess, emptied the water, pocketed the small scissors, and pulled her T-shirt down over her jeans.

"You're a very cooperative hostage."

"You have the gun, and you've already killed one person and tried to kill another."

"So the SEAL survived." It was a statement, not a question.

"To testify against you on both counts."

"They can't try me if they can't find me."

"If you die from that wound, they won't have to go to the trouble."

His face went stony again. "You don't want to test me."

The look in his eyes made her insides shudder.

"Moira, I need you up here," Sam said from the hatch.

She forced herself to climb slowly up the steps, dragging in a deep breath of the clean sea air while she looked out into the bay. Sam squeezed her arm, his gold-flecked brown eyes intense. "Go raise the sails and set them. If he starts shooting, hit the deck."

Moira moved to the port side of the boat. Thomas appeared from below, moving slowly while holding the left side of his belly with one hand and the gun with the other.

THOMAS TURNED HIS attention to Moira while she cranked the sails up.

"You've trained her well," he said.

Sam rushed him from behind, forcing him forward toward the port side of the boat and, with all his weight, shoved his father down on the wood rail. Thomas yelled in pain as Sam forced his head down, trying to throw him overboard. Thomas dropped the pistol and grabbed the rail. The Glock skittered across the deck.

Thomas twisted and thrust his elbow back, hitting Sam in the jaw. Sam punched him in the side, aiming as close to the injury as he could get. Thomas bent at the waist, gagged, and fell to his knees, somehow still managing to lunge for the Glock.

Moira stepped on it and shoved it back with her foot.

Sam pounced, driving Thomas down on his belly, and twisted his arms behind his back. He ignored his father's groans and tightened his hold. He resisted the urge to pound his father's face into the deck because he could still see the fear and sickness on Moira's face that were there when she joined him from the cabin.

"Go below and get me something to tie his arms." She scooped up the Glock and rushed below, returning with a rope and a knife in moments.

While he tied his father's arms and secured him to one of the cleats aft, she used the sat phone to call the Coast Guard. Her voice shook just a little here and there, but she held it together.

When she closed out the call, Sam opened his arms to her, and she met him halfway while they clung to each other.

"There really is three hundred thousand dollars in a backpack in the cabin below," she said.

Unsurprised Sam said, "Money stolen from his clients."

"He really is a psychopath."

"Yeah, he is. And hopefully he'll spend the rest of his life in jail."

He tilted her face up. "I'm sorry you were trapped below with him. I couldn't think of any way to get him up here but to go along with what he wanted."

"I know. It's okay. We're okay."

DETECTIVE HART AND Buckler exited the cabin behind the forensic team one last time and strode to where Sam and Moira sat on the padded bench aft against the bulkhead. Moira nestled in close with an exhausted sigh. It had been at least two hours since they came aboard.

"We have all the physical evidence of his stay on the boat, plus the Glock and the money. I'm sorry for the mess we're leaving behind," Detective Hart said.

Sam raised a hand and brushed it aside. "It's nothing we can't clean up."

"It'll take some time," Buckler added.

"All that's left is for you to come in and sign your statements in a few days," Detective Hart added.

"We can do that."

"Whenever you're ready." Hart frowned. "Your dad won't be out of the woods for some time, it seems. That ricochet did some serious damage."

Moira's arms tightened around Sam, offering whatever comfort she could give. He had purposely used his father's injury against him in the fight and likely caused more damage.

"Congratulations on your marriage," Buckler said.

"Congrats," Hart echoed.

They stepped up on the rail and onto the dock.

"Do you think they tag team everything they do?" Moira asked.

Sam laughed. "Seems they do."

"Are we going to try again tomorrow?"

"Fuck, yeah. This is our honeymoon."

"I dread looking inside the cabin. Your father trashed the sleeping berth, and that forensic team was down there a long time."

"I'll look." He eased away from her and disappeared downstairs.

He was back in a second and jerked his cell phone out of his pocket. "I'm calling in the team. Seven SEALs can get more done in half an hour than most people can in a week."

She covered his phone's screen with her hand. "Tomorrow will be soon enough. Let's go home. As long as we're together, that's the only honeymoon I need."

"You deserve more, Moira. I wanted to give you more, but…we'll probably lose our reservations for docking at our other stops."

"We can call when we get home." She pressed close and held him. "Your father said you were as hard as he is, but he's wrong. You grieve for your fallen teammate, something he'd never understand. You love me. He would never know the first thing about how to love anyone."

He cupped her face and tipped it up. "The guys call me Hard-Ass Harding because when we're on a mission or training, I have to be all business, and my word is law. Their lives are in my hands. With you, I can set that aside and be *more* than the soldier, I can just be a man who needs love and all that comes with it. Every moment you were down there with him… If he'd hurt you…"

He kissed her as though it might have been the last time, leaving her breathless. "You're home to me, Moira. When I walk off the plane, I'm coming home to you."

"And I'll always be waiting for you."

EPILOGUE

U SING THE TABLET controlling the drone overhead, Hawk scanned the desert and watched the strategic movement of teams as they shifted across the rough terrain from one position to another. The exercise in navigation and battle strategy was going well.

It felt good getting out in the field again. He could breathe here. Being able to get out of the office and observe the men in action as an evaluation had relieved some of his dissatisfaction.

"Hawk One, this is base," a voice said on the radio. Lieutenant Gantry had given him his own call sign since he and one other officer were observing six of the teams.

"Hawk One here," Hawk replied.

"You have an emergency message from your wife relayed through Master Chief Marks. She says, it's time."

"What?" Shock tore the word loose though he'd heard the message.

"She says it's time."

Shit! Two weeks early. And he was a hundred and fifty miles away. *Shit!* For a moment excitement and panic charged through his system at the same time.

"Master Chief has transport on its way."

Thank you, Langley. That eased the panic.

"I'm sending someone to take over your post. I'll give you

some coordinates off the reservation and direct the bird to that location."

"Roger that, base. I'm ready for those coordinates." He punched them into the GPS as the communications officer gave them to him.

Hawk beckoned to Seaman Reynolds, who had driven him here. The young SEAL had dark red hair and freckles and looked about seventeen, but was probably early twenties. "You up to being a taxi for a few minutes, Reynolds? I need a ride off the range."

"Sure, sir."

As soon as his relief arrived, Hawk handed over the drone control pad and radio, grabbed his backpack, and he and Seaman Reynolds jumped into DPV Desert Patrol Vehicle. Reynolds took the wheel and the vehicle flew down the hill, leveled out, and shot out onto the road leading away from Camp Billy Machen.

After twenty minutes, the young SEAL stopped the DPV on a bare spot next to a deserted road with nothing coming or going either way and shut off the engine.

"You don't have to stay, Seaman."

"I don't mind, sir."

Though he had been silent nearly the entire time they'd been together, Reynolds asked, "May I ask your advice about something, sir?"

As he discussed several duty stations and career and training paths open to the young Seaman, his need to be somewhere else—*right now* squeezed his stomach into knots of anxiety.

When the distinctive whomp-whomp-whomp of a chopper became audible in the distance, he gave a sigh of relief. It rose over one of the hills like a giant red dragonfly, settled over their position, hovered, and then dropped slowly down onto the empty road.

"Good luck, Reynolds," Hawk yelled above the sound.

"Thank you, sir."

Hawk raced to the chopper, hunched down beneath the beating blades, and tugged open the door. He stared into the familiar face of a Navy helicopter pilot who'd come in after them more than once during deployments. Hawk hopped in and buckled up "What the hell have you been up to, Chunk?"

"You're lookin' at it, Lieutenant Commander." The chopper rose in the air, leveled out then buzzed forward. "I already know what you've been up to." He waggled his eyebrows. "I heard your wife is having a baby today. Getting a little long in the tooth for that, aren't you?"

"There's no expiration date tattooed on my equipment, Chunk."

The big man laughed.

ZOE GRIPPED THE chrome bars of her bed as another contraction hit. They were getting seriously close, and still no Hawk. She took a cleansing breath as the pain eased and tried to relax.

The woosh, woosh, woosh of the baby's heartbeat played like reassuring music from the monitor next to her.

It had been three hours since she left the physical therapy unit and rode the elevator up to labor and delivery, where they put her in a bed for observation. Had she known she was in real labor, she'd have called Hawk right away. Now she had and he was a no show. *Where the hell is my husband?*

A nurse came in, slipped on gloves, and checked her progress. "You're at five already, Zoe. Maybe another couple of hours if you continue to progress like this. You can have the epidural whenever you need it. Just push the button."

She nodded, and, in the grip of another contraction, nearly asked for it then. Instead she rode it out. She reached for her cell phone and texted Hawk 9-1-1. If that didn't get him wheels up, nothing would.

THEY WERE FIFTEEN minutes out when Hawk felt his cell phone

vibrate and jerked it out of his pocket. The 9-1-1 on the screen sent a spike of adrenaline through his system, and his skin prickled.

"Chunk, I need you to get this bucket moving."

"Roger that."

Langley was waiting for him when they landed at the small airstrip. "Send me a bill, Chunk. I gotta go."

"This one's on the house."

"Thanks."

He bailed out of the chopper before the blades had even stopped moving, and, hunkering down, rushed across the lot to meet Langley.

"Get a move on, Lang. Zoe's 9-1-1'ed me."

Langley screeched out of the parking spot and pulled out into traffic.

"WHERE THE HELL *is* he? I need him." The pain was getting more intense. She tried to breathe with it, but all she could do was grip the bedrail and hold on. She'd waited too long to ask for the epidural.

"He'll be here, Zoe." The young nurse, Shelley, said as she allowed Zoe to grip her arm.

Her water broke, and she was overwhelmed by the need to bear down.

The nurse hit the button on the bed. "We need a doctor in here."

LANGLEY BRAKED TO a stop as close to the front door as he could get. Hawk leaped out, barely hearing Langley's "Good luck" as he ran toward the entrance, raced to an elevator, and hit the button. He jumped out on the labor and delivery floor and skidded to a stop at the nurse's desk. "Zoe Yazzie?"

An older woman said, "Room 409. You'd better hurry."

Hawk jogged down the hall, looking at the room numbers, pushed open the door to 409—and walked into chaos.

"PUSH, ZOE. PUSH." The nurse was saying in her ear, and counting while Zoe held her breath and bore down. She was trying, and had been for nearly thirty minutes, and at this point her entire body ached, and she was exhausted.

The door flew open and Hawk rushed into the room and straight to the bed. He touched the nurse's shoulder, and she moved out of the way. "I'm sorry I'm late, baby."

He slid in behind her and she gripped his wrists. "Let's do this."

"You're an asshole for being late."

"Yeah, I am. I'm sorry."

He was her rock, her comfort. He gave her strength. And she was still going to kill him later. Another contraction hit, and the urge to push swelled with it. She caught her breath and strained with all she had while he counted.

"The baby's crowning," Doctor Chapman announced.

"Deep breath, baby," Hawk encouraged.

It became a mantra, deep breath, push, and the count. Three more tries, and she felt the baby's head leave her.

"One more time, Zoe," Doctor Chapman urged.

The baby's shoulders came through, its body slid free, and the release and relief brought tears to her eyes."

"You have a beautiful baby girl, Zoe!" Doctor Chapman announced, her smile covered by a mask but still visible around her eyes.

"A girl," Zoe repeated. She remembered holding a baby girl in the nursery and feeding her. Her throat closed with an emotion so strong it was hard to breathe.

Their baby girl gave a lusty cry as the doctor lifted her onto Zoe's stomach, Zoe's arms went around her, holding her close.

Hawk eased out from behind her and eased her down to lie back.

The baby's skin was pale compared to A. J.'s, but her hair was thick and as dark as her brother's. Even with her eyes swollen from the journey she just completed, she looked very much like her father. A feeling of love and contentment rolled over Zoe.

"A girl was what you hoped for, wasn't it?" Hawk asked, and bent to kiss her.

"Yes," she said and reached up to touch his cheek. "I love you, even though you're an asshole for being late."

Everyone in the room laughed, even him.

The baby's eyes opened and seemed to look at him. "Hello, Grace." He called her by name. "Seeing her face for the first time...I can't find the words to describe the feeling."

The emotion in his face triggered a similar memory for Zoe, then another. The memories flew past like the pages of a book, flipping faster and faster. A. J. as a baby like Grace. Hawk holding him for the first time with the same look of love and wonder in his eyes. A. J.'s first steps. A. J. running into his father's arms.

When she could catch her breath again. She reached for Hawk's hand and drew it to her cheek. "We've built a lifetime of memories in the past year, and eventually I'm going to remember the rest, too."

THE END

FOR MORE INFORMATION ABOUT TERESA REASOR

Website: www.teresareasor.com

MILITARY ROMANTIC SUSPENSE
BREAKING FREE (Book 1 of the SEAL Team Heartbreakers)
BREAKING THROUGH (Book 2 of the SEAL Team Heartbreakers)
BREAKING AWAY (Book 3 of the SEAL Team Heartbreakers)
BREAKING TIES (A SEAL Team Heartbreakers Novella)
BUILDING TIES (Book 4 of the SEAL Team Heartbreakers)
BREAKING BOUNDARIES (Book 5 of the SEAL Team Heartbreakers)
BREAKING OUT (BOOK 6 of the SEAL Team Heartbreakers)
BREAKING POINT (A SEAL Team Heartbreakers Novella)
BREAKING HEARTS (Book 7 of the SEAL Team Heartbreakers)
BREAKING CHAINS (Book 8 of the SEAL Team Heartbreakers)
BUILDING STRENGTH (Book 9 of the SEAL Team Heartbreakers)
BUILDING FAMILY (Book 10 of the SEAL Team Heartbreakers)

SEALS IN PARADISE SERIES
HOT SEAL, RUSTY NAIL
HOT SEAL, ROMAN NIGHTS
HOT SEAL, TAKING THE PLUNGE
HOT SEAL, MIDNIGHT MAGIC

PARANORMAL ROMANCE
TIMELESS
DEEP WITHIN THE SHADOWS (Book 1 of the Superstition Series)
DEEP WITHIN THE STONE (Book 2 of the Superstition Series)
DEEP WITHIN THE MIND (Book 3 of the Superstition Series)
WHISPER IN MY EAR
HAVE WAND, WILL TRAVEL (Book 1 Have Wand, Will Travel)
ONCE BITTEN, TWICE SHY (Book 2 Have Wand, Will Travel)

ADVENTURES OF A WITCHY WALLFLOWER (Book 3 Have Wand, Will Travel)

HISTORICAL ROMANCE
CAPTIVE HEARTS
HIGHLAND MOONLIGHT
TO CAPTURE A HIGHLANDER'S HEART: THE TRILOGY

The Highland Moonlight Spinoff Trilogy in parts
TO CAPTURE A HIGHLANDER'S HEART: THE BEGINNING
TO CAPTURE A HIGHLANDER'S HEART: THE COURTSHIP
TO CAPTURE A HIGHLANDER'S HEART: THE WEDDING NIGHT

SHORT STORIES
AN AUTOMATED DEATH: A STEAMPUNK SHORT STORY
CAUGHT IN THE ACT: A HUMOROUS SHORT STORY

CHILDREN'S BOOK
WILLY C. SPARKS, THE DRAGON WHO LOST HIS FIRE